TIMELESS *Regency* COLLECTION

A Midwinter Ball

TIMELESS *Regency* COLLECTION

A Midwinter Ball

Heidi Ashworth
Annette Lyon
Michele Paige Holmes

Mirror Press

Copyright © 2016 Mirror Press
Print edition
All rights reserved

No part of this book may be reproduced in any form whatsoever without prior written permission of the publisher, except in the case of brief passages embodied in critical reviews and articles. These novellas are works of fiction. The characters, names, incidents, places, and dialog are products of the authors' imaginations and are not to be construed as real.

Interior Design by Rachael Anderson
Edited by Donna Hatch, Heather B. Moore, Jennie Stevens, and Lisa Shepherd
Cover design by Rachael Anderson
Cover Photo Credit: Owen Benson, Photographer

Published by Mirror Press, LLC
ISBN-10: 1-941145-82-5
ISBN-13: 978-1-941145-82-1

TABLE OF CONTENTS

Much Ado About Dancing   1
by Heidi Ashworth

Sweeter Than Any Dream   95
by Annette Lyon

An Invitation to Dance   195
by Michele Paige Holmes

OTHER TIMELESS REGENCY COLLECTIONS

Autumn Masquerade
Spring in Hyde Park
Summer House Party
A Country Christmas
A Holiday in Bath
A Season in London

Much Ado About Dancing

Heidi Ashworth

For my much loved
maîtresse de danse
~Marie-José Rebboah~

OTHER WORKS BY HEIDI ASHWORTH

Miss Delacourt Speaks Her Mind
Miss Delacourt Has Her Day
Lady Crenshaw's Christmas
Lord Haversham Takes Command
Miss Armistead Makes Her Choice
A Timeless Romance Anthology: Winter Collection
Power of the Matchmaker
O'er the River Liffey

One

Enrosque—A Twist

England, Midwinter 1817

"All the county knows my annual house party to be among the most anticipated of the year," Mrs. Smith of Dance Hall announced to those within the reach of her voice. "What's more," she said with an airy wave, "within months of everyone's departure, there are a greater number of marriages announced in the newspapers than is usual. I am wrong to crow," she said with a finger to her nose, "but I am persuaded it is on account of my most excellent dancing lessons."

Miss Analisa Lloyd-Jones favored her hostess with an indulgent smile. "I shall be astonished if even your incomparable lessons have the power to procure a husband for an old maid such as myself."

"Old maid!" her hostess countered, her eyes round with what Analisa surmised to be as much apprehension as incredulity. "You can't be more than eighteen. Never fear, we shall marry you off this year, see if we don't."

"I shall be twenty come the fall," Analisa replied brightly. "Though, I confess I am not in the least sorry to have remained a spinster. Now that Colin has gone to India with his wife and baby, Papa and Mama are not entirely on their own." She stood and walked to the side of her friend, Miss Emily Everitt, who busied herself with a piece of embroidery.

"Analisa, you mustn't sacrifice so for your parents," Emily said as she jabbed her needle into the canvas she held before her. "I am determined that I shall not."

A chorus of "Nor I," was sung out by the girls seated on the various chairs and sofas scattered about the first-floor salon. Such a noisy utterance proved to be too much for Mrs. Smith, who shook her head in protest as she moved briskly from the room.

"Come now, ladies," Analisa said with a laugh. "We all know for what we long. We shall be churlish and ill-humored until we retire to our rooms and dress for the evening's enticements. Let us begin."

Miss Mary Arthur's embroidery hoop clattered to the floor as she rose to her feet with alacrity. "I feared I should be expected to squander the entire afternoon stitching brown reeds around a lake," she said with her matter-of-course panache.

"Either that or be forced to primp through our supper," Emily murmured. "I am persuaded Mrs. Smith has forgotten what it is to be young. She may don a wig if it pleases her," she said with a sniff, "but the creation of my near-best coiffure requires a great deal of time to achieve."

"Then come," Analisa insisted as she drew Emily to her feet. "Let us make our way above stairs before Mrs. Smith returns and insists on inventing something else with which to keep us occupied."

With cries of appreciation, the remaining young ladies

sprang to their feet and allowed themselves to be ushered through the door and up the stairs to their bedchambers. As the eldest among them, Analisa imagined herself a hen gathering her chicks. Immediately, she banished the image from her mind; she knew it would only lead to peevishness if she pictured herself a spinster amidst so many fresh-faced maidens. Indeed, it was best not to dwell on the fact that if she did not marry soon, she would, come May, be expected to embark on her fourth Season. It was a humiliation not to be borne with any grace.

She released the sigh she refused to air in the company of the others and made her way to her chamber door. Though an accommodation of many charms, its beauty failed to distract from the folded piece of parchment lying on her dressing table. It bore her name scrawled in the self-same hand as had the monthly missives Lord Northrup had sent her for nigh on two years. Why her Papa had seen fit to have this one forwarded to Dance Hall, she could not fathom. He was well aware that she had long given up on reading the earl's letters; they always proved to sink her into a black mood. She was tempted to ignore this one as she had most of the others, but a quiver of misgiving caused her some hesitation. With a shaking hand, she took up the folded parchment and broke the seal.

> *Miss Lloyd-Jones, to Whom I Have Remained True,*
>
> *I have longed for even a line from you during my months abroad but have received not one. Perhaps your neglect for my comfort is fit punishment for the wrong I have done you in warning away your previous suitors, as well any who might have made their intentions known after my departure. What more can*

I do than to most humbly beg your pardon? It is my intention to call on you in the very near future. I anticipate our meeting with delight and pray that I find you in good health.

 Yours, As Ever,
 Northrup

  It was as she feared; the earl had returned to England. Analisa sank onto the bed as the parchment fluttered from her hand. Dance Hall was a matter of miles from her country home; if Lord Northrup had done as intended, he had surely been informed of her whereabouts. A deep and abiding hope for a substantial storm filled her heart. She went to the window, and her heart sank at the sight of a cloudless, blue sky.

  Suddenly faint, she sank into a chair before her legs entirely failed her. She was strengthened by the thought that followed; if the weather held, Mr. Charles Wainwright would surely attend the practice ball, known as the Folly Bally, to be held directly after supper. She suspected that he admired her, a sentiment that was steadfastly returned. His rich brown locks and eyes so dark they appeared to be black haunted even her dreams. For the past year, she had whiled away the hours imagining every detail of the gown she would don for their wedding or conjuring the possible appearance of their sure-to-be numerous children. And yet, despite long looks of admiration too numerous to count, he never had so much as bespoken a dance.

  She entertained hopes that a house party would encourage his attentions, all of which she was determined to receive with as much wit and charm as was at her disposal. The very notion caused her spirits to soar until, with a groan, she discerned why he had failed to so much as engage her in conversation in all the time she had known him: Lord Northrup had forbidden it.

Visions of the far too many balls she had endured from her chair as she hid her humiliation behind her fan rose into her mind. She supposed Lord Northrup was responsible, as well, for the lack of gentlemen callers, gifts of flowers, and invitations to ride in the park, all of which had dried up like the Red Sea at parting these last two London Seasons.

An incipient rage threatened to overtake the last shreds of her equanimity as she contemplated all she might say to Lord Northrup, and at the first opportunity. She rose to her feet and paced the floor as she worked out each insult, only to cast aside one after the other. It would never do for her to be overheard speaking with such animosity. She would be most distressed if, as a result of her loose tongue, Mr. Wainwright were to form an unfavorable opinion of her.

She took a deep breath and examined her reflection in the glass; she mustn't allow her secrets to be revealed in her face. She was distracted from her scrutiny when her abigail, Ruby, scratched at the door. Analisa bade her enter, and together they began the process of doing up her hair for the evening's Folly Bally.

"Miss," Ruby said as she took up a lock of mahogany hair and twisted it this way and that. "Beggin' yer pardon, but are the fine gentlemen to stay the night elsewhere as they did during last year's house party?"

"But of course. Mrs. Smith is nothing if not an eccentric hostess," Analisa said with a fond smile. "She does not approve of young ladies and unwed men sharing a roof. She feels certain this can lead to no good. I must, however, give her credit for her many successes; her parties result in a veritable crop of marriages."

"If only the weather hadn't been so dreary this

Christmas, she might o' held the party anyway, and mayhap a storm might have come out of nowhere and snowed in the boys and girls together for the duration. Ain't that the fun of a house party?"

"I, for one, Ruby, am grateful she waited; more of the guests can make use of the roads now that the weather is so fine. The men shall also be able to find shelter nearby after tonight's Folly Bally as well as after the Grand Ball."

Ruby took up a brush and sighed. "It's not only the swells who enjoy a bit o' fun during a house party, miss. I should have liked it better gettin' snowed in, with, case in point," she said grandly, in imitation of her mistress, "Mr. Wainwright's valet tucked up under the eaves. He is so very handsome. And," she added with a sharp look for Analisa in the mirror, "we all know how you admire Mr. Wainwright, and it ain't only that he is a younger son of a duke and was a hero in the Peninsular war!"

"I am more than familiar with the charms of Mr. Wainwright, Ruby, and, what's more, you forget yourself in saying such things." Analisa refused to reply to Ruby's ensuing comments. Instead, she watched as the girl gathered a portion of Analisa's rich, dark hair at the crown of her head and coaxed a row of ringlets to fall on either side of her brow. A cunning arrangement of flowers and feathers was secured to the back; Analisa thought it perfectly charming. All that remained was to don her best white muslin gown and a simple strand of pearls. Her newly created silk gown that even now lay between sheets of silver tissue was in reserve for the true ball that was the culmination of the house party.

"You look a gem of the first water," Ruby said with a sigh of pleasure.

"Let us hope the gentlemen share your opinion." Analisa noted her wry smile as it beckoned to her from the glass. "I have managed to elude their compliments for nigh on two years."

The girl furrowed her brow. "That is just modesty talkin', miss, for it can't be true! Even so, you have never looked more beautiful."

Analisa smiled and bade Ruby quit the room to rest; she would be required in the wee hours of the morning to help her mistress out of her finery. Once the girl had gone, Analisa again studied her reflection in the mirror. She hoped she was not vain, but she was more than pleased by what she saw. The new hairstyle lent her a regal air, and the ringlets along her brow brought out the gray in her fine, almond-shaped eyes to perfection.

Satisfied she looked her best, she collected her fan and crossed the room. The gaze that met hers when she opened the door was as surprising as it was wished for. Mr. Wainwright, in his chocolate brown coat and froth of white cravat, was never a more welcome sight. It was all Analisa could do to prevent herself from throwing herself into his arms.

"Mr. Wainwright, how unexpected! What are you doing up here?" Her heart beat hard in anticipation of his reply.

"I could not resist the chance to have you to myself for a moment before the pandemonium sets in. But, shhh," he added as he put a finger to his lips. "You and I are both aware that I shall be tossed out on my ear should I be discovered."

"Well," she managed to say in spite of the breathlessness his proximity induced, "I should be most sorry were that to happen. That is to say, *all* of the ladies," she stammered, "shall, quite naturally, be regretful should they not have the opportunity to dance with you."

He made no reply except to flash a dazzling smile composed of brilliant white teeth and hold out his arm. She took it, feeling as if she were in a dream, one in which his pure masculinity was deeply impressed upon her. The blood that beat in her ears drowned out all other sounds as they moved down the hall to the top of the staircase. In her excitement, she felt incapable of observing a thing past the tip of her nose. Meanwhile, said article was treated to the pleasant aromas of cologne and starch that wafted from the linen at his throat.

They made their way along the staircase to the first floor. As they peered down at the ground floor passage, he put his finger again to his lips and indicated she should descend to the front hall where the young ladies awaited the gong to announce supper. Analisa found it took a mighty force of will to move away from him. After only a few paces, she could not refrain from turning to look over her shoulder. She saw that he had already made his way nearly to the door of the ballroom where the men were made to wait until they were allowed into the dining room.

She realized she could now breathe quite naturally but somewhat mourned the disorder of her sensibilities caused by the presence of Mr. Wainwright. Perhaps, if she had had the opportunity to stand so near him at any point in the past, she might have kept herself better in hand.

She achieved the front hall to find she had dallied too long and was quite alone. The footman opened the door to the dining room, and she entered to find a sea of girlish faces. Each was stamped with a curve of the lips that led her to fear they knew her secret. "Good evening," she said in astonishingly unexceptional tones. "You all look so beautiful! Perhaps it shall be best if I return to my chamber directly after supper as I haven't the slightest chance of catching the eye of a single gentleman."

Analisa was gratified by the number of smiles that broke

out at her words; she supposed the sole incidence of muffled laughter must have been expressed by one of the younger girls who had never known Analisa to have been favored by any gentleman. It led her to realize just how old and hopeless she must appear to them, and she felt the smile slip from her face.

She forgot all of her discomfort, however, once she was seated in a chair that faced the door in anticipation of the appearance of the men. She owned it was an unconventional means of courting, but the stir of emotions it created was intoxicating. Finally, after some unexplained delay, the footmen flung wide the doors, and the men began to file into the room. There were unrestrained sighs of approval from the young ladies as each gentleman paused to be momentarily framed in the doorway. More than one young man blushed at the intense scrutiny with which he was met, and all appeared to be somewhat dazzled by the high tide of emotion.

One gentleman, however, seemed untouched by the panoply, a circumstance not the least surprising to Analisa. He entered the room with a confident air and strode to stand as close as he was able to a chair directly across the table from where she was disposed. He looked even finer in his brown suit coat than before, his locks curling about his face and his black eyes shining.

"Gentlemen," Mrs. Smith pronounced with a ringing clap of her hands. "Tonight there are very few rules and even fewer strictures. Sit by whomsoever you choose; whether it be across the table from the lady of your admiration or right beside her is of no consequence. As long as you are under my watchful eye, you may spend as much time with your lady as you choose. You may even dance with her as often as she accepts your invitation to do so."

A chorus of approval went around the room at this last pronouncement. However, her decree that all of the gentlemen must depart in their various conveyances the moment the ball drew to a close was met with an equal number of masculine groans.

"Now, gentlemen," Mrs. Smith cried over the objections, "if you have cherished hopes of staying the night under this roof, you shall be sorely disappointed."

A renewed babble of discontent rose into the air, but Mrs. Smith was not to be denied. "The rules," she rebuked, "were clearly printed on your invitations. Do not attempt to do other than follow them to the letter! This is not my first house party, I do assure you. However, you must all be silent before we may begin," she added with an arch look that appeared to be the old woman's feeble attempt at severity.

As Analisa turned to hide her mirth, her eye was caught by Mr. Wainwright, who seemed to be every bit as amused. When his gaze fell in a pointed manner to the chair in which he intended to seat himself, she felt her delight swallowed up by the self-conscious flush that rose in her face. She nodded, none too gravely, in return, pleased that he had not chosen an unseemly dash round the table to take a seat at her side.

"Are we all at readiness?" Mrs. Smith asked. "Very well, then. When I arrive at the count of three, you may take your seats. One, two, three!"

The room erupted into mayhem, prompting the footmen to cower in the corner as men dashed to and fro. So consumed were some in the pursuit of chairs closest to those they most admired, they narrowly avoiding knocking heads with another. Two unfortunate fellows found themselves chest to chest, the buttons of their coats caught together as their owners did their utmost to charge off in opposite directions.

Analisa laughed as merrily as the others, even as she contemplated the mortification she most certainly should have felt if Mr. Wainwright had behaved in such a fashion. Instead, he calmly stepped to the chair he desired and laid his hand upon it. When the chaos had sufficiently died out enough to allow him to pull out the chair, he seated himself with grace and aplomb.

It was only when the uproar had descended to a low rumble that Analisa became aware of a curious deflation of her emotions. It took but a moment for her to discover the reason: Lord Northrup had not come. How his failure to appear should have the power to darken her mood, she could not say. To her chagrin, it could neither be denied.

Chapter Two

Pas de duex—A Dance of Two

Analisa had never enjoyed such a meal. More to the point, she had never before been so openly admired by a man whose favor she returned so precisely. In spite of the lackadaisical rules, one could hardly shout words of affection for all to hear; it was Mr. Wainwright's cleverly worded messages that made the meal the most delicious she had yet known.

"I have chosen my seat well," he confessed whilst the fish was being served. "The view is excellent."

"Oh? I hadn't realized there were any windows on this side of the room." She turned to behold naught but a footman bearing a platter of carp.

"Have I claimed the presence of a window?" Mr. Wainwright quizzed with a lift of his well-shaped brow.

Analisa smiled. "No, I suppose you have not."

Upon the appearance of the fruit and sweets, Mr.

Wainwright was once again in fine form. "I do so enjoy dancing, do you not, Miss Lloyd-Jones?"

"Why yes, immensely." He did not immediately reply and remained silent for so long she began to babble. "Mrs. Smith is adamant that her dancing lessons are the foundation of her successful house parties. She is so confident of this that she dubbed her home Dance Hall upon the death of her husband."

"In light of such passion," Mr. Wainwright remarked in earnest, "I intend to dance as many sets as possible." The manner in which he then turned his gaze down table provoked Analisa's heart to sink. To her delight, he turned his gaze to her again and said, "I daresay there is one who shall agree to dance them all with me."

Stunned at the soaring of her spirits, she felt almost giddy. "I am persuaded there are many in the room willing to be the *one*." Privately, she wondered how one, whomsoever she might be, was to know whether or not it was herself to whom he referred.

When all had been consumed, the company trooped from the room, each arm in arm with his or her current *amour*. As the couple farthest from the door, Analisa and Mr. Wainwright were last to depart. With a smile, he once again held out his arm, and she took it with a heart full of anticipation.

As they moved up the stairs and down the passage towards the ballroom, she was again very aware of how he seemed to tower over her. Yet, unlike before, she felt perfectly well. What she was now experiencing was not a dream but a beautiful reality brimming with delights for all of the senses. Strains of sweet music drifted through the air above the mingled sounds of intimate chatter and sumptuous fabrics brushed against limbs. The walls, covered in peacock blue *moiré* silk beckoned her into a world of beauteous frivolity. The floor they walked along was of gray-streaked marble, polished to an impossible shine, and the chandeliers overhead bore crystals of such clarity they might have been drops of pure water.

Against this backdrop was the square jaw and dimpled chin of her escort who smiled down at her with affection. Analisa felt a long denied sensation—that of having been finally restored to her former self: a poised, assured, and desirable young woman. In turn, the anger she had felt when she learned of the prohibition Lord Northrup enacted upon his departure was mollified; she was not unwanted and despised after all.

Finally, they entered the ballroom, one of the most elaborately embellished she had ever beheld. It had been redecorated since the prior year's house party, and Analisa was positively overcome by the plethora of peacock-inspired flourishes. Her gaze was filled with feathered figures in every variation of blue, green, and lavender one could possibly imagine. Then her gaze fell to the two and twenty people who did little to fill the vast room.

She was delighted to see that Emily and Mary each basked in the glow of their mutual admirers and that there was nearly an equal number of gentlemen as ladies in attendance. So, it was with some astonishment that, as she and Mr. Wainwright promenaded down the length of the ballroom, Analisa noted two gentlemen standing together in the far corner of the room. One was turned to face her; he seemed older than most of the assemblage and bore a shrewd gleam in his eyes she found rather alluring. He was handsome as well—fair of hair with full lips and large eyes. To her surprise, they seemed to widen when his gaze met hers.

He stared at her with recognition, of that she felt certain though she knew him to be, without a doubt, a stranger. Or perhaps what she deemed recognition was mere admiration, an expression from which she had benefited far too little as of late. She knew that to respond would mark her as fast, but a smile sprang to her lips in spite of her wishes.

Without taking his eyes from her, he leaned into his companion and spoke a word or two into his ear. The other man, taller than the first and broader in the shoulder, turned his head, somewhat hesitantly, to look where he was bid.

Analisa was persuaded she did not see correctly. She knew this man, and yet she did not. His formerly freckled skin was slightly bronzed, he had grown at least an inch, and what had been a shock of ginger atop his head had grown into a mop of russet locks that cascaded along his brow most becomingly. The rich blue of his coat was echoed in the hue of his eyes, and for the first time since she had known the young Lord Northrup, his arms and legs appeared to be in perfect proportion with the remainder of his frame.

There was something of his initial expression that she supposed to be pure wonder, but she knew it could not be so; surely he had come to Dance Hall expressly to find her. He turned fully round, and she was struck with the elegance of his deportment, one that implied an assurance not echoed in his eyes. However, the manner in which his jaw was gripped tightly with suppressed emotion was just as she remembered.

To her dismay, she realized Mr. Wainwright had never ceased his advance into the room. As such, she stood face-to-face with the Earl of Northrup and his companion long before she felt inclined to do so. Now that she was upon him, Analisa could see there was more flesh on his bones than she had believed possible. Silently, she owned that it flattered him. If only there were a way to signify that he should resist looking at her with a gaze that burned holes into her very soul.

"Callerton, Northrup," Mr. Wainwright said with a nod for each. "I am persuaded Miss Lloyd-Jones is known to you, Laurie, but I take delight in presenting her anew." Her escort favored her with a glowing smile. "This is Mr. Callerton and, as I am persuaded you are aware, this is Lord Northrup."

As Mr. Wainwright's gaze vacillated between her face and the earl's, she felt somewhat perplexed. Her beau's manner lacked the covetousness she would have preferred to his show of triumph. Unable to fathom what it could mean, she began to feel no small amount of apprehension.

"Mr. Callerton, I am pleased to make your acquaintance," she forced herself to say exactly as she ought. "I expect you are a friend of Lord Northrup's," she added with a fleeting glance for the earl at her side. "As Mr. Wainwright has said, Lord Northrup and I are somewhat known to one another."

This statement prompted smiles in Misters Wainwright and Callerton so broad one might accuse them of smirking. In dismay, she looked to ascertain the breadth of Lord Northrup's smile only to find that his expression was positively grim.

She gasped as the truth dawned upon her. "I fear I have been somewhat dull-witted. I now comprehend that you see me as an object of scorn." She felt her face flame with the humiliation that scorched her breast. "And to think I was foolish enough to believe you sincere in your attentions, Mr. Wainwright."

"I could never scorn such as you! And I am most sincere in my admiration," he said with an inclination of his head. "But, alas, you have been deemed sacrosanct for years. I confess, I regret it, but I must leave you to your earl as his claim is a prior one." With a sweeping bow, he took himself in the direction of the others.

Lord Northrup cast Analisa a look of regret. "Allow me to beg your pardon on Mr. Wainwright's behalf. He shall soon have reason to repent of such audacity," he promised in a voice that rumbled deeply.

Analisa felt it a vast improvement over the high-pitched whine in which he spoke the last time they had conversed. However, she hadn't a moment to further examine her feelings regarding his threat before Mr. Callerton attempted to desert her as well.

"I find I must cry off," he said with an expression too woeful to be fully genuine. "It is a long way to a warm bed for me."

"Not at all," Lord Northrup replied. "The Lloyd-Joneses shall be best pleased to put you up at Dun Hafan together with myself."

Analisa quickly considered. Mr. Callerton was very pleasant and if he proved to have money besides, her papa might favor him over the earl. "Do say yes," she insisted. "It is true, my father shall be delighted to serve as your host, and tonight is the most frolicsome of balls, I do assure you." She gave him a bright smile, one she hoped hid the apprehension she feared showed in her eyes as she risked a glance up at Lord Northrup. He turned his head away before she could read his expression, but the very air between them felt heavy with dread.

Mr. Callerton's countenance bore a more natural smile than previously. "You are most kind. I find I am happy to remain, after all. I would be honored to bespeak a dance, should Laurie approve."

"I am certain he shall," she replied in hopes that her bewilderment did not show in her face. She had thought Mr.

Callerton to be the Laurie mentioned by Mr. Wainwright. "Though, at present, I cannot comprehend how the composition of my evening should be any concern of Laurie's," she added firmly.

Mr. Callerton's eyes grew wide, and he turned his gaze to Lord Northrup. Analisa would dearly have loved to gather the courage to verify what she saw in Mr. Callerton's expression but found it far more comfortable to avert her gaze and bite her lip in apprehension. Lord Northrup was infamous for his temper, but what had caused it to flare at this moment, she could not guess.

Mr. Callerton was clearly in little doubt as he quickly murmured his apologies, turned on his heel, and fled.

In years past, Analisa had found that an angry Lord Northrup was one she could twist round her finger with ease. "Shall we dance, then?" she suggested as she whirled about to face him.

To her chagrin, his response was not at all what she had anticipated. In days of old, he would have complied though his anger would have yet been palpable, his manner grudging, his words explosive. Then, as they danced, his fury would subside, and his customary admiration of her would resume. Instead, she encountered a cool expression that indicated an unwillingness to comply. When he grasped her elbow to draw her into the shadows, no words of rage followed, though his earlier open admiration had vanished.

"I had hoped our first exchange should consist of words far more pleasant," he said. "However, I find I cannot refrain from informing you of my meeting with your father." He spoke with a calm that belied the apprehension he seemed at pains to conceal. "He has agreed there is neither a reason nor the need to breach our marriage contract."

"Has he?" A white-hot rage threatened to overwhelm

her. "You may speak of contracts all you wish, but I doubt there was ever any such document."

"Nothing in writing," he admitted, a bit ruffled but all the bolder for it. "A contract spoken between two gentlemen is as worthy as any that is written." He stared at her intently as if he expected an immediate reply. When none was forthcoming, he released her arm and stepped back a pace. "Do pardon my outburst."

If he deemed this an outburst, he had, indeed, changed. Sensing a weakening of his self-possession, she straightened her spine. "He informed me that you asked for my hand. However, my brother interceded on my behalf. Papa must have had his doubts, as he allowed Colin time to find me a more suitable match."

"And has he done?" Lord Northrup asked with an aplomb that indicated he well knew the answer.

"No," she said as she attempted to look away. She found that she could not; there was something terribly compelling about this new Lord Northrup that bade her look on. "Colin found himself a wife, instead. He was then consumed with wedding preparations and everything that follows. Almost directly after the baby arrived, they sailed for India to meet his other grandparents."

"Then there are none who would take my place." It was a statement of fact.

Words of censure rose to her lips. They vanished when she noted the softening of his expression as he gazed at her.

"Fools, they, each and every one."

Startled, Analisa forgot her qualms and dared to see what dwelt in his eyes. The look they shared was not in the least discomfiting, despite the seeming disappearance of the musicians, the room, and everyone in it. He did not speak, and yet, as he chained her gaze in his, he conveyed a message, one she failed to comprehend. She knew her eyes spoke of nothing in return, and when he looked away and down at the floor, she realized he knew it too.

The spell broken, the words she had previously called up spilled, unbidden, from her mouth. "Lord Northrup, I have remained unwed for reasons of which you are very well aware. Your actions towards me have been monstrously unfair."

He made no reply, but a crease appeared between his brows as he continued to stare steadfastly at the floor.

"I have always known you to believe yourself undeniably worthy of whatsoever you desire."

The crease deepened, but he made no attempt to mount a defense.

"In light of such, you thought it perfectly unexceptionable to warn away all of my potential suitors. It seems, at the risk of inviting your wrath, they have complied."

He lifted his head, and his gaze flew to her face. To her surprise, there was something in his eyes she had never before seen—uncertainty or perhaps even remorse. No, it was something softer yet—hurt. The mere notion squeezed her heart with such force that she gasped in pure astonishment.

The crease between his brows reappeared. "Pray, do not pity me."

"For what should I pity you?" she asked, astounded. "Indeed, why should any pity a man with youth, money, and power in his grasp? With but the lift of a finger you might have nearly any girl in the room and beyond to wife. What I cannot comprehend is why you should wish to shackle yourself to the one who cannot like you."

He looked, for a moment, as if he had been struck, and the scalding across his face that she had long expected finally appeared. Then he laughed, ruefully, a small smile curving one corner of his mouth. "I have long admired you for your unrestrained conviviality. I had not thought there could be an end to it." The humor drained from his face. "Am I so despicable, then?"

His words shamed her, but her anger would not be denied. "Not at all." She was astonished to find she spoke the truth. "As I have said, there are none here who would despise you in the least. And yet, they have not suffered at your hands as have I." She disguised her words with a brittle smile. "You have made me the unwitting subject of a joke between who knows how many gentlemen of my acquaintance. You have created a state of affairs that has made it undesirable, if not impossible, for any man to deign to so much as invite me to dance. For nigh on two years I have suffered this indignity."

He opened his mouth to utter what she feared would be a hateful retort, but he snapped it shut again, his eyes dark against his drained-white skin. She knew by the staccato of his breath that he labored under the effects of an intense emotion, but still he said nothing.

Thoroughly alarmed, she looked about the room for a source of aid. None seemed aware of her peril and, as each couple waltzed by, she saw how each delighted in the company of the other. Their happiness prompted in Analisa such a profound sense of sorrow that her eyes filled with tears. She struggled to regain her composure, but the tears only came faster and, mortified, she turned to flee. To her astonishment, she felt her hand caught in another's, and she was whirled expertly into the dance.

Blinded by tears, it was a few moments before she knew of a certainty in whose arms she was held. That it was Lord Northrup who had taken pity on her should have been a humiliation past bearing. Instead, her heart filled with gratitude; she had wished to dance with anyone save her father for ever so long. Her grief drifted away to be replaced with sheer happiness, and a bubble of laughter rose into her throat, such that she could not contain it. Heads turned at the sound, and she laughed again.

She took in the expressions of those who passed by, all of them smiling, even the gentlemen who had reason to fear Lord Northrup's wrath. She felt as if she were flying in his arms and realized he had become a most accomplished dancer. She had no objections when he, refusing to release her, bespoke the next set. It was the Quadrille, the steps of which allowed her to dance with other gentlemen as well. It was if the desolation of nearly two years melted away, little by little, until it disappeared altogether.

Just as she decided that she was perfectly content to dance with Lord Northrup all night, the set came to an end. To her bemusement, he escorted her to a chair in a corner of the room and indicated she should sit.

"You no longer wish to dance, my lord?" she asked in full expectation that he would insist she rest whilst he procured her some refreshment.

"I have had my fill of dancing," he said, not unkindly. "I trust you shall enjoy the remainder of your evening." He gave her a deep bow, then turned and walked out of the door.

Analisa looked about her with apprehension; she doubted she would find anything in the evening to now enjoy. The others had been paired off since dinner, leaving none to invite her to dance. Just as she concluded that she truly must retire, Mr. Callerton appeared at her side.

"Will you honor me with a set?" he asked, his eyes twinkling with mirth.

Instantly, Analisa felt her mood lighten. "Why, yes, Mr. Callerton, and as many others as you should wish." She laid

Much Ado About Dancing

her hand in his, and together they danced all night and into the morning.

Three

Ferme—A Closed Position

With a sigh of pure content, Analisa lay abed and contemplated the shadows that gamboled along the counterpane. Permission to lie-in was one of the best-loved features of a Mrs. Smith ball, and Analisa reveled in the knowledge that she was missing out on nothing of import. As promised, her hostess had swept the men from the house the moment the orchestra had begun to pack their instruments. The other girls were almost certainly still abed as well.

She smiled as she anticipated what remained of the day. Once the young ladies had taken sustenance and gathered in the salon, the etiquette lesson would commence. It would consist of only the girls; the gentlemen would be denied the house until the following day. Idly, Analisa wondered if Lord Northrup would carry on with the house party or admit defeat and return to his home. If so, he would not be present for the infamous dancing lesson, though she hardly dared imagine the self-important earl under the instructive thumb of Mrs. Smith.

When her stomach could no longer be denied, Analisa willed her rebellious body to rise. She proceeded to wash on her own as Ruby had been given the day off. It was a relief to don a comfortable round gown and arrange her hair in a simple knot at the nape of her neck. Upon descending to the breakfast room, she found herself sipping hot chocolate and reading the morning paper, the latter an indulgence her father did not countenance, when Lord Northrup stepped in through the door from the garden.

Analisa nearly dropped her cup. "My lord, what brings you here?" She knew she sounded as aghast as she felt, but it seemed fitting.

He looked about. "Is it only you, then?" he asked, a bit taken aback.

"I beg your pardon," she said in tones both frosty and bright. "Is there someone, in particular, you should have preferred to encounter?"

"No, of course not." He had the grace to look discomfited as he swept his hat from his head with an uncharacteristic lack of self-possession. "I arrived at half past eleven in expectations of finding the party below stairs for a late breakfast. I was informed the household was still abed, so I made a visit to the stables. As Dance Hall is rather thin of thoroughbreds," he explained, "I determined that a ramble would be a promising means of whiling away the time until the young ladies should arise. As I have never before attended a house party at Dance Hall—one would think the very appellation of the establishment might serve as warning for even the least discerning," he said with an accusing eye, "I am unfamiliar with the area; I promptly found myself fairly lost."

With a start, Analisa realized she still held her cup aloft.

She joined it gingerly with its saucer on the table as she considered her response. "My lord," she said slowly. "There was a detailed accounting of scheduled activities enclosed with your invitation. I am sorry to say the gentlemen have not been invited to any of today's events. I do hope you are not angry."

"I assure you I am not," he said shortly. He rolled his hat under his arm and turned his gaze here and there as if he knew not where to look.

"I must commend you for your patience." Indeed, she had never seen him so content to be still. "Perhaps I might be of some assistance. Pray, tell, for whom are you waiting?"

"Waiting? Ought I to be?" He allowed his gaze to rest on her a moment before he turned away again.

"I couldn't say, but it appears you are looking for someone. Might it be Mr. Callerton? Surely you brought him along with you this morning."

"No. Should I have?" he asked. He favored her with a questioning look that amounted to what she deemed an untoward interest.

"Why, yes. I suppose if you thought you were meant to be at Dance Hall, you might have assumed the same would apply to him."

"Yes, I see," he mused as if the thought had never entered his mind. "He was still abed when I left Dun Hafan. I can only assume he excels at reading schedules of the sort enclosed in invitations."

She softened the laugh that rose into her throat with a smile. "Very well, I suppose there is naught to be done about it now." A suspicion began to make its way into her mind, one that suggested the earl knew well enough he was not meant to be on the premises until the morrow. "However," she said as she stood as if in dismissal, "I regret to say that Mrs. Smith will never allow the presence of a gentleman for today's lesson."

He looked down as if to formulate his reply. When he looked up again, his face lit with pleasure. "Why, here is she of whom you speak. Perhaps she shall reconsider."

"My lord! What has brought you here today?" Mrs. Smith asked, pure delight peppering her words, while the young ladies in her wake stifled their giggles behind her back.

"It seems I have erred. Mr. Wainwright persuaded me, along with Mr. Callerton, to attend your house party to which he was invited. However, he failed to avail us of the rules. I should not have wandered about so freely if I had known I was not expected. I credit my eagerness to your hospitality; the ball last night was one of the most pleasant I have had the privilege to enjoy."

As her self-proclaimed suitor, Analisa felt he should have, at the very least, cast a furtive glance in her direction along with such words. It was curiously deflating that he had not.

"I am honored, my lord." Mrs. Smith's face was pink with pleasure. "Pray, pardon the lack of a personal invitation; I should have been delighted to issue one if I had been made aware that you have returned to our shores. But, hold a moment! I have had the most splendid thought! You must remain and assist me with today's etiquette lesson."

"I am honored," he said with a slight bow. "But I believe I am truly meant to be elsewhere."

"Perhaps, but you are wanted *here*, my lord. Your sojourn to the Continent qualifies you as a fine etiquette instructor, if your dancing is any indication. Doubtless you did not notice my presence last night," Mrs. Smith said with a coy smile, "as I took great pains to remain unseen. However, I see all," she claimed with a wag of her brow. "You are a beautiful dancer. As you might have heard hither and yon, it is the dancing at Dance Hall that does the deed."

"And what deed is that?" He attempted but failed to hide the shock in his expression.

"Why, the coming together of a man and a woman," Mrs. Smith pronounced as she advanced into the room while Emily, Mary, and the others followed eagerly in her wake. "They meet, they dance, they fall in love. It is a simple as that."

"I would that it was so, Mrs. Smith." He produced the hat from beneath his arm and placed it on his head. "If an act as commonplace as a waltz had such power, it . . ."

"It what, my lord?" Mrs. Smith gazed at him, her head tilted to one side like one of her stuffed birds, while the young ladies looked on, equally expectant.

Analisa found that she too was most anxious to know his reply. However, the silence stretched out until even the girls refrained from whispering amongst themselves. At long last, a tiny smile tugged at a corner of his mouth, and he dropped his gaze to the floor. "Very well, then," he said as he again removed his hat. "I shall be pleased to assist your lesson. That is not to say they are in dire need of such," he added with a glance that brushed the face of each young lady present. "The salons of Venice were peopled with dolts compared to the pretty manners I witnessed last night."

"*Bravissimo*, my lord!" Mrs. Smith cried as a chorus of sighs and titters bloomed at her back. "Girls," she said, spinning about, "go on up and we shall be with you presently."

The young ladies swarmed from the room, their excited chatter a hum in the air. Emily proved to be more sedate in her departure, but Mary gave Analisa a roughish moue over her shoulder.

Analisa barely restrained a moan as she sank into her chair. "I am utterly humiliated on their behalves. If that is the comportment that compels a man to wed, then I am doomed for a spinster, indeed."

"Never say so, Miss Lloyd-Jones!" Mrs. Smith scurried to put an arm about Analisa's shoulder. "I am afraid the earl," she said with a wave that indicated Lord Northrup at her side, "is too generous in his assessment. Most of these young ladies would do well to emulate your polished manners."

Analisa smiled her gratitude, but could not bring herself to rise and follow the others. "I shall be along in a moment; please do proceed without me."

"Oh!" Mrs. Smith cried in a small voice. "If you insist, but I shall be down presently to retrieve you in the case you wallow overlong."

Miserable, and on no account she could discern, Analisa waited for Mrs. Smith, followed by Lord Northrup, to quit the room before she laid her head upon the table. As she allowed herself to know fully all that she had lost in the past irretrievable months, tears gathered in her eyes. The latest Season's crop of debutantes were silly, to be sure, but they were young. Doubtless they would all soon marry, whilst Analisa merely grew a year older. She wondered whom Lord Northrup would wed once he gave her up, then wondered why the very notion should smite her heart. It was all too perplexing.

With a sigh, she sat up to draw a handkerchief from her pocket and felt a hand on her shoulder. "Dear Mrs. Smith, you are so kind," she said, dabbing at her nose. "What can I have done to deserve you?"

"Mrs. Smith is correct." The words were spoken in far

too deep a voice to belong to the animated hostess of Dance Hall. "Despite your beauty, it was your unfailingly pretty behavior that first led me to believe you should make me an unexceptionable wife."

Mortified to be discovered weeping, and gravely doubtful of the earl's words, Analisa shot to her feet. "Again, you make sport of me! Allow me to tell you what I think of you. I freely admit your capacity to arrive at conclusions with such remarkable speed is most commendable. However, if I am not too bold, I must insist that it is precision that you lack."

He looked at her in some surprise. "You truly do not believe you should make me an unexceptionable, nay, an excellent wife?" When she did not reply, he uttered a grunt of exasperation. "Miss Lloyd-Jones," he said, pressing her into her chair, "we are meant to marry." He took up a chair opposite her and leaned forward, his expression earnest. "I wrote you letters; your father has verified that you received them—one each month totaling twenty-one in all. I made no secret of my intentions, neither my expectations. There is only a date to be selected and the license to procure, and we shall be man and wife."

Despair flooded her heart, but she refused to wring her hands in his presence. "How can this be?" she asked with a show of false courage. "You claim to find me possessed of characteristics desirable in one's wife. And yet, you were only too happy to be rid of me so early in the evening. I wonder, had you comprehended how your departure last night threatened to leave me bereft of a dancing partner?" It was a small thing compared to the whole of it, but it needled her. "Wasn't your sojourn on the Continent long enough for me sit out every dance?"

He gave her a questioning look. "Matters should prove

different once our betrothal is made public. In the meantime, you know as well as I that it would not be seemly to dance with you more than twice of an evening."

Analisa studied his countenance whilst she contemplated her reply. He looked a bit lost. "Truly, Mr. Wainwright has not informed you of the rules of this house party," she said in disbelief.

"Have I not said as much?"

"Then you haven't come here this morning fully aware you should be the only man present?" she asked, alert to any token of deceit.

"I was aware that I should arrive before Mr. Callerton," he said slowly, "but I deemed it equitable; he went to great lengths to inform me of how he monopolized your evening after my departure last night."

"Oh!" she cried. "How rag-mannered you must think me!" Her skin bloomed with heat, and she knew it had turned scarlet from head to toe. "But, as you must realize, all the others had paired off already." She noted that he looked as nonplussed as ever and pressed on. "At Dance Hall we are allowed to dance with whomsoever we choose, as often as we choose. It is Mrs. Smith's intent for the ladies and gentlemen to pair off. She believes it is a feature of her house parties that results in so many marriages. It is also the explanation as to why she does not allow the men to spend the night here, and for reasons that are all too apparent. However, that is one rule that has not seemed to escape your notice."

"I wonder how it possibly could. The butler would not allow us across the threshold without making it absolutely clear that we should be booted out the door the moment the ball was at an end. Besides which, I have no desire to put myself forward as one in search of a wife. What other purpose should I have to attend the ball but to see you? Once my two dances with you were at an end, I felt it best to take myself off."

He was so patient, so kind; it was all too bewildering. "What you must think of me! It is no wonder you quizzed me about my manners," she said in a small voice.

"I have done no such thing. I spoke the pure truth when I commented on your admirable manners. However, dancing most of the night with Callerton, well, I do confess I thought it ill done of you. I most willingly beg your pardon."

Analisa forced aside the gratitude that swelled in her heart. "And I must do the same. But, I must ask, with whom had you expected me to dance? You have them all terrified to so much as speak to me."

"Have I?" He gave her a measured look. "Callerton danced with you, and what is more, he seems to have survived it unscathed."

Analisa laughed. "Time will tell. If he is not present tomorrow, I shall deem him rolled up in a ditch somewhere between here and Dun Hafan never again to be seen."

It was the earl's turn to laugh. She admired how it enlarged his eyes and made his countenance glow.

Her heart light, she decided that twitting Lord Northrup was pleasant work, indeed. "Do not say you granted Mr. Callerton permission to dance with me prior to last night. It would be a humiliation past bearing. And, oh! Not Mr. Wainwright as well? I have been utterly deluded. I thought perhaps he loved me, just a little," she said with a sad smile.

"But of course he does," he said, his smile fading. "As do . . . others." He dropped his gaze to the tabletop and studied a scratch in the gleaming wood with an intensity the men of her acquaintance most usually only afforded a horse at auction.

"Others?" she asked in astonishment. "I had not thought

it possible." The pain of many months spent in doubt as to her worthiness to wed threatened to overwhelm her once again. Instead, she trained her thoughts on the way in which a ray of sunlight caught his hair afire, motes of dust dancing in every direction like so many tiny sparks. He looked up too suddenly for her to turn away, and his gaze caught in her own. As much as she wished to, she could not look away; his eyes were so beguiling, so blue, and so very wounded.

"I am persuaded you know of what I speak," he said, his brow furrowed. "You have had my letters."

She did have them, somewhere, but she was reluctant to tell him the truth: that after the first few missives, she had declined to read most of the ones that followed. She knew he deserved to know of it, but she pushed the notion of confession from her mind together with the import of his words.

"Let us speak no more of it at present," she suggested. His lack of an immediate reply to this proposal felt nearly as disconcerting as the bouts of angry exhortation to which he had treated her in the past. "We had best join the others," she urged as she rose to her feet. "Mrs. Smith will be fretting."

He rose as well. "Miss Lloyd-Jones, it seems that you spoke true last night; indeed, you cannot like me. To wed you against your desires . . ." He gripped and re-gripped the brim of his hat. "The very notion is repugnant to me. When last we met, I was young and self-important, too enamored of my position to consider you anything but delighted to be my wife."

Analisa knew him to be correct. Indeed, when last they met, he was a boy to whom she had often been tempted to read a catalog of his faults. The man that stood before her was older and even wiser, one who no longer hid behind a defense of pure arrogance. She found that she had no wish to injure him and chose her words with care. "Yes, very young, and I so heedless and contrary," she said breezily. "I often do just as I please. Father supposed you would take me in hand, but Colin agreed that I should only lead you a merry dance."

He looked down at the hat between his hands, the air thick with words unspoken. Finally, he sketched a bow and paced to the door. She watched him go, her heart a jumble of emotions, foremost among them the desire that he remain by her side. To her astonishment, he turned around when he gained the door and regarded her with an unwavering gaze.

"Miss Lloyd-Jones, I attended the ball because I wished to speak with you of our future together. More than that, I wished to see you; it has been so long since we have met." He paused and allowed himself to gaze openly upon her hair, her eyes, her lips. "When I discerned your distress, I felt it as my own. My only wish was to see you happy. You wanted to dance, and so I took steps to ensure that you did so. Your happiness made me happier," he said with a somber smile, "than I have felt in recent memory."

"I know not what to say," she said, feebly.

"No, you must say nothing, only hear me out," he insisted. "I left Dance Hall last night firm in the belief that I had indeed become a better man, a man more worthy of you. And yet, I find that I have not changed at all; until a few moments ago, I fully anticipated that you would like the man I have become every bit as much as I had expected you to like the boy I was before I went away."

She wanted nothing more than to afford him some comfort, to insist that he had indeed changed, that she did like him better than she had in days past. However, in the end, there was nothing she could say that would not wound as much as enlighten. She bent her head to hide the tears that sprang to her eyes, and when she again looked up, he was gone.

Four

Fouette—A Series of Turns

Analisa waited a moment before opening the door to peek into the passage. She neither saw nor heard anything of Lord Northrup and found that the knowledge restored her equilibrium. She dried her eyes and plumped her cheeks as she made her way up the stairs and into the salon where she supposed the girls were deep into their etiquette lesson. Contrary to the excitement and lively chatter she expected, Analisa encountered a scene of orderly calm. The girls were quietly seated, hands in their laps, their pretty ankles crossed beneath their chairs. They watched someone in the center of the room with a degree of attention she had believed to be beyond their capacities.

To her astonishment, it was Lord Northrup. Next to him stood Emily, her hands clasped in his. Analisa felt her mouth fall open; she had thought him to have quit the premises altogether. As for Emily, the glazed expression of adoration on her face prompted in Analisa the avid desire to scratch out the eyes of her dearest friend.

"Mrs. Smith," Analisa said in a voice that wavered. "Pray, pardon my tardiness."

Mrs. Smith nodded, indicating that Analisa should find an empty chair and be seated. Such a task proved difficult in light of the fact that her legs had turned to water.

"I do hope you are feeling more the thing, my dear," Mrs. Smith empathized, prompting the girls, as one, to finally drag their attentions from Lord Northrup to stare at Analisa. She knew not where to look—certainly not at Lord Northrup, who gazed at her with what she supposed to be an unbearable pity. Neither could she bear the sight of Emily, who continued to look at the earl as if he were the only man in England.

"Here we are," Mrs. Smith said as she studied a piece of parchment through a pair of horn-rimmed spectacles. "We have just touched on the rule that proclaims a lady must always rest her hands palms up. We have also gone over when and how and which length gloves to wear. However, we shall not retrace our steps, Miss Lloyd-Jones, on your account; I am persuaded you have much experience in these matters."

Audible whispers, many of them full of mirth, leaped across the room like a flame to oil, in spite of Mrs. Smith's bewildered disapproval. Analisa, however, was not in any doubt as to the cause of their laughter. Her cheeks burned; it would be more charitable if Mrs. Smith refrained from continually alluding to the fact that Analisa was not a chit fresh from the schoolroom. Though she knew that her lack of masculine admiration was due to Lord Northrup's instructions, the others did not. Clearly, they thought her an object of fun.

"Now then, ladies." Mrs. Smith clapped her hands, and

the girls returned their attentions to their hostess. "We are now to discuss what is to be done if a gentleman were to take you by the hands, as demonstrated by Lord Northrup. He does it very well, does he not?" she asked, her face beaming. "Why I have never thought to invite a gentleman to the etiquette class before now, I do not know."

The young ladies in the room came undone at this, and it was more than a few moments before Mrs. Smith regained order. Meanwhile, Lord Northrup continued to clutch Emily's hands with a tenacity Analisa felt to be entirely needless. Her thoughts dwelt on the notion that, if he did not take care, one might suppose he had feelings for Emily. The very idea was absurd, silly, and entirely impossible. Why it made Analisa wish to take a pair of scissors to every one of Emily's gowns, she could not begin to fathom.

With a start, Analisa realized she had long depended on Lord Northrup's feelings for her. When she had bemoaned her lot as the least admired young lady in all of England, she comforted herself with the knowledge that he admired her, and above all others. Now, as he smiled into the eyes of her erstwhile, dearest friend, Analisa felt as if the last vestiges of wind had been lost from her sails.

"I commend you, ladies, on your attentiveness," Mrs. Smith pronounced. "Lord Northrup, do proceed."

Exactly what it was the earl was meant to do, over and above smiling at Emily like a loon, Analisa could not discern. For this, she need must get closer. "Mrs. Smith," she called, throwing her hand aloft. "I should like to assist."

Her hostess looked a bit taken aback, but she soon recovered. "Of course, Miss Lloyd-Jones, how have I not thought of it?"

Analisa rose, the weakness in her knees banished, and

briskly made her way to the center of the room. "You may sit down now, Emily," she hissed.

"Not at all, Miss Everitt, you shall remain just as you are," Mrs. Smith proclaimed.

Analisa thought Lord Northrup's smile grew broader at the words, but she was unable to see properly what was happening as Mrs. Smith had taken her by the hand and dragged her in the opposite direction. Once Analisa was placed a few feet from the one she had hoped to replace, their hostess addressed the company at large.

"I must enlist the services of another." As there was no lack of volunteers, the time it took to choose one and have her situated next to Analisa seemed a short eternity, one in which she imagined Emily and Lord Northrup stared into one another's eyes.

"Now, Lord Northrup," Mrs. Smith adjured, "please carry on if you will."

Analisa could not help but feel that he and Emily excelled at their commission, whatever that might be, and required no prompting. However, she dared not say so.

"Miss Lloyd-Jones, you shall take Miss Gibbons by the hands just as the earl has done." Mrs. Smith took hold of one of Analisa's hands in preparation to mold it into the desired shape.

"Mrs. Smith!" Analisa said in low tones. "I am hardly an infant."

"There, there, dear, you shall get it right in no time, you shall see."

With a determined smile, one to replace the roll of the eyes she would have dearly loved to execute, Analisa grasped Miss Gibbons's hands in her own and stood exactly as she supposed Lord Northrup and Emily, now behind her and out of her line of vision, were so doing.

"Exceptional!" Mrs. Smith smiled her pleasure. "Now, young ladies, I wish you to imagine this as you with the young man of your choice. I dare say your thoughts have all alighted on a gentleman; you shall require no assistance in so doing, I am persuaded. If there are two or more of you thinking of the same man, it matters not; you shall keep his identity a secret. There are many to choose from, though I daresay it should prove difficult to think of any but our very own Lord Northrup, so handsome and pleasing is he in his manner as well as his appearance."

Another chorus of giggles rose into the air.

"Mrs. Smith, shall we not proceed?" Analisa whispered.

"What is that, dear?" her hostess asked. "Do speak up!"

Analisa suppressed a groan. "I am concerned for Emily. Her arms must be growing fatigued," she hedged, "being as high in the air as they are."

"As they are being held in such strong, masculine hands, I do doubt it. Now, Lord Northrup and Miss Lloyd-Jones, who shall play the gentleman in this sketch, I wish you both to behave as if you are whispering sweet nothings into the ear of your young lady."

Analisa immediately heard a slight rustle as the earl leaned closer to Emily. Analisa knew she was expected to do the same, but she stayed rooted to the spot upon overhearing his words. They were in Italian, but having been instructed in a number of foreign languages, she translated the words with little difficulty: *To live without loving is not truly living.* She burned with indignation; it was patently unfair of Lord Northrup to encourage Emily when he hadn't the slightest intention of pursuing her hand.

"Miss Lloyd-Jones," Mrs. Smith chirped. "We are waiting!"

With a start, Analisa dipped forward and muttered some nonsense into Miss Gibbons's ear.

"What was that?" Miss Gibbons said with a gasp. "I couldn't make it out."

"Miss Gibbons, your actions are the very picture of what one must *not* do when presented with just this predicament," Mrs. Smith pointed out. "As we can see, Miss Everitt is the very essence of proper comportment. See how her eyes shine and her cheeks blush so prettily? Now, it would not be *de rigueur* to signify that one has heard the words of one's admirer. No, no, no, that would not be maidenly in the least. One might even choose to turn one's face away and gaze at the ground, taking care that one's profile is displayed to full advantage, just so." She put her fingers to Miss Gibbons's pallid face and turned it to the side. "And yet, one does not wish to discourage one's *amour* if one wishes him to approach one's father with an offer of marriage. It is a matter most delicate."

"Shall we make another attempt, Mrs. Smith?" Lord Northrup asked.

"Yes! The very thing! We shall look to both of you young ladies to demonstrate the correct response this time, shall we not?" Mrs. Smith warned.

Once again, Analisa found it impossible to obey before she heard Lord Northrup's compliment. He spoke in a louder voice than previously. As such, she could only assume it was his wish to be overheard making love to Emily.

"Today I touched a rose and knew it had been created in imitation of your silken cheek."

Analisa longed to verify her suspicion—that Emily's "silken cheek" blushed as prettily as before. It was the slight intake of breath, executed to perfection by Emily, that caused Analisa's blood to boil. In a miff, she leaned forward to whisper her message into the ear of Miss Gibbons and said what first came to mind: "You go too far."

"What was that?" Miss Gibbons gasped. "How can I have done?" she wailed, wringing her hands. "I have done nothing that might shame any creature!"

"That will do, Miss Gibbons." Mrs. Smith fairly pushed her into the nearest chair, taking no care to determine whether or not it was already occupied. It was, and Mary Arthur, Miss Gibbons splayed across her lap, was having none of it.

"You are crushing me, Yvette!" Mary ground out. "You would do well to avoid sweets in future."

Miss Gibbons burst into tears upon this pronouncement, and the recurrent babble rose into the air.

"Do find your own seat, Miss Gibbons!" Mrs. Smith called out above the commotion exactly as if she was not the cause of this particular fracas.

Just as Analisa resolved to step forward and assist in restoring order to the room, she felt a presence at her side.

"It is said," came the voice of Lord Northrup, husky in her ear, "that silk was born of man's desire to recreate the touch of his lover's lips."

Analisa felt her eyes grow wide as she restrained the urge to confront him; it should only prove to place her lips, silken or otherwise, in alarming proximity to his. Unaccountably, all of her hostess's admonitions fled, and she turned her face as far from Lord Northrup as possible, her chin held high.

"Tut-tut, Miss Lloyd-Jones," he said, his voice low. "Mrs. Smith would not approve. You are merely in need of further practice. Never fear, I have saved my favorite till the end. God," he murmured as he stepped so close that his chin grazed the top of her ear, "made the rose as a rehearsal for his final masterpiece; that of Woman."

Each puff of air from his lips sent tendrils of her hair aquiver followed by a renewed weakness in her knees. However, she refused to afford him another excuse to find her lacking and looked down in as demure a fashion as even Mrs. Smith could wish. It spared her the humiliation she might have endured if she had indulged her impulse to look up into his eyes.

"Ladies! That is quite enough!" Mrs. Smith insisted, but it seemed to Analisa as if the words came from a faraway place and time. The reality of Miss Analisa Lloyd-Jones consisted only of herself and one other—the man who stood so near that a sigh too deeply taken should prove sufficient movement to throw them together. There was naught to feel but the heat of his chest at her shoulder; to smell but his heady cologne; to hear but the flow of his breath against her hair.

She felt she should faint if her gown should as much as brush against him. Her body began to tremble as her muscles tired of their rigid state. When she felt the earl's hand at her wrist, his touch so light she first thought it but a feather, she nearly jumped in alarm. Slowly, as if not to cause her any dismay, he moved his hand until it covered hers. She could not recall when a man other than her brother or father had touched her ungloved hand, and she trembled anew.

When he stepped away, the air that rushed in at his absence was like a burst of winter on her skin. The voices of the others in the room suddenly made their way to her ears and, somehow, she, the earl, and Emily all stood in their former positions.

"Let us resume our lesson, ladies," Mrs. Smith admonished. "Miss Arthur, you shall demonstrate to us the manner in which a proper young lady offers an apology to another young lady. And Miss Gibbons, you shall do the same. Be warned, it needs must be contrite!"

Analisa attempted to attend to Mrs. Smith's instruction to no avail. Instead, Analisa marveled at how Emily felt a mere shadow, one that did little to fill the space between Analisa and Lord Northrup. It was if he yet stood by her side, his breath warm on her skin, his hand caressing hers. Measuring the distance from the corner of her eye, she determined that to feel his presence was quite impossible, and yet she was assailed with sensations she had only felt when he was in her orbit.

Without warning, she somehow became aware that the room had once again broken out into chaos, and that Mrs. Smith was greatly distressed.

"I have never been so ashamed of the rackety manners of a group of girls at one of my house parties," their hostess proclaimed. "I am sorry to say that I regret allowing Lord Northrup to join our lesson; his presence is surely the catalyst of this bickering and weeping." She paused for breath and more than one sob was heard to hang in the air. "Well!" Mrs. Smith huffed. "That is quite enough! Each and every one of you, upstairs, now!"

Farthest from the door, Analisa lingered as the others departed. Each dipped a curtsy for the earl, and he favored them with a courtly bow in return. Emily stood at his side, hands clasped regally as if she were his countess bidding their guests good night. Mrs. Smith hovered at the door to offer a bit of advice or praise to each girl as she departed and so was not availed of this piece of nonsense.

Finally, Emily was the only young lady in the room other than Analisa. Lord Northrup offered her the very same circumspect bow he gave the others, but she would not be discouraged.

"Lord Northrup," she said in breathy tones, "I am persuaded you should make a most satisfactory dancing partner at lesson on the morrow."

"Is there a dancing lesson tomorrow to which the gentlemen are invited?" He smiled in genuine pleasure.

Analisa's thoughts divided into several themes at the sight: one as to how blue were his eyes when pleased, and two, what manner of cad could encourage the attentions of a girl not five minutes after secretly making love to another.

Convinced that her father must learn of the earl's perfidy, she resolved to write him a letter at her first opportunity. Still, she lingered even after Emily had finally removed herself from the room. Analisa refused, however, to grant the earl anything more than the curtsy required by Mrs. Smith. Lord Northrup bowed in return, his back to his hostess. This action left him free to hold out his hand in quest of Analisa's.

She hesitated to oblige, but when he lifted his gaze to hers, she found she could not deny him. With a genuine show of reluctance, she placed her hand within his reach. He did not kiss it as she both hoped and feared but clung to it a bit longer than was seemly. Apparently, his store of sweet nothings was exhausted for he said nothing before he turned away to bid farewell to Mrs. Smith.

Analisa watched him walk through the door and down the hall to the head of the staircase. Once he descended the first few steps, the last sign of his dark red curls disappeared from view. Only then did she notice the gift he had left her; in the center of her palm lay the velvet-soft petal of a red rose.

Five

A la Seconde—Second Position

In the morning after breakfast, Analisa read and approved the letter she had written the night prior. She affixed a seal to the parchment, blew on the red wax until it hardened, and turned to her abigail. "Ruby, take this below stairs and arrange for it to be delivered to Father at once. Tell the messenger that he should wait for Mr. Lloyd-Jones's reply."

"Yes, miss." Ruby curtsied. "Have you asked that your papa should send you the earl's letters, then?"

Analisa gave the girl a warning look, softened by an indulgent smile. "The contents of my letter are entirely my affair."

"Yes, miss, o' course, but I was only hoping that you should finally read them."

"I agree, Ruby, but only because I do so despise being ignorant of what I am expected to know." She did not add that she had also informed her father of the earl's weakened stance as to their betrothal contract. "Additionally, I have hinted at the possibility of a proposal from a gentleman other than the earl."

"Oh, miss!" Ruby exclaimed. "I do hope you told him about the particular attentions of Mr. Wainwright and Mr. Callerton. I should be pleased to take up residence in the home of either gentleman."

"Whosoever would not?" Analisa stood in hopes it would hasten Ruby in the execution of her task. "I do believe either should make me a most comfortable husband. I have told Father as much."

"Certainly your papa should have no objections to Mr. Wainwright," Ruby said eagerly. "But Mr. Callerton is a bit of a mystery, is he not?"

"This is true. Father shall look into the matter, I have no doubt. Needless to say, he shall know nothing of it save you get below stairs with the letter and have it dispatched forthwith."

"Yes, o' course, miss," Ruby said, her eyes wide with the weight of her responsibility. "I shall make a great to-do about it in the servant's hall and insist they send their fastest manservant."

"That will do, Ruby," Analisa said with a fond smile. "Now go!"

Once the zealous maidservant had departed with the letter, Analisa cast about for something to occupy her time until the coming dancing lesson. Her eye fell on the rose petal where it lay on her dressing table, and she wondered where the earl had come by such. Donning a bright red, hooded cape, she set out to comb the garden for a rose bush that had survived the storms of winter.

At present, the weather was mild with no snow having fallen the past fortnight; nevertheless, she was skeptical that a rose bush might have burst into bloom in the interim. She skirted the house as she assumed that the bushes closest to shelter were most likely to bear blooms. To her disappointment, she found little more than berries.

She continued her search, persuaded that Lord Northrup had pocketed the petal during his walk about the house the morning previous. As she came round the far corner of Dance Hall, she encountered a greenhouse made almost entirely of glass. Doubtless it harbored a rose bush or two.

To her delight, she found an outer door and took the cold, smooth latch in her hand. She pulled it and was besieged by waves of warm, moist air mingled with the aromas of numberless blooms. Enchanted, she breathed deeply of the orange and lemon blossoms, then removed a glove so as to run her fingers along the rows of herbs to release their pungent aromas. Eventually, a melodic splash of water came to her ears. She pushed back the hood from her hair and wandered about until she found her way to a fountain, its pool stocked with brightly colored fish. Across from it was the door into the house proper, flanked on either side by a potted rose bush. Each bloomed with a riot of deep red petals.

The bright blooms were so tempting; what had possibly induced the earl to pilfer only a single petal? She reached out to finger the velvet buds, taking care to avoid the thorns. Lost in her private world, she was greatly startled when she suddenly sensed a presence by her side.

Thinking it to be one of her friends, she whirled about to discover Mr. Callerton regarding her, his eyes dancing with pleasure.

"Oh my! I'm afraid I must look the very picture of fright." Her heart beat so with apprehension that she feared it could be seen as it knocked against the folds of her cloak.

"You are a picture, indeed—one painted by a great master." He folded himself into a deep bow. "What other explanation could there be for such brilliant color in your cheeks?"

"Oh," she breathed as her hands flew to cover the marks of her distress. "It is over warm in here, is it not?"

"Indeed." He paused and looked about him for a moment. "There is a settee just to the other side of those palms. Let us sit." He did not wait for her response before he took her arm in his and led her thither.

Gratefully, she sank onto the high-backed bench and busied herself with the removal of her other glove. She could hardly believe her good fortune in stumbling across Mr. Callerton less than an hour after dispatching a letter to her father. She opened her mouth to broach an acceptable subject on which to converse but was taken aback when Mr. Callerton seated himself a mere few inches from her person. To her further dismay, he reached out to pull the string of her hood without so much as a by your leave.

Free of its moorings, the lush red cloak slid down her arms to puddle about her. Before she could surmise what he was about, he deftly flicked the soft folds from her lap, an act that left her in no doubt as to his experience handling women's garments. As she was not in the least wishful of a husband utterly lacking in worldly wisdom, she set aside her constraint and studied him with renewed interest.

"Many thanks," she said with what she hoped was a glowing smile. "I shall now recover from the heat soon enough."

"Not too soon, I pray." He took her chin between his thumb and finger and made a show of studying her face. "That blush upon your cheek is so lovely; I am persuaded that I have never seen its equal."

Analisa felt unable to respond with her chin yet his captive. To her relief, he released her in response to a beseeching glance. Unfortunately, he dropped his hand instead to her thigh, a circumstance any number of beseeching glances failed to rectify.

"Have you toured much of the Continent?" She would rather have asked him when he intended to remove his hand, but she had never before been properly courted. As such, she dared not say anything that should spoil her chances of receiving an offer of marriage.

"Yes, of course. It is where the earl and I first became acquainted. Has he not written to you of me?"

"Let us not speak of Lord Northrup," she proposed with a coy smile, one she prayed would deter him from posing further questions to which she did not possess answers.

"But of course." He lifted his hand from her thigh and laid it against her cheek.

"What brings you here so early today, Mr. Callerton?" she asked, while, swiftly, she placed her gloves where his hand had once been. "The gentlemen are not expected for the dancing lesson until this afternoon."

"Would it be scandalous to confess my only object was to see you?"

The lecture from the etiquette lesson the day prior came forcibly to her mind; her instructor would have been most appreciative of the maidenly constraint with which Analisa looked away.

Mr. Callerton laughed and dropped his hand to her shoulder, whereupon he began to rub his thumb along her collarbone. "Though I had not expected to find you on your own. Hasn't Mrs. Smith intentions for you?"

"I daresay the younger girls are enjoying another etiquette lesson, but I have excused myself. I pray I am not too bold when I say that there is little Mrs. Smith can teach me. It has been long since I left the schoolroom, after all." Analisa prayed that her words evoked visions of a tree full of ripening, rather than rotting, fruit. "Now, pray tell, for what purpose have you come in search of me?" She realized the moment she so longed for had possibly arrived and her heart again began to take up a lively beat.

"Very well, then, I shall admit the truth: I have thought of nothing but you since the other night. Is that something of which I should be ashamed?" He smiled and gazed directly into her eyes in so easy a manner, she felt not the least discomfited by it.

"Not at all! Need I be ashamed to confess that I have had you in my mind not an hour past?"

He raised his brows in what looked to be some astonishment. "I am delighted to hear you say so, but, I must say," he added with a chuckle, "I am relieved that Laurie is not present to overhear our *tête-à-tête*."

Analisa felt her brow crease in confusion. "Pray forgive me, am I meant to know this Laurie?"

"Why, yes, of course! Lord Northrup—you don't suppose his friends call him such."

"Yes, I had supposed they had done. He became a lord at such a tender age, he was already Lord Northrup when first we met."

"I'm afraid you have it rather backward," Mr. Callerton explained. "His name is Gabriel—Gabriel Lawrence."

She was enthralled by how different the earl's given name sounded in contrast to his title. "I do believe it suits him. Why ever should anyone wish to call him Laurie?"

"I suspect he picked it up at school. Boys are merciless upon these matters, which is precisely how I became known as Dora."

"Dora! Surely you jest, Mr. Callerton."

He smiled and drew his hand along her shoulder, bringing it to rest at the base of her neck. "Not at all. It's the worst they could do with my given name of Theodore."

"It is a lovely name," she said pleasantly enough, though she wished he might keep his hands to himself. "I do believe it suits you."

"Ah, but do I suit *you*, Miss Lloyd-Jones?"

Finally, they were coming to the matter at hand. "Am I to be pumped for clues on the state of my heart?" she quipped.

Mr. Callerton plucked her hand from her lap and held it between his own. "Ah, but the heart is not the matter under discussion, is it, Miss Lloyd-Jones?"

"By that, I surmise you refer to the supposition that claims with whom one aligns oneself is as dependent on practicalities as it is on mutual attraction." Analisa heard an echo of her father's harsh sentiments in her words but knew she was correct; one could not hope to enjoy a successful marriage with a man she did not like. Conversely, one might very possibly be attracted to the handsome stable boy but as a husband, he would never do.

"I perceive that you begin to understand me," Mr. Callerton said in tones so low it threatened to undermine her equanimity.

His manner was so varied from that whilst they danced a few nights prior that Analisa found she could not predict his intentions. His eyes, curtained as they were by a row of thick lashes, harbored nary an inkling of his thoughts. "I believe that I do, Mr. Callerton, but one mustn't speculate. If there is anything you wish to say to me or perhaps a question you wish to ask, I assure you, I am eager to learn what it is."

He looked up to meet her gaze, and a slow smile spread

across his face. "It is only that I fear to cause you any astonishment. I would not have you alarmed on my account."

She shifted about to face him more fully. "I believe you will find me more prepared for your question," she prodded, "or whatever it is you have to say," she added with a bright smile, "than you suppose."

He gazed at her in silence, but the growing light in his eyes spoke volumes. She owned it was pleasant to be so admired but found she was impatient to hear his offer of marriage. To that end, when he guided her face to his, she closed her eyes and relented.

She had never before been kissed, had no experience with which to compare, but she felt his was a competent kiss. His mouth was pleasantly cool against her own and soft as a baby's breath. Sadly, it almost seemed to end before it began. A bit crestfallen, she opened her eyes to find that he looked at her with a hunger that caused her no undue amount of consternation.

"Am I wrong to believe you and I shall rub along together better than most, Miss Lloyd-Jones?" Before she had a chance to so much as nod her head, he gathered her into his arms and pulled her close as if to kiss her again—and again and again if she read his expression aright.

"I must ask you to stop, Mr. Callerton." She ensured that her voice was firm. "There is much to be settled before there can be more between us, do you not agree?"

He withdrew his arms with a rueful laugh. "You are wiser than I presumed, which is all to the good. I shall not tremble in my boots for your sake on account of Laurie."

Analisa felt her ire rise at the implication. "It is true, at times, he has spoken of our betrothal as a *fait accompli*, but there has been no official announcement. There have been times, as well, when he has admitted to doubts that we should truly suit." She thought back on his remarks in the breakfast room when he had admitted how wrong he had been to make assumptions. "I am persuaded that were I to receive another offer, he would consider me released from any obligation."

Mr. Callerton emitted a gusty sigh. "I know him well enough and do not believe he shall concede defeat as readily as you suppose. I do, however, enjoy a challenge and shall look forward to what remains of a most amusing house party."

"He shall not be angry, if that is what you fear. He has proven that he can be a gentleman when he so chooses. And, I might add," she said as she removed Mr. Callerton's hand that had found its way again to her thigh, "that I fully expect you to behave as one as well."

He laughed again as he crossed his arms and held them tight against his chest. "I shall behave myself for now, as long as you promise that you shall be mine."

"But of course I do, Mr. Callerton." She attempted and failed to deny the sense of triumph that rose in her breast. "I do ask, however, that you allow me to inform the earl of how matters stand when I deem it most suitable. Between now and then, whenever that shall be, you must be patient. Matters might prove difficult, even a bit distressing, with the both of you harbored under my father's roof, but I believe it shall all come about in the end."

"I believe the word *excruciating* to be more fitting," he said as he carried her hand to his lips and kissed it. "But I am nothing if not a patient man."

Analisa would not have predicted that matters could be settled so quickly and satisfactorily. She regretted that she did not love Mr. Callerton, but she liked him very much indeed. "You are a man of many superior qualities, and I anticipate the discovering of them with great pleasure."

Mr. Callerton rose to his feet, her hand still in his. "Laurie and I have spent much time together in our travels on the Continent. He spoke of you so often and with such admiration that I imagined you to be quite different than I now find you. He is, after all, such a paragon of rectitude."

"I know not what to make of your observations, Mr. Callerton. However, I am persuaded Lord Northrup admires me for a number of reasons."

"Indeed, I did not mean to imply that you are in any way lacking!" Mr. Callerton exclaimed. "Naturally, he spoke of your beauty so often that I wondered at it. And yet, it was his notion of beauty that I doubted. I believed such a Puritan would define beauty far differently than would I. In this, I have erred."

"Thank you, Mr. Callerton," she said with a smile calculated to charm. "That was prettily said. Now I believe I must return to the house."

"Of course, and from here I shall take your leave."

He helped her to rise, and she felt light as a feather under the strength of his arm. It was very pleasant and spoke of many pleasant days to come. Theirs would not be a marriage of mutual passion, but she found that she expected less of life than she had when she was sought out and fawned over by every eligible man in her sphere. "I look forward to this afternoon's dancing lesson but be warned, I expect Lord Northrup shall insist I spend the course of the lesson with him."

With a twinkle in his eye, Mr. Callerton released her hand and favored her with the deepest of bows. "Until then, my dear."

Six

Chasse—To Chase and Replace One Foot with Another

Analisa remained in the greenhouse until Mr. Callerton made his way outside. Once he had disappeared from view, she heaved a sigh; she felt entirely spent. Taking up her cloak and gloves, she followed the music of the fountain to the entrance of the house. Reluctant to discover what new vexation might await her on the other side of the door, she lingered over the roses. It occurred to her that a few of the buds would make a lovely coronet to wear with her new gown come the ball. Her head full of such agreeable notions, she opened the door to discover the earl in the passage.

"Lord Northrup!" she gasped. She knew it impossible, yet she could not help but feel that her secret was plain for him to see. "The dancing lesson does not commence for some time."

"I fear I have arrived earlier than is seemly," he said as he held his arm out to her, "but I wished to speak with you."

"Of course." She took his arm with no small amount of apprehension. "How did you find me?"

"I nearly did not. The greenhouse was the last place you could be."

"I own I have never before ventured into this part of the house. *I* hardly know where I am."

"Never fear, I shall lead you to safety."

"Thank you, my lord," she replied as she fretted as to whether or not they were likely to encounter her new beau before they gained the front hall. "Was it your friend, Mr. Callerton, who informed you of my whereabouts?"

"I haven't seen him. Is he at Dance Hall?"

"Why, yes, he is," she replied, choosing her words carefully. "He stumbled upon me in the greenhouse, quite by accident. I hadn't even known that is where I was headed."

"Perhaps he followed in your wake." His voice betrayed nothing of the tension she could feel in the muscles of his arm.

"I doubt not the possibility. In any case, we had the liveliest discussion about diminutives of Christian names. Were you aware he was called Dora at school?"

"Yes," he said shortly. "What's more, I might easily contrive to introduce a dozen topics of conversation far more lively."

She was not in the least deluded by his show of indifference. "Perhaps, but there was more said of even greater interest, at least to me. He explained how you came to be called Laurie." She could not help but look up to ascertain his reaction to her words and was delighted to see his ears turn a bright shade of red.

"My father always used my proper name. It has been years now since I have heard it spoken."

"Gabriel is a lovely name, but I like Laurie too," she said with a smile that owed nothing to artifice.

"Perhaps, but 'Lordy Laurie' was a regular taunt I should never wish to hear again," he said darkly.

"To be sure," she said as gravely as she could manage around her incipient laughter. "I suppose you should never forgive me if, in that, I should find anything amusing."

He came to a halt and guided her about so that they stood face-to-face. "I should forgive you most anything, and willingly," he insisted, taking her hand in both of his. "However, you must see that to make light of something so disagreeable is nothing short of cruel."

"Pray forgive me, my lord." She felt her smile slip from her face. "I had no desire to cause you a moment of distress. You never need fear that I shall do so in such a way again."

He made no reply, but she saw clearly the pain in his eyes.

"You were so young a lord," she said slowly as realization dawned, "and vulnerable. To have lost your father when yet a schoolboy, to then be head of the family as well! What a burden to be endured by one so bereft of years."

"Yes," he said, his gaze flickering away from hers as if he felt shame at the very memory.

"Pray forgive me. If I had but thought . . ."

To her astonishment, he pressed her captive hand to his chest and covered it with his own. "Analisa," he said as if the weight of her name felt foreign on his tongue. "Have you truly read my letters? Not the ones at the beginning," he instructed, shaking his head. "Those aren't of any value. The ones I wrote once I arrived in Italy and after, those are the ones to which I refer. I fear perhaps they have gone missing."

"Not at all," she was glad to confess. "I received them, one each month, regular as clockwork. It was something upon which I knew I might always depend." She was surprised to realize that she had, indeed, depended on the arrival of his letters. It allowed her to suppose that, even if every other man had forgotten her, one had not.

"Then you must remember that day, the one of which I wrote; I shall never forget what you did."

She hung her head, unaccountably terrified that he should read her expression and learn the truth.

He took her chin in his free hand and drew it up. "You do remember," he prompted, searching her eyes, his own full of hope.

She was painfully aware that she dared not delay her confession any longer but she could think of nothing but the manner in which his heart pounded under her hand. She could not work out what it could possibly mean.

"I do believe this is the moment Mrs. Smith would have me turn away in maidenly modesty." Her words were meant to serve as an amusing distraction, but, to her astonishment, her voice shook and, despite every effort to do otherwise, she found it impossible to look anywhere but his lips. Most alarming of all was the manner in which her heart beat in tandem with his, hard and ever faster.

"Analisa," he whispered as he lowered his head to hers. "So long have I waited for you."

His kiss was that of a man parched with thirst, his lips hot, demanding and too much occupied to bar the groan that rose up from his throat. Quite unlike the kiss bestowed by Mr. Callerton, it was long and lingering. He did not drag her into his arms nor take liberties that implied he thought her his; rather, he plundered her lips as if they were stolen treasure he could no longer resist or deny.

To her chagrin, nothing had been said in Mrs. Smith's etiquette lesson as to what manner a young lady should espouse when having her lips scorched and her knees buckled. Analisa rather thought she was meant to favor his impertinence with a resounding slap, but her right arm was trapped against his chest, and the other hand, of its own accord, crept up to rest where the curls met the back of his cravat.

When, finally, he lifted his head, hers was swimming so that it proved difficult to think. The smile he offered was as sweet as any she had seen, and she returned it too quickly to allow her time to consider what it might cause him to believe.

"Your father had a message from you before I left for Dance Hall. I was present when he sent your mother to your room in search of letters. Perhaps I am wrong to yet entertain expectations," he said, his words belied by the manner in which his eyes fairly danced. "However, it has given me great hope to know that you wish my poor scribbles near you."

Analisa had never been so grateful for one of Mrs. Smith's lessons for there was not a better moment to look away with maidenly constraint. She was most grateful, also, for the support his arm gave her when he took hers up again to proceed towards the front hall. Weak with fear that he had indeed assumed too much, she fretted that her guilt showed on her face. Having no wish to meet a living soul, the main portion of the house was achieved sooner than she had hoped. Her fears were realized when she spied Emily lingering by the front portal.

"Ah, Miss Everitt," the earl announced in so steady a voice Analisa could not help but wonder at it. "Many thanks for your efforts in locating Miss Lloyd-Jones. As you see, I have found her."

"My lord, how clever of you! But, Analisa, you were meant to attend the etiquette lesson. I was growing anxious on your behalf."

"I went to take a turn about the garden, and when I finally found a door into the house, I became disorientated." Her voice sounded strange in her own ears and more than a little breathless.

"Dearest, you appear to be burning with fever," Emily said. She stepped forward and laid a hand against her friend's cheek.

"Do I?" Analisa replied weakly. "It is nothing. 'Twas exceedingly warm in the greenhouse."

"Greenhouse?" Emily echoed.

"It is quite lovely," the earl replied. "Perhaps Mr. Wainwright would be best pleased to explore it with you, Miss Everitt."

"Mr. Wainwright. But of course," Emily said with an arch look for Analisa.

A prolonged silence fell before Lord Northrup again spoke. "Miss Lloyd-Jones, I wonder if you would be good enough to escort me out onto the drive. There is something I would like to show you."

Analisa noted the gleam in Emily's eye and knew they were of one mind; Lord Northrup meant to renew his proposal of marriage. "I should be happy to do so, my lord, if it requires but a moment," she said in tones meant to dampen his intentions. "It shall be time, soon, for luncheon, followed by the dancing lesson."

Her admonition apparently caused him no concern as he motioned the butler to open the door, after which her suitor took her by the hand and led her out onto the drive. Analisa's heart sank within her; his disappointment at her betrothal to another would now prove greater than it might have less than an hour ago.

"My lord," she began, unsure of what should follow.

Immediately, he stopped and turned to her, his face

wreathed in smiles. For the first time in her memory, she believed him comelier than any man of her acquaintance.

It was at that moment Mr. Callerton burst from the house, Emily in his wake. Analisa knew not whether to be relieved at the delay of the inevitable or apprehensive of what was now to come. As she snatched her hand from the earl's grasp, a rider appeared on the path from the gatehouse and proceeded towards them at great speed.

Mr. Callerton seemed to take notice of naught but Analisa. "Miss Lloyd-Jones, you are utterly charming," he proclaimed as he edged the earl to one side and took her hand in his. "I so enjoyed our little *tête-à-tête* this afternoon."

She watched Mr. Callerton bend over her hand and kiss it as if it were happening to another girl entirely. Rather, it was the earl who claimed all of her attention. Her heart hammered in trepidation as, slowly, a crease appeared between his brows, and the smile fell from his face. She was never to know his further reaction to Mr. Callerton's behavior for in that moment the rider forced his mount nearly to Analisa's side and, with a spray of crushed limestone, ground to a halt.

"You fool!" Mr. Callerton placed himself as a barrier between Analisa and the restive horse. "You have put the lady in some danger."

"I beg your pardon," the rider said as he slid to the ground, "but I was told to deliver this without delay." The rider held out a packet just as Mr. Callerton reached for it, and the ensuing collision sent the entire bundle of papers tumbling to the ground. The rider lost no time in attempting to collect them, but Mr. Callerton would have none of it. The manner in which he pushed the boy away was so proprietary as to be brash.

"Why, Miss Lloyd-Jones, how extraordinary." Mr.

Callerton turned to her, his hands full of packets of parchment, most with seals unbroken. "These look to be Laurie's letters to you from our days on the Continent. Perhaps *now* you might read what he wrote of me," he suggested with a broad smile.

Quickly, she looked to the earl, her heart quailing within her as he plucked a sampling of parchment from Mr. Callerton's hand. In disbelief, Lord Northrup shuffled through the still-sealed letters until, finally, the anger she had so feared since his return became agonizingly apparent.

"What am I to make of this?" he demanded with far more restraint than she had dared to expect.

"As you have surmised, I sent for them. I wished to read them," she began, hoping to explain.

"How can that be? You gave me reason to believe that you *had* done!"

"I have done no such thing," she returned, indignant.

"What you, indeed, have not done was to read my letters followed by your audacity in leading me to believe that you had. And for what purpose should you wish to read them now? To glean from them my assessment of Mr. Callerton?"

Analisa was lost for a reply that would not serve to deepen his anger. Worse, any response she made should only serve to sink her further in his esteem; it was that from which she shrank the most.

"The words I spoke," he ground out as he shook his head in disbelief, "would have remained unsaid if I had but known the true state of your heart." He looked at the ground in dismay, the crease between his brows dark and thunderous. "And in my earnest belief that my feelings were finally returned, I . . ." He pressed his lips together in refusal to air the words that would make the others privy to what should prove to be her shame. "And you allowed it!"

"Lord Northrup," Analisa cried, aghast. "You rather make it sound as if I am expected to be the keeper of your virtue. Do you expect the same from others or is it only I who must ensure that behavior be pristine?"

He frowned in apparent bafflement. "Others?"

She looked him directly in the eye, fulminating as it was, and lifted her chin. "You traveled for nearly two years on the Continent, to Italy and other places as well. I find it difficult to believe that in all of that time you had none for companion but Mr. Callerton."

His face drained white as his eyes opened wide in comprehension. "There have been," he said in clipped tones, "no *others*. That I cannot say the same of you . . ." Jaw gripped tightly against what he might have said, he pushed past Mr. Callerton and threw the fistful of letters in his possession to the ground. Then he swung himself onto the messenger's horse and galloped away.

Mr. Callerton dropped the balance of the missives to join their fellows in the limestone gravel. "I fear Sir Rectitude shall be in a fury for a good while yet," he said as he once again possessed himself of Analisa's hand. "I expect he shall never forgive you. In the end, however," he said with a wink, "it shall clear the way."

"Mr. Callerton," Analisa said slowly. "The dancing lesson shall not commence for several more hours. I would be pleased if you were to leave until expected."

"But of course," he replied with an inclination of the head.

Analisa hardly noticed his departure, so intent was she on the diminishing figure of the earl as he galloped into the distance. She waited until he was well and truly gone before she fell to her knees and allowed the sobs to rise from her throat. When she had plucked every one of his letters from the ground, she stood to discover Emily still in the drive, transfixed in astonishment.

"Analisa, my darling, what has happened?" Emily begged. "How is it possible that anything of note *has* happened? We have only been parted since breakfast."

"Emily, you must swear to me that you shall never tell a soul."

"What might I possibly say?" Emily asked as she went to Analisa's side and put her arms about her. "Though, I shall admit that I am trembling in fear for you."

Analisa relaxed into Emily's arms. "You are my dearest friend, and I swear to tell you all. Only, we must not be overheard."

Together, they entered Dance Hall and made their way to Analisa's chamber. Once she had locked away the letters in her portmanteau, she gave Emily her full attention.

"Lord Northrup kissed me."

"Oh, indeed something *has* happened, and it is terribly exciting! Mrs. Smith would suffer an apoplexy if she knew of it," Emily pronounced with a roll of her eyes. "But I do not see how that has led to such a dreadful altercation."

"I do! Oh, Emily, I have made such a muddle of things," Analisa moaned as she collapsed onto the bed.

"Then, dearest," Emily said as she laid her head on the pillow next to her friend's, "you had best start at the beginning."

"I confess I hardly know where that is. He has always behaved as if I was his due, and it just as unendingly vexed me."

"He vexed us all," Emily said with a sigh. "He was always such a little jackanapes."

"He was no such thing," Analisa insisted, though she

refrained from asking herself why it hurt to hear him made such an object of fun.

"But of course he was! And yet, you were always kind to him, always saw the matter as if looking through his eyes, just as you are doing now."

"Perhaps, but kindness is not love, Emily. He has expected me to *love* him. It has been quite intolerable. Why, he is nothing but a boy—that rusty hair, those freckles! And he ever so tall and thin as a rail!"

"Analisa Lloyd-Jones, now it is you who are the jackanapes! He is a man grown, and his hair is no longer rusty. I don't know precisely how you would name it," Emily mused, her eyes wide with enthusiasm. "But it's so glorious that I wish nothing more than to run my fingers through it the moment I lay eyes on him. Naturally, he is still quite tall, but he has grown into his height, and wonderfully so! And now that his face is no longer as white as a ghost's, one barely perceives the freckles."

Analisa forced down the tremor of anxiety that rose in her heart at Emily's exclamations of delight. "Yes, you are quite right. I suppose my words were meant to explain why I have not read his letters—why I have not wished to—before now."

"Is that what has made him so angry, then?"

"Yes. I was afforded a number of opportunities to tell him the truth and I did not. I was apprehensive," she said with a wan smile. "But that is not all that has made him angry. I can't say how he could possibly have divined the truth about Mr. Callerton, for *he* has kissed me today as well."

Emily's brows rose nearly into her hair. "Analisa Lloyd-Jones! Do remind me to beg off of etiquette lessons in future!"

Analisa chuckled ruefully. "It was not as if I refrained

from attending in pursuit of my first kiss. Rather, I wished to be alone so as to ponder. The other morning, the earl and I came to a bit of an understanding. I made it known that I had no desire to marry him, and he conceded that he was wrong to assume I had done. He gave me reason to entertain hopes that if I should invite an offer of marriage from someone else before he had a chance to post betrothal notices to the papers, he would consider our marriage contract null and void."

"Why have you not spoken of this to me?" Emily demanded.

"I don't know," Analisa said with true regret. "I suppose I felt that you were hoping for an offer from him, yourself."

"Don't be ridiculous! How could I have been ignorant of his intentions towards you? You have spoken of it often enough. But, pray tell, what does this have to do with his letters?"

"He wrote of what he wished me to know," Analisa replied. "His feelings about events that occurred in the past, I believe. That is why I had them fetched; I meant to read them all tonight so that I need no longer lie. But, Emily, that is not all; Mr. Callerton has offered marriage."

"Egad! What are you to do?"

"I shall marry Mr. Callerton. Only . . ."

Emily reached across the counterpane and took her friend's hand in hers. "Only what?"

Analisa sighed as tears started in her eyes. "The notion of causing grief to the earl has precipitated such a dampening of my spirits. And yet, I cannot help but feel that Mr. Callerton shall make me a more comfortable husband, one who shall not expect me to love him in ways that I do not. Does that make me insufferably self-indulgent, Emily?"

"Not insufferably so, I don't believe, but very possibly

foolish. One does not feel downcast over the pain of a man for whom one does not care. And, in all fairness, Lord Northrup offered for you long ago."

"It is true, but when Father informed me that the earl had asked for my hand, I could not refrain from weeping. Even Colin thought it a bad match. He knew Lord Northrup could never manage me, and I agreed."

"Yes, dearest, but since then you have transformed into a woman. No longer are you the petted and adored debutante of every ball, demanding, albeit good-naturedly," Emily added hastily, "to have her way in any disagreement. You are meeker, more biddable, and it is all to the good."

"I suppose I should feel vilified by your words," Analisa remarked. "However, to my astonishment I find that it is only his opinion of me that matters in the least."

Emily reached out and brushed away the tears that streamed down Analisa's face. "Perhaps your path shall be made clear in the reading of his letters."

"Yes," Analisa replied. "They have waited long enough."

Seven

Jete—To Leap

Analisa, Lord Northrup's letters in hand, settled herself on the bed against a quantity of lace-trimmed pillows. Quickly, she put aside the few she had read upon his initial departure two years prior; there was no need to reread such self-important, objectionable words. Then she carefully broke the seal on each of the folded pieces of parchment and arranged them accordingly by date.

> *Frankfurt, September 1815*
> *Miss Lloyd-Jones,*
> *I write to assure you of my safe arrival into Germany. I would not have you unduly alarmed for my safety and have made the assuagement of your fears my first order of business upon obtaining my room. I look forward with great anticipation to the day when our presence in one another's company shall be contiguous, and we might travel together as far and*

wide as we wish. I have not as of yet received any of your letters and can only assume that I have traveled too far and too quickly for them to find me. Have no fear; I am persuaded they shall catch me up in due course.

Yours, As Ever,
Northrup

Analisa put this letter aside with distaste; it served as an excellent reminder of the earl's former arrogance. With a sigh, she chose a missive with a later date.

Geneva, February 1816
Dear Miss Lloyd-Jones,
I have yet to receive from you a single line. To my regret, I begin to suspect that it has naught to do with the quantity of snow outside my window. Switzerland is excessively cold, there being little to do in such weather but sit in my rooms to read and nurse my melancholy. Often, I wonder why I simply do not return home to you. I should have done so already but remain at the behest of your esteemed father, whose letters have found their way to me without the least trouble. It is his belief that you require more time to become accustomed to the notion of marriage. I agree that you are quite young and are in need of some seasoning. As such, I have conceded to his wishes.

Your Impatient Suitor,
Northrup

Analisa thought back to the previous winter and found that she could only agree with her father's wise assessment, though the earl's created in her a less favorable impression.

She skimmed a few more letters from the previous spring, ones filled with diverting descriptions of people and places that would have proved just as delightful when they had arrived. However, she was in search of those that revealed what it was he wished her to know. Recalling that he had indicated that she should forego all others but those written from Italy, she found the first, dated June 1816.

> *Dear Miss Lloyd-Jones,*
>
> *Germany and Switzerland are countries of dramatic beauty. I enjoyed them both exceedingly but find that the air of Genoa is the gentlest I have known since leaving England's shores. Words are not adequate to describe the vibrant colors or the deliciously slow pace of life. I find I am drawn to it—I, who have been so eager to complete every quest. For the first time, I am reluctant to return to England. It is not that I do not yearn to see you; it is only that I begin to perceive that the man I have been is, perhaps, not the manner of man who can make you happy. I can now perceive that I have been too commanding, too jealous of your attentions to others, too sure of myself and what I have to offer. I pray that I possess the capacity to improve myself into someone with whom you can consider sharing your life.*
>
> *As Ever,*
> *Northrup*

It was some time before she put aside the parchment upon which that letter was written. Indeed, she read it over and over in search of the phrase that had most caused her heart to swell. Unable to determine which, she moved on to a number of letters in which he wrote of his thoughts as he:

roamed the hills, wandered the countryside, lingered in the museums, surrendered to music, learned how to dance with grace and execution, and visited with the native children as they played in the square. Reading such, it was not in the least difficult to know what was written on the heart of the man Lord Northrup had become.

Finally, there were only two letters remaining, ones she hoped spoke of the events to which he alluded with such insistence.

> *Florence, December 1816*
> *Dearest Miss Lloyd-Jones,*
>
> *It was always my father's intention that I tour the Continent upon achieving manhood, just as many young men of my stamp have done. Indeed, I have met some such in my travels. He was wise to set me on this course before he shed this mortal coil, for I find that there is a most imperative broadening of the mind that can be afforded only by travelling beyond the shores of one's birth. As I walk through the streets of the city and observe the mothers and fathers with their children, their goats and sheep by their sides, I see that they are a simple people, a poor people, but they are the happiest people I have yet beheld. Prior to leaving England, I believed I knew enough, if not all, to make me as knowledgeable as one might ever wish. I felt my country the pinnacle of any known to man, my family the pinnacle of the county, and I the pinnacle of that family. Though a nobleman only, I felt myself destined for greatness. The longer we are parted, however, the more I comprehend that the greatest achievement to which I can aspire is to make you happy.*
>
> *Your Northrup*

Analisa's happiness was a matter that had never before been addressed by anyone outside of her family. Well aware that her parents had little idea of how to go about it, she owned that her brother was the only person who had set himself to the task with any degree of charity or ability. She had often longed to be loved as Colin loved his Elizabeth but had given up the notion as one so rare and unlikely that she had no hopes of it finding her. As such, the earl's words penetrated her heart and filled it with such a swell of joy, it threatened to burst from her chest. Eagerly, she plucked the last letter from the counterpane and read.

Calais, January 1817
My Dearest Miss Lloyd-Jones,
How I long to see your face. I shall soon return to you a man changed from the one you once knew. I pray when that day arrives you shall find in me someone you can love. I shall never forget the moment I knew that I loved you and always should.

He loved her. It was an unlooked-for sentiment—one she had never thought to consider. She had always felt he regarded her merely as a possession to which he was entitled, not a soul to cherish. Savoring the first few lines of this letter, she read them over and over again before she moved on to the remainder of the letter.

I was ten and three years of age, the sole emotional support of my mother, head of my household and family, and a titled lord. Like other boys of my station, I attended a boarding school where I quickly learned that all must pay the price set by the older students. The most recent term had ended, and the young people of the county were at home. We had all been invited by the Duchess of Beaufort to a party to celebrate her daughter's birthday. Present was one of the boys with whom I attended school. He was a strapping lad, sixteen years of age, exceptionally nimble-witted, and dangerously so. His sole aim all the weary term long had been to make my life a misery.

He found me at the refreshment table, and when he referred to me respectfully by my title rather than to call me "Ginger-Gabe" or worse, the dreaded "Lordy Laurie," I felt somehow safe from his former abuses. He led me to the stream that he insisted bore a treasure hidden in its depths. When I failed to discern anything out of the ordinary, he proposed that I lie on the bank so as to improve my scope of vision. Had I known he would hold my face under the flow of water, I should have resisted. Pray, believe my most honest exhortations when I say he had no wish to put a period to my existence; he merely wished me to believe he did. I was only too happy to oblige and knew the end was near when, suddenly, he released me. I rose shakily to my feet and turned around to find, standing before me, a girl younger than myself but already noble in her bearing, with long dark hair and magnificent gray eyes.

I wanted nothing more than for her to believe I was not so weak, so craven, as to allow such violence to my person. And then I looked into her eyes and knew she had seen too much. She smiled at me, held out her hand, and said, 'Come, return to the party. The lemonade is more refreshing than the water of the stream.' How I loved her for it. That very day I made it my utmost concern to learn her name and family. I confess it came as some relief to discover that her father was not a nobleman, for it gave me the utmost confidence there would be no objections when I was ready to make her mine. After all, I was an earl.

When I returned again to school, matters were different. There were still the taunts and the misery, but there was also a grudging respect. It seems that my tormentor had concealed himself so as to witness this girl's kindness. It inspired in him, as it does daily in me, a desire to be a better man. On my darkest days, I found I could always call to mind her ready smile; her warm laughter; the feel of her hand, gentle on my arm; the myriad virtues that followed her about every moment of every day. To secure her hand for my own before I left England's shores was the wisest choice I have ever made. I had pictured my life with her present for too many years and could not risk leaving her at the mercy of society and its vagaries.

To that end, my dear Miss Lloyd-Jones, I wrongly threatened all those who might seek your hand within an inch of their lives if they did not leave you be. My reputation as a man with a wild temper was such that they feared me. Letters from your father attest to the truthfulness of this; he writes that none dare to appear as if they are courting you, fearing I shall learn of it and return home to wreak my vengeance. To my undying shame, he reports that while your friends enjoy the company of suitors, you are often on your own and suffer from melancholy. Please know that this knowledge has caused me ceaseless torment since I first learned of it.

When I have returned to England, I pray I shall

find that my sins are not beyond the reach of your forgiveness. If you find you can indeed absolve me of the wrongs I have done you, I humbly beg you to write and tell me what is in your heart. I know well enough it is more than I deserve, but, should you wish to do so, I ask that you have it delivered to my home. In that way, I shall have your absolution in my hand the moment I arrive. Until then, I must content myself with my hopes and dreams.

 He Whose Heart is Forever Yours,
 Gabriel, Lord Northrup

  A vision of the earl arriving home in quest of his letter rose into her mind; how his heart must have smote him when no letter was to be had! Tears wet her cheeks as she considered how he had arrived at Dance Hall, injured heart in his hands, in hopes he might yet earn her forgiveness. How unkind she had been—how impatient. How arrogant to assume him too self-indulgent to be alive to the truth of her wishes and feelings.

  He said that he loved her, not for her wealth and consequence, but for her kindness, her faultless comportment, and her virtue. She imagined his devastation when he realized her deceit. Worse yet was Mr. Callerton's revelation. It can only have led the earl to believe she had behaved in a manner so unworthy of his love.

  Taking the bundle of letters in her arms, she rolled onto her side and shed tears of bitter regret. She knew not how long she wept, only that she was forced to swallow her tears in order to deny Ruby entrance when she rapped at the door. When, sometime later, Emily tiptoed into the room, Analisa feigned sleep. After she placed a shawl over her friend, Emily left as quietly as she had entered, but Analisa heard her in conversation through the closed door.

"She is asleep. I believe she might be ailing."

"In that case," came the voice of Mrs. Smith, "it is best that we leave her be. If she is to miss this afternoon's dancing lesson, let us hope she is in top form for the ball tomorrow night. This is her third Dance Hall house party, and I fear my reputation shall suffer irreparable damage if she does not accept an offer of marriage before the week is out!"

Eight
Ballet Blanc—A Dance in White

Analisa awoke to merry birdsong. It was so cheerful, it took her a moment to realize that someone rapped at her door. "Come in," she called as she quickly gathered the crumpled letters and placed them under a pillow.

Emily appeared on the other side of the door. "I thought you should never awake!"

Analisa smiled. "As you can see, I have done. Have I slept through breakfast?"

"Not quite, but you have slept through last night's supper."

"And the dancing lesson," Analisa said slowly. "I suspect I am not in good odor with Mrs. Smith today."

"Quite the opposite," Emily assured. "She wants you well and rested for the ball tonight."

Analisa rose and contemplated her reflection in the mirror. "I suppose I am well enough, but my appearance is another matter entirely." She sat at her dressing table and picked up a brush. "Did Lord Northrup return for the lesson?" she asked as she studiously avoided Emily's reflection in the mirror.

"No, he did not. It was most remarked upon."

"And Mr. Callerton?"

"Yes, he was there. He danced with several of the girls. As for myself, I took the lesson with Mr. Wainwright. I find him most charming, do you not?"

"Yes, I do," Analisa said with a wry smile. "And I think he shall make you very happy."

The smile faded from Emily's face. "Are you certain it shall not injure you were I to marry him? I know you hoped for an offer from him before you became a young lady with two other men fixed on marrying you."

Analisa replaced the brush with a sigh. "There is only Mr. Callerton, and he is one I can never love. As for Lord Northrup, even if I were to consent to honor our betrothal, I doubtless shall not see him again."

"Analisa," Emily said quietly, "do you love the earl?"

"I do not know that I do." Analisa rose from her chair and began to pace the room. "And yet, I do not know that I do not. I begin to remember the times we spent together when we were younger before he had become so insufferable. And now he is not in the least insufferable and is so very kind and truly wishes for my happiness above his own. And, Emily," Analisa said as she whirled about to face her friend, "he loves me. I had not looked for that, not from any, and most especially not from him whom I thought so caught up in his consequence that he could love none but his own self. It seems that he has truly changed, and I, rather than return his feelings, have given him a disgust of me." She squared her shoulders in determination. "I do not believe I can continue with the house party. I shall write to Papa and have him send the carriage."

"Pray, do not be heedless," Emily begged. "Perhaps Lord Northrup simply requires time on his own to think. If you were to send a message to your father, asking for some trifle or another, mayhap the earl will return with it."

Hope sprang to life in Analisa's breast at her friend's words. "I do believe you are correct. I should then have the opportunity to speak with Lord Northrup, to explain everything, before the others arrive for dinner," Analisa said with renewed enthusiasm. "But what if Mr. Callerton were to insist on coming along?"

"Choose something small that the earl may manage on the horse. He needs must return Mrs. Smith's mount anyhow. Perhaps he will think ahead and bring his evening clothes along as well, so as to change for the ball."

"Emily, you are quite, quite brilliant! I shall ask for my pearl drops and suggest that Papa send them with the earl as soon as can be."

Analisa hastily scratched out a message, and Emily took it directly to the downstairs maid to arrange delivery. Within a very short space of time, all was sorted, and Analisa felt peace for the first time since she had learned of Lord Northrup's return to England.

After breakfast, a meal that did little to quell Analisa's sudden pangs of hunger, she went to the greenhouse to choose the buds for the coronet she planned to wear for the ball. This pleasant task was followed by luncheon, a merry meal attended by only Mrs. Smith and the girls of the house party, all of whom were in high spirits.

When Analisa returned to her chamber, it was, ostensibly, to rest up for the ball. In truth, she wished to be alone so as to hide her growing agitation. The hours that passed whilst she waited for Lord Northrup to arrive were the longest of her life. When a rap came at her door a mere hour prior to the dinner bell, she ran to throw the door wide.

A house maid curtsied and held out a small parcel. Analisa reached for the box and opened it to reveal the expected ear bobs. "Wait," she called to the maid who had already hastened down the passage. "From whom did you receive these?"

The maid turned and curtsied again. "Miss, it was from the same messenger who was sent to deliver your most recent missive."

"Thank you," Analisa said in a voice that was faint in even her own ears. Pushing the door shut, she leaned her forehead against it and burst into tears. At length, when she finally wiped dry her eyes, she noticed a small piece of parchment beneath the ear bobs. With trembling fingers, her heart throbbing with its last hope, she retrieved the note and read the woefully few words written thereon.

Be patient, my child. He is a man wounded but one who loves you well.

"Thank you, Papa," she whispered, her heart swelling. Perhaps he knew how to make her happy, after all.

There came another rap at the door, followed by the appearance of Emily. "What has happened? Has he come?"

"No, he has not. However, this arrived with my pearls." Analisa held out the message for Emily.

"Then you have cause to hope!" she cried upon reading it. "Clearly, he has spoken with your father, who has persuaded him to stay. He shall be at Dance Hall tonight, I know that he shall!"

Analisa embraced her friend. "I pray you are right," she murmured into Emily's shoulder. "However, his presence is no assurance that he yet wishes to marry me. Either way, what am I to say to Mr. Callerton?"

"You shall not marry him, then?"

"No," Analisa said with perfect surety. "I fear I am quite spoiled for any man but he who wrote those letters. If, after all, he does not want me, I shall remain a spinster." Analisa leaned back to look Emily in the eye. "Perhaps I ought to take up residence with Mrs. Smith and assist with her etiquette lessons until I am old and gray and too deaf to take note when someone deigns to whisper in my ear."

Emily laughed merrily. "You shall do no such thing. You shall wed Lord Northrup as you were always meant to do. Now, I shall repair to my room to make my toilette, and you shall do the same."

This time, when Analisa shut the door, her heart was sounder than the last. She went to the washstand to cool her face and bid Ruby to enter the room when she rapped on the door. The first task to which they attended was the dressing of Analisa's thick hair that they artfully arranged into numberless looped braids softened by ringlets. It required an inordinate amount of time to accomplish, and Analisa had never been more pleased with the result.

At last, the moment arrived to don the ball gown Ruby had pressed and hung in the cupboard earlier that morning. It was the loveliest creation Analisa had ever seen in the pages of Ackermann's Repository, but the reality was positively breathtaking. She stared at herself in the pier glass and could hardly believe that the vision in silver tissue was she. As she pulled the soft gloves up over her elbows, she realized there was something amiss. "Ruby, where is the coronet I asked you to fashion for my hair?"

"I shall just fetch it, miss. I thought if I took it from the cold of the larder too soon the buds would only droop the sooner."

As Ruby quit the room, Analisa studied her reflection

with more care. The red rosettes on her dancing slippers were perfection, but the row of ribbon blooms in a faded, softer shade of red seemed suddenly too juvenile. Impulsively, she took a pair of scissors from the dressing table and snipped the threads that held the garland to the hem of the dress.

"Miss, what have you done to your lovely gown?" Ruby cried when she returned with the coronet.

"Do you not like it? I believe it makes for a more sophisticated hemline. And, see here," Analisa said as she pulled a few buds from the coronet. "I shall make a little bundle of these and pin them here, at my waist." What she did not reveal was that she wore the red buds in hopes that, from them, Lord Northrup would divine the truth of her feelings.

"You shall be the most beautiful lady in the room, miss," Ruby pronounced as she affixed the rosy crown, "but not if you keep frowning as you are so doing."

"Yes, you are quite right." Analisa attempted to smile as naturally as ever but did not favor the result. With a sigh, she turned from the pier glass and began to move about the room.

"Now, miss, you shall have your hem torn or worse before the ball has properly begun."

Analisa barely registered Ruby's words of caution. "Perhaps I had best refrain from going down to dinner and ask for a tray in my chamber, instead. I don't believe I shall be able to eat a thing, at any rate."

"You must eat, miss! You shall need your strength for the dancing."

Analisa hardly noticed the girl's reply, and it was some time before she noticed that Ruby had slipped from the room. With a flutter in her stomach, Analisa realized it was time to descend the stairs and enter the dining room. In need of courage, she picked up the note from her father and read it again. Suddenly, his words took on a different meaning, and she despaired in the case they referred to Mr. Callerton rather than the earl.

The flutter in her middle became a feeling of dread as she forced herself to open the door and move down the passage. Other girls were doing the same, and she was grateful to descend the stairs on the arm of Emily, who looked positively resplendent in her cream gown.

"Matters shall work themselves out," she insisted. "All shall be as you wish."

Despite her doubts, Analisa gave her friend a warm smile.

In the end, supper was a sore trial. Mr. Wainwright sat across from Emily and showered her with the compliments to which he had treated Analisa less than a week prior. Meanwhile, Mr. Callerton sat by her side and continuously attempted to place his hand on her thigh under cover of the table. This led her to view him with such distaste she wondered how she could have ever thought him clever or even handsome. The final blow came with the failure of Lord Northrup to arrive. When queried, Mr. Callerton insisted he had not seen the earl at Dun Hafan since he had returned to the house on Mrs. Smith's horse the evening prior.

Once dinner had been consumed, Analisa realized she had no other choice but to enter the ballroom on the arm of Mr. Callerton. Her heart sinking, she mused on how different matters stood from the night of the Folly Bally. It had been a night full of heady promise, all of which had burned to ashes in a matter of days. She felt utterly listless and far more cheerless than she could remember.

As Mr. Callerton promenaded her down the length of the room, she watched the expressions of her friends. Emily's face was aglow, Mr. Wainwright's too; Mary Arthur's full of happiness as she danced with her new beau. Analisa lifted her chin in an effort to banish the envy that ate at her heart. It was then that she beheld the man who stood alone at the end of the room, his back turned to her.

She thought perhaps she was dreaming; it was so like the night of the Folly Bally. Only this time, Mr. Callerton was by her side, and the man at the end of the room, as much as she wished him to be, could not be the earl. And then he turned.

She knew this man, and yet she did not. Gone was the petulant boy, the one with the freckles and the rusty hair she had never quite been able to dismiss. In his place was the man whose heart she had come to know through reading the letters he had so faithfully written to her, one who had earned her love.

Just as before, his eyes opened wide when he saw her, and as she looked into their blue depths, she comprehended the message written in them. She saw pain and regret, but there was also burgeoning hope and a bottomless well of love. Every muscle in her body was poised to run into his arms, but Mr. Callerton had tightened his grip on her.

"Why, Laurie, I should have thought you slunk off in defeat by now," Mr. Callerton drawled. "I believe I made it clear that Miss Lloyd-Jones has chosen me."

The moment Analisa had most feared had arrived. "Mr. Callerton, please do not."

"I have warned you, Callerton," Lord Northrup said in a low voice. "I shall not allow you to tell such lies of Miss Lloyd-Jones."

"Lies?" Mr. Callerton crooned. "I have offered, and she has accepted. Where is the lie in that?"

"It is true." Analisa turned to face Mr. Callerton. "I have made you a promise, but find I cannot honor it." Too apprehensive to note the reaction of either man, she regarded the marbled floor.

"See how she plays the innocent maiden," Mr. Callerton chided, "when, in reality, she is a—"

His accusation was stopped cold in his mouth when the earl swung his fist and landed it on Mr. Callerton's face with a bone-jarring blow.

He immediately released Analisa and threw a hand to his nose. "You cur, you have no right!" he cried. He looked wildly about the room for aid, but the others danced closer to the music and seemed not to notice anything untoward.

"It is you," Lord Northrup grated, "who have no right to disparage the good name of the woman who is soon to be my wife!" He grasped Analisa by the hand and pulled her towards the door. "We are leaving!" He drew her through the nearest door, along the passage, and down the stairs at a pace that threatened disaster for her dancing slippers.

"But what of Mr. Callerton! I do hope he hasn't sustained a serious injury," Analisa cried, but she received no reply. She supposed he was too angry to speak, and she felt her apprehension rise. "Where are you taking me? Do not say we are to mount a horse and ride, pell-mell, through the night."

Lord Northrup turned and caught her by the shoulders. "Would you, if I asked it of you?" He locked his gaze in hers, expectantly.

The apprehension dissolved as she gazed back at him, at the ruddy locks she longed to touch, the mouth she longed to feel on hers, the deep blue eyes whose pain she longed to banish. "Yes, anywhere," she heard herself say and knew that it was true.

He ran his knuckles, rough from their recent abuse, along her cheek and gave her a brief smile. Then, gathering her under his arm, he led her down the same passage they had traversed the day before until they reached the door into the greenhouse. "Here we shall be safe from Mr. Callerton's scandalous accusations."

Analisa followed him into the warmth and could not help but note how much warmer still was the hand that enclosed hers. "My lord," she began hesitantly. "I must confess to you what I have done."

He took both of her hands in his and pulled her close. "My name is Gabriel."

Analisa swallowed the lump that rose in her throat. "Very well then, Gabriel. Mr. Callerton was speaking the truth. He asked me to marry him, and I promised him that I would. I very much wish that I hadn't; you must believe that."

He seemed not in the least disconcerted to learn the truth. "Has he hurt you?" he asked urgently. "Pray tell that he has not taken liberties. I shall never forgive myself if, in addition to my other sins, I should have failed to protect you."

"Protect me?" Analisa frowned in bewilderment.

He drew her by the hand to sit on the selfsame bench she had shared with Mr. Callerton the day prior. "It is I," he said earnestly, "who has brought you to his notice, I who must answer for his appalling behavior."

"It was only a kiss," she said quietly as the tears started in her eyes.

"That is all?" he asked with a baffling intensity.

"Yes," she assured him, "but I had thought it of no consequence as we were soon to be married."

"Shush," he murmured as he gently put a finger to her lips. "It is not your actions I excoriate but his. And mine."

"Yours? But why?"

He renewed his grip on her hand. "I might have refrained from inviting such a man to come home with me, one whom I had known for only a short time and whom I had no business introducing to gently bred young ladies. Certainly," he said with another squeeze to her hand, "not to you."

"I confess, I do not understand."

"Then I shall enlighten you," he said, his face darkening. "Mr. Callerton's intention was to set you up in a cottage far from all you know so that he might call on you when he was of a mind to do so."

"He never spoke of such," she insisted. "Though I don't think it in the least odd that, once married, we should live in the country or that he should sometimes stay in town."

"Analisa," the earl asked, somewhat impatiently, "did he once speak of when your marriage might take place? Has the word so much as passed his lips?"

"Yes, of course," she insisted as she thought of the exchange between herself and Mr. Callerton. "I was in no doubt of his intentions; he clearly wished to marry me."

"My dearest Analisa, it is to your credit that you see only good where there is naught but evil. Mr. Callerton is the sort so vile as to see evil where there is only good. He still has not arrived at a realization of the truth: that you did not comprehend his true objective."

"No!" She felt the blood drain from her face. "How could he believe me such that I would ever agree to . . .? Oh! It is insupportable! Has he told you this?" she asked, aghast.

"He said enough when I saw him after I arrived at Dun Hafan last night for me to have suspicions. I confess I was tempted to believe the worst of you after all that has passed between us. I have never known such a difficult night but, come the dawn, I knew how mistaken I had been to doubt you for even a moment." He possessed himself of her other hand and trained his gaze on the pair of them in his. "And still, my pride was such that I could not bring myself to warn you of Mr. Callerton's perfidy as soon as I might have done. It is yet another wrong requiring your forgiveness."

"Gabriel." His name in her mouth was like music. "It is I who need beg *your* forgiveness. You have saved me from a fate I dare not even contemplate, while I have done naught but trifle with your emotions and lead you on a merry dance. And all of this in the face of your steadfast care for me." She knew she ought to have spoken of his love but wished to hear the word first from his lips.

He shook his head. "You are not to be repudiated. You are too young to be expected to know your own heart."

"And yet," she said gently, "you claim to have known yours since you were a boy."

His head jerked up at her words, and he searched her face eagerly. "You have read my declaration? Dare I hope for such?"

"For that," she said softly, putting her hand to his cheek, "and more."

He favored her with the intensity of his gaze, then seized her hand in both of his to press a lingering kiss to the center of her palm. He raised his head, his hair glowing in the light of the candles, and put her hand to his chest so she might feel the thundering of his heart.

It wasn't until he briefly lifted his other hand to touch lightly the crown of roses that she saw how he trembled. "You have turned my paltry gift into an abundance," he murmured. "I thank you for that—for the good tidings it bore. I knew not how you would receive me tonight. I very nearly faltered but knew that if naught else, I must warn you of your peril. When I saw you on his arm, I feared you should not heed me. And then I espied these buds in your hair, and I took heart."

"It is your courage I regard most highly," she said softly.

"The courage to wait for me, then to leave me—to come to Dance Hall upon your return to England when you had no reason to hope."

He looked down at her hand still against his heart. "During the course of my travels, there were times when my courage failed, when I did all in my power to repress my feelings, to conceal them, or, at the very least, control them. I even wished, at times, for a means to erase the words I had sent off across the sea. For a while, in Switzerland, I thought my dreams useless, that I had no choice but to endeavor to forget you." He looked up with a smile and cupped her chin in his hand. "In the end, these sorrows only served to strengthen my desire to make you mine."

She felt her eyes well with tears of happiness. "I fear I have wronged you in so many ways and do not feel worthy of such devotion as yours. And yet," she confessed, lifting her gaze to his, "I find I am in want of more."

"Devotion," he said, taking her by the shoulders and drawing her up to stand in the circle of his arms, "only follows where love leads."

She felt her heart turn over in her chest, giving rise to a constriction of her throat. With nary a thought for the admonitions of Mrs. Smith, Analisa slid her arms up along his shoulders so as to indulge her desire to twine her fingers in the curls at the nape of his neck. "And, where, precisely, is that?"

She saw something flare in his eyes just before he dragged her hard against his chest and kissed her with a tender passion that exceeded her expectations.

"Analisa," he breathed, "my darling girl, it leads to you." He ran his lips along her cheek and across her brow. "Will you, at long last, give this weary traveler the home for which he longs?"

In answer, she drew tighter her arms around his neck and guided his mouth to hers. Such was her absorption that she did not hear the approach of Mrs. Smith until the moment she parted some palm fronds at their side through which she thrust her head.

"Well! I have never seen such a display of improper behavior at one of my house parties!"

"It is nothing over which you must brood, Mrs. Smith," the earl insisted. "We are betrothed."

"Oh!" she cried as she threw her hands to her mouth. "I thought I should never see the day. But, as we all know," she said gaily as she waved an arm over her head in parting, "it is all on account of my famous dancing lessons."

"As you may recall, we did not attend the lesson," Analisa said with a laugh.

"Nevertheless," Mrs. Smith called over her shoulder as she bounced through the doorway into the house. "As a matchmaker, I am a qualified success!" Whereupon she shut the door behind her with a snap.

Lord Northrup laughed and, relaxing his hold, looked down into Analisa's face. "We *are* betrothed, are we not?"

"Well, indeed, I cannot be sure," Analisa drawled as she broke out of his embrace and sat again upon the bench. "I do not recall that you have properly offered for me. As I have learned, to my sorrow, innocent young ladies are in danger of suffering from misapprehension."

His answering smile was full of joy, and at that moment she knew she could never love anyone as well.

"I shall depart for London in the morning to obtain a special license, whereupon we shall be married whenever you desire. Only, my love, do bear in mind: it is already overlong that I have waited for you."

She cocked her head and considered. "I think I should

like Colin and Elizabeth to attend our wedding. I shall ask Papa to insist they return from India immediately."

"If that is what you wish," he replied with remarkable patience. "Now, come." He took her hand and drew her to stand once again in his arms. "Let me love you, and perhaps you shall change your mind about your brother."

As Lord Northrup bent to kiss his betrothed, Mrs. Smith watched through a crack in the door. "At long last, my reputation is restored," she murmured, and with a most excellent pirouette, she returned to the ball.

ABOUT HEIDI ASHWORTH

Heidi Ashworth is the award-winning author of the bestselling Miss Delacourt Regency Romance series. A San Francisco bay area resident, she is an unapologetic anglophile and dreams of when she can return to England. In the meantime, she enjoys spending time with her husband and three children, in her garden and dreaming up new stories.

Visit Heidi on-line:
Blog: HeidiAshworth.blogspot.com
Website: HeidiAshworth.com
Facebook: Facebook.com/authorheidiashworth
Pinterest: Pinterest.com/ashworth0763

Sweeter Than Any Dream

Annette Lyon

OTHER WORKS BY ANNETTE LYON

Band of Sisters
Coming Home
The Newport Ladies Book Club series
A Portrait for Toni
At the Water's Edge
Lost Without You
A Midwinter Ball
Done & Done
There, Their, They're: A No-Tears Guide to Grammar from the Word Nerd

One

North Yorkshire, January 1824

When Mrs. Wallington announced over breakfast that the residents of Pine Park would soon host guests, her daughter Olivia gave the news little thought and simply took another sip of her morning tea.

Her mother removed her reading glasses and laid the letter on the corner of the table. "It will be pleasant enough to see Andrew, I suppose," she said in a tone that sounded like she referred to a pebble in her slipper rather than to her newly wedded and only son.

Olivia set her teacup onto its saucer with the quietest clink she could manage, knowing her mother disapproved of young girls making noise, even typical ones made in the course of a meal. This included "young girls" of eight and twenty, who were no longer young or girlish. She waited an extra three seconds before speaking to be sure of not interrupting anyone.

"Will Emma be joining him?" she asked.

Mother's right eyebrow lifted. "He used the plural pronoun *we*, did he not? I assume that means we should expect more than one individual." She raised a hand to cut off any protestation, as if Olivia would have made herself a mark in such a way. At a very young age, she'd learned that staying quiet was typically the safest and easiest course. She should have heeded her own advice by not mentioning Emma at all.

"I'm quite sure," Mother went on, "that Andrew wouldn't refer to himself, his valet, and his driver as *we*. Attendants are to be expected, of course."

"Of course," Olivia said with a nod.

Both Mother and Aunt Matilda turned their attention her way, and Olivia immediately regretted speaking. She gave them an uncomfortable smile and reached for her teacup.

"You seem unhappy, dear," Mother said.

"What?" Olivia said, looking up from her tea. "No, not at all." She held her breath and vainly hoped she wouldn't become the object of conversation.

Aunt Matilda agreed with her sister. "You appeared unquiet just now."

Olivia wanted to declare the truth, but she knew all too well there was never any convincing Mother that her sister could possibly be wrong. In this situation, a full explanation—that her uneasy expression had stemmed from dreading this very type of examination—would only exacerbate the situation.

True to form, Mother took her sister's words seriously; she looked Olivia up and down as if inspecting her for flaws.

It was Aunt Matilda who spoke next, however. "I suppose it must be challenging to know that a beautiful woman, newly married and younger than oneself, will be staying under the same roof." She tilted her head in the most maddeningly patronizing fashion.

Mother finally looked away to spoon marmalade onto her toast. "You must learn to manage your envy, dear. Emma is family. While she is our guest, dwelling in melancholia over one's station in life would be most unbecoming. Spinsterhood must be a *terrible* cross to bear."

After a moment of feeling so stunned that she could not move at all, Olivia had to use every energy to keep herself from revealing the frustration building inside her.

They pity me. Pity!

She prayed that the only sign of her anger, had the older women been paying attention, was a slight flaring of her nostrils, an immediate reaction she hadn't been able to contain. She clasped her hands tightly in her lap and ordered herself to not answer their wildly erroneous supposition. Anything she said now beyond a simple reply would only make matters worse.

"Yes, Mother," she said quietly.

Olivia had never been one to accept pity or charity of any kind; one might correctly say she'd inherited the Wallington pride. She did not have a particularly happy life, but she'd found a way to keep her inner imagination and fancies alive while keeping her mother and aunt relatively content at the same time. *Relatively* being the relevant word.

To her relief, Aunt Matilda mentioned some gossip she'd read in the society papers, which shifted Mother's attention elsewhere.

As they talked, Olivia couldn't help but think how wrong they were about what she felt for her new sister-in-law: excitement and anticipation. She hoped they might become friendly with each other. Perhaps one day, they would even call each other sisters. The thought created a delicious twist in Olivia's middle. Imagine having a sister, someone to confide in, a female in the family closer to her age than two and a half decades her senior—in short, someone who understood life as a younger woman. Emma might well be a ray of sunlight in the middle of the rather dreary and predictable existence Olivia lived one day after another under the watchful and overprotective eyes of Mother and Aunt Matilda.

Olivia cut her sausage into small pieces and deliberately chewed each one as slowly as possible. A chewing mouth was a mouth incapable of speaking. As long as she continually ate, she could keep quiet, holding opinions to herself. It would also be easier to not ask questions of her mother and aunt, as curiosity tended to be frowned upon. After one bite, she took another, aware of the silence lengthening—a sign that one of the older women would seek out a topic of conversation uncomfortable for Olivia at best and *about* Olivia at worst.

Mother reread the letter in silence. Olivia looked from her to Aunt Matilda. Her mother was only a hair worse than her sister; they were both difficult, abrasive women who found little joy in life except in finding things to criticize or complain about, and nine times of ten, they nocked their bitter arrows and aimed in Olivia's direction. She could do nothing as the center of their targets but do her best to deflect the arrows. The alternative was to leave the house, with its food, warmth, and clean clothing. Unmarried as she was, she had no choice but to stay under this roof and endure their tongues. She'd long since passed the time when even the most optimistic in their social circles thought Olivia would ever marry, and she'd come to accept her fate as a spinster.

Rather, she'd become resigned to it, which wasn't precisely the same thing.

Had life continued at Pine Park as it had at Landerfield, Olivia wouldn't have minded her position any more than she used to. But ever since arriving three months ago, her mother had grown particularly acerbic. After the wedding, Andrew took his lawful and rightful position as head of Landerfield, with Emma now running the household instead of Mother.

Father had died more than five years previous, and Andrew could have sent them all packing then. Even with his wedding pending, he'd tried to convince them to stay. But Mother had the temperament of a matriarch. Staying at Landerfield as a guest, even a family guest, while yielding the reins of running the estate to a younger woman, the new Mrs. Wallington, had been an unbearable concept. Mother felt entirely displaced and made no secret of her feelings about it. She was increasingly vocal about them, and Aunt Matilda's presence didn't help matters. Instead of offering comfort, she eagerly fed the unquenchable appetite of her younger sister's disdain and bitterness.

Unjustly so, seeing as how Olivia's father had made ample assurance that his widow would be cared for until the end of her days, and how Andrew had been abundantly generous, providing a nice carriage, a new horse, and new furnishings for Pine Park, all without Mother making a single request to that effect, and all after she'd proudly declined the offer to stay.

No, Pine Park wasn't Landerfield, but it was a respectably sized house. They had several servants on staff, and, provided they didn't spend money recklessly, they would have a comfortable, if not, extravagant life. Olivia finished her toast and sat back with the remainder of her tea, wondering how soon she could leave the table without being rude.

"Hmph," Mother said, folding the letter after reading for at least the third time. "Hmph."

"Wh—" Olivia said, then clamped her lips together. No

asking questions of Mother. That was akin to trying to pet a tiger. One was liable to get her hand bitten clean off.

Aunt Matilda, however, picked up where Olivia left off. "It does make one wonder, doesn't it?" she said, then took a dainty bite of toast.

"Wonder what, pray tell?" Mother asked, looking sincerely interested. Had Olivia voiced the same question, Mother's tone would have been accusing. Olivia rested her hands in her lap and lowered her chin, silently waiting for breakfast to end.

"One has to wonder," Aunt Matilda said, "if Andrew is so happy in his marriage after all, if he comes scrambling back to his mother the moment he returns from his wedding tour."

Olivia's eyes widened at that. How did Aunt Matilda dare to say such things against Mother's only son? *Because she is Aunt Matilda,* she reminded herself. *She can say anything, and Mother will agree.*

Plenty of evidence existed to support the fact that Aunt Matilda, and only Aunt Matilda, could voice anything critical regarding Andrew. Had Olivia dared such a thing, she would have been sent from the table and given the silent treatment for a week, during which time her mother and aunt would pretend not to see her and refuse to say a single word her direction or hear a single word from her.

Come to think of it, that would be preferable at times, she thought, and had to restrain a smile, but the humor threatened to turn the smile into a full laugh. Olivia brought her napkin to her mouth to hide the curve of her lips. *Why have I feared such a fate? Perpetual silence would be bliss.* The laugh forced itself out in a quick burst. Olivia held the sound in, and she still had her mouth covered, but her shoulders shook twice before she could control herself.

"Olivia. Is something the matter?" Mother's voice sounded far more like a reprimand than an inquiry into her daughter's health.

She managed to tamp down the laughter and nod, lowering her hand and napkin at the same time. Her face felt hot, but she wouldn't smile for all the diamonds in the world, not now. Laughter would lead to questions, and Olivia was painfully unable to lie. Rather than tell her mother what she found so amusing, she relied on her regular method of coping: silence.

She took another piece of toast in the hope that chewing would help hide her amusement and imagined herself elsewhere—walking through fields of clover or strolling among the rolling grasses of the moors. She lived half of her life in imagined places she'd never been, places where she could always express her true opinions, go anywhere she wished, for as long as she wished. During such fancies, she voiced every opinion she'd kept silent on, from the decor of the parlor to suggestions on replacing the Wallington family china with something more modern.

She never spoke of these dreams, which kept her company during otherwise unendurable hours of complaints, insults, strained silences, and awkward visitors in the morning or for tea, although the latter hadn't occurred at Pine Park. Mother had yet to make or receive any social calls since leaving Landerfield.

But Olivia never stopped living in her imagination, and such dreams were her companions and only friends during recent nights of long, dark winter evenings, which she spent embroidering on the scroll-end sofa while her mother read aloud from the Bible. Currently, she read from the book of Leviticus and refused to skip over any of the descriptions of sacrificing animals, no matter how tedious. Evenings were the hardest to endure, for Olivia knew that young women for leagues around went to balls, had Seasons, were invited to house parties, and more.

Olivia had never been given a single Season, and she'd forgotten the last time she'd been invited to any kind of social gathering. Most people knew her mother's opinion of such things and supposed—quite correctly, alas—that she wouldn't approve. But Olivia would have liked to receive invitations, even if it meant sending regrets. Perhaps one day, she would even have the opportunity to accept an invitation. But that couldn't happen if they never presented themselves.

As the older women continued discussing the merits—or lack thereof—regarding the new Mrs. Andrew Wallington, Olivia let her waking dreams begin earlier than usual. Her eyes strayed to the window, and as the morning sun angled in, showing dust motes twirling in the air, she slipped into the most cherished of her frequent imaginings: the shadowy figure of a man who danced with her, found her beautiful, walked with her, talked with her—and welcomed every moment in which she spoke her mind, which she did with cleverness and wit, of course.

Unlike the other details in her mind, her beloved's features never had fine detail or color. She couldn't be sure of the shade of his hair or his eyes, or even of his height beyond a general knowledge that he stood taller than she did. The details didn't matter; being loved by him made her deliriously happy, even if her rational mind knew that he and the world he lived in were all imaginary, certainly nothing a grown woman should be indulging in like a child at play.

For the next twenty minutes, she deliberately abandoned all thought of her family's pity for her spinsterhood; after all, in her dreams, such pity was impossible, as she was neither melancholy nor a spinster. In her mind, she walked the moors with her shadow man, one hand through the crook of his arm, save for when the wind kicked up and he slipped his arm about her waist to draw her close to keep her warm.

Two

"You really shouldn't have gone to the trouble of planning a ball on my account," Edward Blakemoore said from the couch in the library. He'd only recently arrived at Dunstead Manor to visit James Clement, a friend from Eton days who'd become almost a brother.

"I assure you, *I* didn't go to any trouble at all," James said, standing at the sideboard. He poured the two of them drinks, then handed Edward one of them before taking a seat on the other side of the couch. "It was entirely Fanny's idea. Winter has been lonely for her in the country so far from London. When she heard you were coming, she grew so excited at the prospect of a ball to brighten the dreariness of the season. I didn't have the heart to tell her that you aren't the kind of man who seeks out large crowds." James grinned and swallowed some brandy.

Edward acknowledged the truth of the statement with a

sigh and swirled the amber drink in his glass. He dreaded the prospect of playing the role of gentleman houseguest and eligible bachelor. While technically both, he certainly didn't enjoy being viewed in any kind of light that cast him as a trophy to be won, let alone in a village where most women were far below the station he was expected to marry. Besides, he had no desire to marry, though his family considered it his duty. Instead, Edward intended to manage his late father's estate to the best of his ability. Then, upon his own death, the estate would simply pass to his younger brother, who had already married and produced two heirs of his own.

"Come now," James said a bit overly cheerfully. "Why the long face? If your brows furrow any deeper, you'll end up with a permanent crease between them."

At that, Edward lifted one eyebrow—no longer furrowing it—and stifled a chuckle. "Since when do you care about *wrinkles*?"

James tossed back the last of his drink and set the glass aside. "An unexpected effect of marriage, I suppose."

"Yet another reason to avoid the state," Edward said.

"Why are you so against marriage?" James asked. He crossed his legs and arms, almost as if he'd begun a debate he intended to win.

Edward sighed and set his untouched drink on the side table. "I have nothing against the institution." He quickly held up a hand before his friend could interject. "Nothing against women, either."

"Oh?"

"Truly," Edward said. "I simply do not find any joy in the prospect of making what is tantamount to a business arrangement with a member of the fairer sex simply for the sake of passing my father's estate to the next generation."

"Ah," James said. "So that is why you detest balls. They

represent the potential beginning of a distasteful *business* arrangement."

"I suppose so," Edward said, his gaze landing on the mahogany desk. "I hadn't thought of it in those terms precisely, but yes. If I could find a woman I genuinely cared for, and who genuinely cared for me—if I could find a woman with intelligence and opinions and cleverness—"

"Careful what you wish for, my friend," James said with a laugh. "Such a woman might be entertaining for an evening, but are you sure you'd want to yoke yourself to someone so outspoken for life? Wouldn't that become onerous?"

A smile slowly crept across Edward's face, and he turned to James. "No," he said with sudden realization. "Not at all. It would be refreshing to have someone who is my intellectual equal, who challenges me, makes me think and question my own opinions, who doesn't sit meekly in the corner, agreeing with everything her husband says." He shuddered. "*That* would be an unbearable fate. So tell me. Does Glenworth and its surrounding areas have any such women I may look forward to meeting at your Fanny's winter ball? Or must I brace myself for an evening of smiling and bowing stiffly, behaving with perfect civility, yet bored to the point of torture?"

James stood and took both of their glasses back to the sideboard. "Alas, I know of no such young woman—excepting my own dear Fanny, of course." When he returned, he leaned back on his desk and studied his friend. "I wish you could find someone to make you truly happy, Edward. Someone like my Fanny. I assure you, what we have is far more than a business arrangement."

"Are you happy, then?" Edward asked. He'd witnessed dozens, if not hundreds of marriages over his lifetime but could not recall a single couple who definitively had regard for the other beyond respect and civility. If he were to marry, he would first need to love. He simply wasn't sure if such a thing was possible outside of fairy tales.

"I *am* happy. Very happy." A simple statement, but the words lit up James's entire face—and Edward found himself suddenly envious, wanting to know what such a life would be like, feel like.

He could feel his throat tightening with the yearning to have something more. The moment had become too serious, too introspective. Something must be done to lighten it, posthaste.

"Very well," he said in a boisterous tone and stood. He clapped a hand to his friend's arm. "I'll attend your ball, and I'll do so with a smile on my face. I cannot promise that I will enjoy every minute of the evening, but I will do my part to ensure that your dear Fanny's ball is a success." His tone softened as he added, "I wouldn't want to disappoint her."

"Thank you. The ladies in attendance may not be the type to catch your fancy, but Fanny will appreciate your efforts to make them feel welcome." James gave the crooked smile Edward had known since they were both young boys. "And for that, *I* thank you. My happiness hinges on Fanny's happiness. Your attendance will make her—and therefore me—quite pleased."

Somehow, Edward's attempt at lifting the mood hadn't lasted. The tension in his throat was turning into a knot, which he cleared with a swift cough. "Anything for a friend from Eton," he said, then headed for the library door. "I think I'll go out to the stables to check on Topaz." He opened the door but paused before leaving and looked back.

James was still smiling. "You're a good man, Edward Blakemoore."

"Let's not let that kind of story get out," Edward replied.

He winked and left, heading for the stables. He'd ride his horse about the grounds of Dunstead Manor to shake the sense of melancholy that had descended upon him so suddenly.

Odd, he thought, walking through the corridors. *I've never wanted a wife until today. Unfortunate that the odds of finding the kind of woman I'd want—and her wanting me in return—are almost nonexistent anywhere, let alone in Glenworth.*

Edward had to ride for over an hour to shake the cloud hanging over his head. He returned, dressed, and entered the dining room feeling much more like his regular self. But the cloud returned all too quickly, for throughout the meal, he watched James and Fanny interact in a manner he'd never noticed before. It was all simple things—a tender look, a sincere comment, a kind gesture. Each seemed to communicate a wealth of meaning and love between Mr. and Mrs. James Clement.

Never had Edward felt so extraneous, so unneeded.

Never had he so wanted what another possessed. Due to the station he'd been born in, he'd lived a life wherein anything he wished could be obtained, whether through hard work, clever negotiation, or plain old money.

Now he found himself with a yearning greater than any he'd ever experienced, yet for something that no amount of work, wits, or wealth could give to him.

Three

Another morning meant another breakfast, almost a twin to the one from the day before. It was no wonder that Olivia was pulled from her typical reverie after Aunt Matilda decided she'd had enough to eat. Olivia didn't mind the interruption, as she would be able to quickly return to her imaginary life on their morning walk.

Her mother and aunt both believed that a healthy constitution required exercise, perhaps a remnant from their own upbringings, so even in the dead of winter, they walked through the frozen gardens. Though at this time of year, the walks tended to be much shorter. Not that her mother or aunt would admit to that.

Every time they went out, Olivia felt sympathy for the poor gardener, Mr. Tracy, who had to keep a path clear for them no matter how deep the snow had fallen, then sprinkle it with gravel to decrease the likelihood of one of the women slipping and falling. Most gardeners had much less to do in the winter months, but she suspected he might have more, for in addition to keeping the walkways clear of snow and sprinkled with rocks, he had to somehow make the gardens look pleasing even when the hedges and flowers were dead.

Wrapped in woolen cloaks, Mother and Aunt Matilda walked ahead of Olivia, who quite happily hung back, gradually letting the distance increase until she almost felt alone. She imagined that her man of the shadows was nearby, hidden by a tree or hedge, and might step around a corner and greet her at any moment. He'd put his arm out. She'd take it with a shy curtsy like a proper lady. They'd walk together arm in arm, and when Mother and Aunt Matilda eventually glanced over their shoulders and noticed, they'd smile and nod to him with a murmur of greeting.

In Olivia's dreams, her mother always approved of him. How could she not? Olivia's imagination had created a man so perfect that even her mother's high standards for a gentleman would be easily met, yet he wouldn't be unpleasantly stiff like a real man of whom Mother approved would undoubtedly be. No, he would be kind and warm and tease just the right amount, so she'd know how much he cared about her—that he loved her so much, he noticed the little things worthy of a lover's joke.

The realm of fancy included all things that made—or rather, *could* make—Olivia happy, and she let herself enjoy such flights of the mind, knowing quite well that more than likely, they would be her only true source of happiness from that time forward. No one in the human realm could be both the kind of man she could desperately love and a man who somehow managed to attain her mother's approval rather than the condescending disdain she kept in reserve for most of the world.

Olivia got so enthralled with her current dream—

dancing at a ball with her man of shadow, looking radiant in a new ball gown, the envy of the other young women—that she didn't notice that the older ladies had turned back to return to the house until she narrowly missed stepping right onto her aunt's boot.

"Excuse me, Aunt Matilda," she said sheepishly—and regretfully, as the world of the ballroom and the shadow man whirling her around the floor vanished like a soap bubble floating through the air and then popping into nonexistence. Was it her imagination, or were their walks getting shorter each day? Perhaps it was the unusually cold winter.

Her aunt sniffed and walked on as her mother shook her head with sad disapproval, as if Olivia were a misbehaving six-year-old. As she turned to follow, she paused to admire the way the snow bordering the shoveled path sparkled as if someone had taken a handful of diamonds and strewn them across the ground.

"Is something the matter?" Mother demanded, pausing in her step and looking back. Aunt Matilda did the same, her eyebrows raised so high it was a wonder they didn't disappear into her hairline altogether.

Olivia blinked a few times, returning, alas, entirely to the present moment, complete with toes that felt pinched and a nose so cold it almost felt as if it were on fire.

How warm my imagination keeps me, she mused.

"I'm fine, Mother." Olivia instinctively nodded, almost as if she were a servant, then picked up her skirts and hurried along the icy path as quickly as she dared, saying, "Coming." She put on an expression of contrite humility as one might put on a garment. This one was certainly ill-fitting, but neither of the older women seemed to notice the unnatural manner in which Olivia held her face.

I certainly feel like a servant at times, she thought,

working hard to keep her shocking thoughts from showing on her face.

As she walked back to the house, her shadow hero had the opportunity to return, complete with his voice, intellect, and enjoyment of things such as science and politics, subjects Olivia found utterly fascinating, but which young ladies weren't supposed to be interested in—or supposed to understand, if her mother's opinion meant anything. In fact, Mother blamed Olivia's passion for mathematics and science for landing her firmly in the position of spinsterhood.

"Intelligent women intimidate a man," she'd said a thousand times if once. "If a man cannot be assured that he possesses the greater intellect, he won't pick the woman as his wife."

If Olivia's lack of marriage offers was any indication, Mother was correct on that point. As Olivia walked along, she kicked a lump of snow with her toe, a virtually silent and undetectable way of expressing frustration and disappointment. Her only way of doing so without raising her mother's ire.

If a man is intimidated by a woman who can think and who enjoys learning, then he is not for me, and I am most certainly not for him.

The thought was true, but not exactly comforting. Olivia had no desire to live out her life as an old maid, stuck with Mother and Aunt Matilda until they died. At that point, she could accept Andrew's offer of living with him and Emma at Landerfield, something she looked forward to, as much as the private admission made her feel a stab of guilt. She didn't wish her mother to die, of course, yet she would have preferred to live at Landerfield with her brother and his new wife, who were much closer to her in age. Olivia imagined that she wouldn't be so lonely living there.

But she had to acknowledge and prepare herself for the fact that her new sister-in-law might not want another woman in her home, especially after they had several children filling the bedchambers, along with nannies and tutors.

Would that I were a man and could study science at a university, become a scientist, and support myself with work in a laboratory. Would that such a dream could come true, ever, for any woman.

Instead, women's fates lay largely in the hands of those who controlled the money—in the hands of men.

The house came into view as Mary, one of the housemaids, came running for them, without a coat or shawl of any kind. "They're here, ma'am," she said breathlessly when she reached Mother.

"*Who* is here?" Mother demanded in a tone as cold as the icicles hanging from the eaves.

Her mother wasn't asking the question out of ignorance, of course. The entire household knew that Andrew and Emma were coming today. No, Mother had asked the question—stressing the first word—as a lesson to poor Mary, who was young and still learning how to be a proper housemaid, including how to announce visitors. No surprise, really, as she spent most of her time in the kitchen helping the cook, but as the house lacked a large staff, Mary needed to learn other duties that went beyond making scones and tea. And Mother had reminded her to announce the names of guests, not only their arrival.

With the safety of her mother's back facing her, Olivia rolled her eyes and laughed silently. Mary wouldn't dare tell if she saw. The lady of the house might not approve of Olivia, but the maid had no right to do so, and Mother would jump to the aid of her blood and dismiss Mary without argument.

Mary definitely noticed Olivia's reaction, and she did look somewhat shocked, but she erased the expression quickly, then cleared her throat.

Mary answered, her eyes trained on the snowy ground and her hands clasped so tightly that her hands were white. "Mr. and Mrs. Wallington have arrived, ma'am. Their luggage is being brought up to the northeast guest chambers, as you instructed. Mrs. Barton is preparing the tea to be served in the parlor momentarily."

"Much better," Mother said with a nod of approval. Her face tilted upward, so she spoke while looking down her nose at Mary. "Tell them we'll be in shortly."

Aunt Matilda shook her head. "So difficult finding good help these days," she muttered, eyebrows raised as she seemed to study the needles of one of the many pine trees for which the house was named.

Mary looked from Mother to Aunt Matilda, wary, like a dog worried that it was about to be kicked. "Yes'm," she managed, and when Mother and Aunt Matilda said nothing more, she gave a quick curtsy and hurried inside, likely to escape them as much as the cold.

The party headed inside, though much too slowly for Olivia's preference, as she was quite excited at the prospect of seeing her brother for the first time since his wedding tour to the Continent. Her mother seemed to be walking even more slowly, as if she knew Olivia was eager to get inside. Being the loyal daughter she was, Olivia remained a few steps behind her mother and aunt. They entered the back door, where Mary waited to help them with their wraps, and then they followed Pierce, the butler, to the parlor. Andrew stood upon their entrance.

"Andrew," Mother said. He stepped forward and hugged her, but, per usual, she stood straight as a board.

When he stepped back, Mother nodded even more stiffly, if that was possible, toward her new daughter-in-law—the woman also known under the roof of Pine Park as the one responsible for robbing Mother of house and home.

Emma stood beside Andrew. "Mother Wallington," she said warmly, a trace of hope in her voice.

Mother hardly acknowledged the greeting; she merely crossed to a settee and sat at the edge of it, almost as if she were perched on the cushion. She certainly couldn't be comfortable, but then again, when had Mother ever indulged in luxuries such as comfort? Poor Emma couldn't have known about the family she'd married into, even if Andrew had tried to tell her about it. No one could fully grasp Mother or Aunt Matilda without experiencing their aloof pretentiousness firsthand.

Unsurprisingly, Aunt Matilda's greeting was formal. Andrew didn't attempt to embrace her; he simply gave her a proper bow and said, "I hope you are well."

"As well as can be expected in winter," Aunt Matilda said, "with burning coal vapors indoors and temperatures that seem designed to kill an old woman with rheumatism."

As Andrew straightened, he seemed unsure how to reply to such a comment. He and Emma exchanged glances, and Olivia thought she caught the barest hint of amusement passing between them. It was gone as soon as she saw it, however, leaving Olivia wondering if it had been in her imagination. Their aunt took a seat beside Mother, at last making way for Olivia to greet her brother. She hugged him gratefully, feeling the warmth of his cheek against her chilly one from the outdoors.

He pulled back and took her hands in his. "It's so good to see you, Olivia," he said.

"And you," she replied. The wedding seemed ever so

long ago, though it had been only a few months. She turned to her sister-in-law. "It is very good to see you too. I hope your tour was pleasant."

"Oh, it was most enjoyable," Emma said. "We particularly enjoyed our stay in Italy."

Olivia wanted to pepper Emma with questions about their travels, but a swift clearing of the throat from her mother cut off that thread of conversation. Feeling a bit chagrined, Olivia retreated to a chair near the fire—as close as she could be to their guests while being as far as possible from her mother and aunt. Such actions constituted the entirety of Olivia's rebellion against their expectations, such as it was. In her waking dreams, however, her rebellion knew no bounds; she did things that would utterly shock and horrify her mother and potentially send Aunt Matilda into a state of apoplexy. The thought forced Olivia to hide an amused smile of her own.

Yet what would Andrew and Emma think of her fantasies? She had a feeling that Andrew wouldn't be so horrified, and she hoped that Emma would be a kindred spirit in the same vein. Not that Olivia had any way to find out; she'd have to broach the topic of shocking behavior and ask in blunt terms what they thought of such things, neither of which she could ever imagine herself doing.

"Oh, come, Mother," Andrew said.

His voice brought Olivia's head up and her mind back to the parlor. What had Mother said? How much of the conversation had Olivia not heard? *This could be very bad indeed,* she thought, eying her mother warily.

But Andrew simply went on, whether before either of the two older women could speak or whether neither had anything to say, Olivia wasn't entirely sure.

"You are and always will be welcome to live at Landerfield," he said.

Mother raised her eyebrows almost as high as Matilda's. She pretended to inspect the stitching on the settee as she replied, "I will not encroach on anyone's charity. You are the rightful master of the estate, and your wife is fully capable of helping you manage it. I am no longer needed or wanted, so we will live here, as your father provided for in his will. It's all quite comfortable, as you can see. We want for nothing."

Nothing save for the status of living and running an estate such as Landerfield, Olivia mused. Her mother seemed to view her son's inheritance and marriage as a personal affront and fall from grace. But what had she expected her son to do? Of course he would marry, and Olivia was grateful he'd found a woman of proper breeding and station whom he respected, yes, but also loved.

"You are welcome to visit any time," Andrew said.

"I should hope so," Mother said with a huff. "Landerfield was my home for thirty years."

Emma gently placed a hand on Andrew's arm, indicating that she wanted to speak. "What my dear husband means, Mother Wallington, is that you are welcome to come and *stay* any time you wish. You are family, and in our eyes, Landerfield will always be your home."

"Fiddlesticks," Mother said, then sniffed again. "This *cottage* is my home now." She said the word as if referring to a rotten piece of meat, although the statement wasn't accurate anyway. Pine Park was smaller than Landerfield, but only Mother would think to call it a cottage.

"Which brings me to a question," Mother said.

Andrew and Emma looked curiously at each other and then at Mother. He finally asked the obvious. "And what is that, Mother?"

"Why precisely have you come to visit? This house is so modest compared with Landerfield—it's practically a food pantry. Christmas is long over, as is Twelfth Night. Travel in the winter is miserable at best. So why now?"

"To visit you and my dear sister," Andrew said, then quickly added, "and Aunt Matilda, of course."

Matilda's entire response was a lifted chin with the turn of her head toward the crackling fire.

Oh, Andrew, Olivia thought. *You have no idea how easy it is to offend under any roof where both Mother and Aunt Matilda reside.*

He looked both surprised and confused. Over the years, Olivia had wondered why he'd been spared the worst of the vitriol, and figured that it was likely due to his time away at Eton, during which his return for visits were a time for celebration, even for Mother. He hadn't been home to be a mark on a target as Olivia had. Yet even if he had, he was born male and meant for great things, while Olivia was the girl destined for spinsterhood. Apparently, Mother's ire hadn't felt a need to aim in Andrew's direction until he'd done something to cause what she viewed as a wound.

Her brother leaned forward. "In addition to the joy of seeing my dearest family, we came now because a neighbor of yours will be hosting a ball on Friday eve." He looked so pleased with himself; he couldn't possibly know that he'd done the equivalent of throwing a burning log into the center of the room.

"Oh?" Mother said in a familiar tone—feigned curiosity with derision hiding beneath the surface. A glance their way showed Olivia that her brother and sister-in-law remained utterly oblivious to any lurking danger. To an outsider, the single word probably did look benign.

If only I could warn him somehow, she thought, but then

questioned her haste in worrying. *Perhaps I've developed a particularly sensitive ear to Mother's moods and assume matters will turn out worse than they really will.*

Andrew's face became animated as he went on, surely thinking that he'd landed on the perfect topic of conversation. "One of my dearest friends from Eton recently bought a home in the area—Dunstead Manor, it's called. I'm sure you remember hearing about my chum James Clement. We became friends my very first year."

When Mother answered, it wasn't to confirm whether she had any memory of anyone with such name. Instead, she latched on to his first comment. "So you've come not to see your mother but to visit an old friend. And to attend his ball."

"Not just to see Mr. Clement. To see Mr. Blakemoore, too," Emma said, her tone clearly trying to be helpful.

Mother threw her a scathing look, then asked Andrew, "And who, pray tell, is this Mr. Blakemoore?"

"Another friend from Eton," Andrew said sheepishly. "He's visiting Dunstead Manor, and the ball is in his honor." Andrew's cheeks had drained of color almost completely, no doubt an effect of realizing his misstep. He forced a chuckle and said, "It's quite amusing, really. Blakemoore has no desire to wed, but his mother insists he look for a wife, so when Mrs. Clement offered to host a ball, it seemed a good way to keep Mrs. Blakemoore happy for a little longer." He smiled, clearly expecting Mother to understand and soften after hearing the fuller explanation.

"I see," she said, her tone every bit as icy as before. "What is Pine Park to you, then? A convenient inn?"

Olivia winced. Had she known Andrew would attempt this line of conversation, she could have told him to avoid talk of a ball and Misters Clement and Blakemoore altogether. But he didn't know Mother as she did, so he went on with further attempts to smooth any ruffled maternal feathers, and Olivia sat there helpless to stop it.

"N-no," Andrew stammered. "I—*we*—wanted to visit you. The timing of Clement's ball is a happy coincidence. We don't have to attend at all, do we, Emma?"

"Of course not," she said swiftly, though Olivia detected disappointment in her eyes.

"We'll stay here with you," Andrew said. "I'm sure you have plans for us—meals and outings and such—and we certainly have no desire to ruin any of that." He finished with a quick inhalation and a sigh, then seemed to hold his breath, waiting for Mother's reply.

She didn't answer at first. Instead, she stared at the grain in the wood floor, and did so for fourteen full seconds—Olivia counted. Any silence lasting more than seven portended an eruption. She braced herself and wished for Andrew's sake that he'd experienced at least a modicum of Mother's outrage over the years so he'd have known to make no mention of Mr. Clement's ball until the time was right.

Mother finally stood in one swift movement. "I have a headache," she announced as Aunt Matilda stood at her side, ready to leave with her. Mother addressed the butler, who stood at the door. "Pierce, tell Betty I need some laudanum."

"Right away, ma'am," Pierce said with a slight bow before leaving to relay the message.

With a great show of pain—Mother excelled at such theatrics, which made certain that anyone in her presence knew of her ailments—she walked to the door, accompanied by her sister. At the threshold, the women paused, and Mother spoke. She didn't turn around, only tilted her head ever so slightly toward her right shoulder and said, "I shall see you at breakfast."

With that, she walked out, leaving Olivia breathing a sigh of relief. Mother intended to punish them with her silence, but sometimes that was easier to tolerate than a string of bitter insults that lasted for days. Andrew and Emma, however, appeared uneasy and anxious.

Four

Emma lifted a palm to her chest and stared at the empty door. "Goodness. That did not go at all as I'd hoped. She hates me. She genuinely hates me."

"Nonsense," Andrew said. He took her hand between both of his. "Mother is merely tired, so she behaved a bit more harshly than she intended to."

Olivia had to hold back a snort. Their mother did nothing without full intention. If she'd offended Emma and given her the sense that she was disliked, then that message was every bit intentional. Olivia held her peace on that subject, however, not wanting to hurt her sister-in-law further. After all, Olivia considered it a point of pride that she didn't inherit her mother's sharp tongue. Or rather, she put her energies into cultivating a sharp *mind* instead, while keeping observations to herself instead of wounding those around her.

Olivia could never understand how her mother could

purposely hurl verbal barbs, whether her aim sent them toward family, friends, or society. Everyone was alike unto Mother in that regard. At Emma's wilted expression, Olivia had to at least attempt to soften the wounds Mother and Aunt Matilda had left behind.

"Mother *is* tired," she began, attempting to agree with Andrew. But then she hesitated. How exactly could she explain why a woman of supposedly good breeding would say such things and then, as hostess, insist on staying in her bedchamber until the morrow, no matter who the guest? In this situation, even Olivia found the behavior baffling. Yes, Mother had felt unappreciated, and she didn't like Emma—not that she'd taken the opportunity to know her—but Andrew, her beloved and only son, had just arrived. She'd never punished him in this manner that Olivia could remember.

"Has she fallen ill?" Emma asked. "She clearly doesn't like me."

"This has nothing to do with you," Olivia said in a rush, realizing only after the words had come out that they weren't particularly comforting. She hurried on in hopes of soothing her sister-in-law another way. "She's offended that the lure of a ball would trump the desire to visit her alone." Olivia shrugged. "And she doesn't particularly approve of balls."

A pity, that. Olivia had once enjoyed balls, but she hadn't attended one in years, not since Mother decided that Olivia was past marriageable age and could therefore stop attending what Mother deemed to be nothing but a necessary evil for finding a spouse. Beyond that purpose, she had no use for them.

"Oh, Mother," Andrew chuckled, shaking his head. "What are we to do with her?"

Emma looked up at him and then at Olivia. "She

disapproves of balls?" she asked warily. "Even for a married woman?"

Olivia leaned forward. "Go to the ball and enjoy every moment. Mr. Clement will be eager to see Andrew again and to meet his new wife, and you shall see Mr. Blakemoore besides. It would be a pity to disappoint them or for you to miss a delightful social engagement simply because Mother happens to belong to a society of centuries past. She believes that balls are where the devil tries to lure people away from the paths of what we should be worshiping: proper etiquette and decorum."

The others couldn't hold back smiles at that, and Olivia found herself restraining a chuckle as well, although she felt quite evil having said such a thing. Mother would be horrified if she ever heard that her daughter had compared etiquette to religion.

"We'll go," Andrew said. "And don't you worry about Mother."

The last seemed to be directed at Olivia, but it was Emma who needed to hear it, so Olivia agreed. "You and Andrew will have a delightful evening. Don't let thoughts of Mother sully a single moment."

"We won't," Andrew said. "But I was talking to you. You will come to the ball with us, won't you?"

"G-go to the b-ball?" Olivia had never been particularly vocal, but she'd also never found herself stammering so much. "M-me? You want *me* to go? To a ball? But I know no one in Glenworth, and—" She almost launched into a speech about her well-known spinsterhood, but Andrew cut her off.

"I know what you're thinking—that balls aren't enjoyable when you're the eldest unmarried lady present."

"It would help if I were widowed," Olivia said flatly, but otherwise found herself speechless. Of course Andrew knew precisely what her concern would be, Mother's protestations aside.

"Do come," he said. "The ball will be the just the thing to lighten your mind and heart in the middle of the dreary winter when we have weeks yet until spring."

She considered the long, gray days of drabness stretching ahead of her, at time when the earth was ugliest because the snow had lost its luster from dirt and smoke, but the tender shoots of new plants and leaves had yet to sprout. A ball would be a nice escape, but it would of necessity happen only in her mind. Mother would have an utter apoplexy if Olivia tried to attend an actual ball without her there as a chaperone, no matter that Olivia was, as Mother regularly reminded her, well past marriageable age.

"James sent invitations to several surrounding villages, so there will be plenty of people who need introductions."

"But Mother would learn of it and be impossible to live with," Olivia said with a sinking feeling. She'd made the mistake of indulging in the fantasy a bit too much; oh, how lovely a ball would be.

Andrew pursed his lips for several moments, deep in thought. "Does Mother take callers?"

"Not recently," Olivia said. "The move to Pine Park hasn't been good for her spirits or her rheumatism, and only a few neighbors have left their cards."

"Then I suppose she doesn't attend many social functions either?"

Olivia's head slowly came up as she began to see what her brother meant. Perhaps her mother *wouldn't* hear of her daughter's attendance at the ball. How would she, when she'd taken steps to ensure the social isolation of the entire household?

A thrill shot through Olivia's chest. Could she really take

part in a ball the way other young women did—dancing and flirting with men who'd deliberately sought her out? The heat of a blush crept up her face as her mind conjured the details of such a magical evening. Oh, how she would enjoy such a night. It would be a memory she would treasure always.

While living at Landerfield, she was known as the gentle spinster sister of Mr. Wallington. Balls meant dancing with one or two older gentlemen, married or widowed, who'd extended the offer out of pity. Dancing as the object of pity was far worse than sitting at the edge of the room without a single partner.

But in Glenworth, no one knew her. With a proper ball gown and hair arranged just so, she wouldn't look like a stodgy spinster. She could behave as if she wore such attire with regularity. She could converse with those in society without Mother's watchful and disapproving eye. She could say anything that came to mind without regard for how it might be taken coming from a spinster's mouth. The idea became bigger and shinier, more tempting than a blueberry scone.

"Perhaps I could . . ." she said slowly, but then she shook her head.

How could she slip into the house afterward without Mother knowing about it? If she found out, Olivia would be punished for months to come. She shuddered. Such an existence would be only slightly better than being thrown into the Tower of London. "I misspoke. I can't go, as *lovely* as it sounds."

Oh, so lovely, she thought with an ache.

"My dear sister," Emma said, "do reconsider, for my sake as well as your brother's. We've both been anticipating the fun we'd have at the ball, and the evening simply would not be complete without your presence."

She called me sister, Olivia thought in wonderment.

Emma reached out and took Olivia's hand, then looked directly into her eyes. "I've wanted to become better acquainted with you, and what better opportunity than at a ball?" she said imploringly. "We are about the same size; you may borrow one of my gowns. And my lady's maid will create something magnificent with your hair. It has such a beautiful shade of chestnut." She turned to her husband. "Don't you think so, Andrew? Her hair is positively stunning. But the severe twist doesn't do justice to the color—or to the delicate lines of your cheekbones."

Olivia was unable to form a coherent answer. No one had ever called her, or anything *about* her, beautiful, let alone *stunning*. She suddenly yearned to go to the ball and to prepare for it under the hand of Emma, almost like Cinderella under the hand of her fairy godmother in the Brothers Grimm story. She'd read the entire volume of stories—one of many books she'd collected secretly—some purchased, others given to her by Andrew without their mother's knowledge.

"I'd love to go to the ball," Olivia said, grateful her voice had returned. "But . . . what about Mother and Aunt Matilda?" She withdrew her hand and addressed her brother. "I don't think you fully understand how difficult they would make things. They'll never grant permission, and if I were to go without approval, well, that might be enough to stop her heart entirely."

One side of Andrew's mouth quirked up in the manner she recognized. He'd worn the same mischievous smile—the one that made his cheeks dimple—many times, such as the day when he'd been no older than ten and had stolen Father's pipe. He'd tried to smoke it behind the stables—and nearly burned the building down in the process.

"Andrew," Olivia said warily. "What are you concocting in that mind of yours?" She didn't quite trust her brother when he wore that expression.

He lifted his hands, palms up, and shrugged. "Who says you *need* her permission?"

She rolled her eyes and was about to explain how the recent display was but a foretaste of what Mother and Aunt were capable of, but he held up a finger and shook his head firmly.

"Who says she must ever be told of your attendance?"

"Are you suggesting I lie to Mother?" Olivia narrowed her eyes. "I couldn't possibly—"

"*You* won't do a thing about it. You will busy yourself with getting dressed under the watchful eye of my dear wife," Andrew said. The newlyweds looked glowingly into each other's eyes for a moment before they seemed to remember that they were otherwise involved in a conversation.

It was Emma who spoke next. "Do say you'll come. I don't know what my dear Andrew is planning, but I'm sure it will do the trick."

Andrew clasped his hands with excitement. "If we can make sure that neither Mother nor Aunt Matilda will have the slightest knowledge about your attending the ball, and if you needn't tell any falsehoods, will you go?"

Olivia licked her lips uncertainly. Both Andrew and Emma smiled as broadly as wolves who'd had their fill in a chicken coop. Olivia considered their words and thought of the excitement a ball would hold for her. Of the additional details she could spin into dreams after an evening at Dunstead Manor. Thus far, they had consisted entirely of fictional events. What if she could relive actual memories again and again?

That might make the coming years at Pine Park almost bearable.

"But how can you be sure they'll never find out?"

"I have my ways," Andrew said. His dimples looked even deeper than usual.

He must already have a plan, she thought.

She took a deep breath to steady herself before saying, "Very well. I'll go."

She felt quite faint from the giddiness over the secret the three of them now held between them.

Five

Preparations for the ball increased, turning Dunstead Manor into a flurry of bustling servants and excited chatter. Edward, in turn, found a growing need to escape the confines of walls, to mount his horse, give her full rein, and gallop through the snowy countryside. Shortly after breakfast, he excused himself to do just that, though he'd already been out on a walk earlier. James and Fanny hardly noticed his exit, so involved were they in sharing a moment of affection between themselves.

Witnessing glowing love was enough to make one want to throw a brick at such a man's head.

Not that James intended to flaunt his love and happiness—not by any means, Edward thought as his valet dressed him a coat, gloves, scarf, and hat fitting for the country winter temperatures. He wouldn't be able to spend as much time outside clearing his head as he did in the summer months, but even half an hour was better than a full day staying indoors, where he would be with James and Fanny, continually reminded of the things he lacked.

When he'd gone on his earlier walk before breakfast, he'd told the stables to ready his horse, so by the time he arrived, a stable hand already held Topaz, fully saddled.

Edward mounted her and took the reins. "I shouldn't be long," he told the stable hand. He adjusted his gloves and hat, then nudged the horse into a trot. He wouldn't gallop, quite yet; that was something he saved for when he felt truly alone—which, he realized with a smile, winter provided in better measure than other months. Somehow, with thick blanket of white, the world seemed hushed and at peace, a contrast to the budding life of spring and the excitement brought by riding through green summer meadows at a dead run. Perhaps a half hour's ride would be enough.

As soon as he turned off the estate's lane, he increased his pace to a good canter, enough to send bitter wind into his face, along with tiny crystals of ice battering his nose and cheeks. He grinned at the sense of feeling so keenly alive. The country road wasn't highly traveled at this time of year, but he did encounter a few townspeople in carriages, which broke the illusion of solitude. When he noted a trail leading off the road, he took the opportunity to ride up it to see where it would take him.

Within minutes, enclosed within white-covered trees, looking like something from a dream, he at last found utter peace and solitude. He encouraged the horse into a full gallop, and she more than happily obliged. Edward had to hold his hat atop his head, and soon his cheeks burned with cold, but he couldn't help smiling.

After a time, Topaz slowed to a canter on her own, clearly tiring. Edward reined her in to a trot and then an easy walk, gradually letting her catch her breath. He patted her neck. "Well done, my girl," he said, stroking her chestnut mane, then sitting back in the saddle and breathing in the frosty air.

That's when he looked about and realized he had no idea where he'd gone or how to return to Dunstead Manor. For all he knew, he could have galloped in a straight line, or in circles, or in figure eights. He turned the horse about and tried to follow his tracks to regain his bearings, to no avail— either someone else had come along, or he'd ridden over his own tracks, obliterating his chances of following them. If he could just find the main road again, surely he'd come across Dunstead Manor easily enough—or at least a passerby who knew which direction to go. The tingling in his nose and cheeks told him that he'd been out plenty long; he needed to find his way back soon, as much for Topaz's sake as for his own.

He tried to follow the tracks again, failed, and grunted with frustration. He'd ridden in this area once before, when the Clements had first moved here, but that was in early autumn, when the leaves had just begun to turn and the trail was still a single brown ribbon leading through the trees, easy to follow. The blanket of snow on all sides made the entire area look wholly new; he could have been in another country altogether and wouldn't have known it.

Topaz nickered and blew out through her nostrils, shaking her head. "I know," Edward said, patting her neck again. "I know."

He was about to make a third attempt at following his tracks when the silence of the wood was broken by a high-pitched cry of surprise—a woman's voice. Edward turned that way and followed the narrow road around the bend, from which he thought the sound had come from. Sure enough, he found a woman on her knees in the snow, scrambling after a fall. Her winter bonnet obscured her face as she gathered items that had scattered back into a basket.

Edward reined in Topaz and hopped off the saddle—then nearly slipped on the ice, just catching his balance by grasping the saddle until he was steady on his feet again. He picked his way toward the woman. "Miss?"

She froze at the sound of his voice, tilted her head ever so slightly his direction—but not so much that he could make out her features—and made a noise that might have been a groan before quickly returning to her work without a word.

"Are you all right? I heard you cry out a moment before."

"I-I'm fine," she stammered, still not looking up as she wrapped a loaf of bread in a dishcloth. "I slipped, is all. Rather embarrassing. I don't usually make such a ruckus when I stumble, but I thought I was alone."

"I can sympathize," Edward said, thinking how he'd been tempted to yell triumphantly at the peak of Topaz's gallop for no reason other than that he could. Now he was quite glad he hadn't done any such thing. He dropped to his knees and reached for several scones that had fallen out of her reach, placing each onto another cloth.

"Thank you for your help, sir, but I can manage," she said, still not looking up.

"I'm happy to assist." Edward was about to reach for more of the mess when her movements stopped completely, making his own pause. He realized that something a yard or two away had caught her attention—a pot lying on its side. She sniffed. "Miss?"

"Don't mind me. I was taking some food to a sick neighbor, and now look; it's all ruined." She gestured toward the pot, which he now noticed had spilled soup all around it, melting the snow.

"I'm so sorry," he said. "If it would help, I'd be happy to

take you home on my horse to fetch more, and from there take you straight to your neighbor's house. You must be half frozen."

"It's not only that," she said with a deep sigh. She gingerly got to her feet and walked to the spilled pot, looking sadly at its interior as she picked it up. "Mother doesn't approve of my bringing food to neighbors, sick or no. This meal took a lot of planning and sneaking about and—" Her voice cut off, and at long last, she looked up at him, brown eyes pulled wide. "Oh, please don't say a word to anyone. If Mother or Aunt were to find out . . ."

"I don't know you, your mother, or your aunt, but even if I did, I would say nothing. You have my word as a gentleman."

She visibly relaxed, her shoulders lowering, along with her chin again. The movement caused disappointment for him, as he'd caught only a glimpse of her features, and now they were hidden again. He wanted to walk over and tilt her chin upward to his so he could study her face.

Pray tell, why do you care about seeing a lady's face? he demanded of himself. *You don't know this woman at all. Must be the sickening lovebirds at Dunstead Manor encouraging my imagination toward silly notions.*

"I'm not from Glenworth," he said when she didn't go on. "I'm visiting a friend. So even if I couldn't keep a secret, it would be highly unlikely that I would reveal information to anyone who could cause you grief. But I assure you, I am quite skilled at keeping secrets." As evidenced by the many larks and pranks he, James, and Andrew had engaged in at Eton—things their families were even yet ignorant of, and would remain so to the grave.

"Thank you," she said, dabbing one eye with the back of a glove. "That is most appreciated. Mother and Aunt have ways of punishing me that—" She cut off and returned to her basket.

"Punish you?" Edward said, alarmed. "How? Are you hurt?"

"Not in the way you mean." She moved with a matter-of-fact practicality, putting the pot inside the basket and hefting the completed load. "Physically, I am quite well."

Not a particularly reassuring answer, Edward thought.

She turned and took a few steps away from him, so he called after her. "Miss? Miss, please. Wait."

She paused expectantly but did not turn around. "Yes?"

"They hurt you . . . in other ways," he said, not asking so much as confirming. He hoped she could sense his genuine concern over how she was treated by her family.

After taking a deep breath and letting it out with a sigh, she nodded.

"How?" He wanted to rush forward, to insist she let him protect her, but that would appear too forward and might even frighten her.

"How do they hurt me?" She laughed lightly, but Edward detected a note of sadness in it. "They wield behavior and words as sharp as any knife. I've sometimes thought that if tongues could wound, my mother and my aunt would be prized weapons for any army."

Humor even in such circumstances—a rare combination. Edward wanted to help this young woman who kept him captivated and piqued his interest.

"I was in earnest," he said. "Come. I'll take you home. You must be freezing. Where do you live?"

She turned toward him and shook her head, but once again her eyes and chin lowered to the snow. "You mustn't come, sir, but I sincerely thank you for the offer. If Mother were to hear that I rode on a strange man's horse, she would—" Her voice cut off, and she seemed to ponder how to go on for a moment. "It would be—quite *unpleasant* at home for some time."

This young woman intrigued him. On one hand, she deliberately flouted her family's wishes, and on the other, she worried about upsetting them for violating the same wishes. Whether from her manner, speech, or the small glimpse he'd had of her face, he could sense that she wasn't so young as to need such strict supervision. She seemed to suffer silently under the pressure while finding innocent ways of rebellion—if one could call delivering food to a sickly neighbor a form of rebellion.

As she turned again to leave, something fell from the basket. Edward used it as an excuse to speak to her again. "Miss, you dropped something." He picked up the fallen dishcloth and handed it to her. Their fingers touched, and he had the surprising desire to hold her hand in his, to look into her eyes and learn about her life. What went on in her clearly quick-witted mind, even though she spent her life with overbearing chaperones?

Look up, he thought, hoping she'd lift her face to his.

"Thank—you." Her voice caught slightly between words as she gently tugged the cloth away. Her cheeks had grown pink, but whether from blushing or from the cold, he couldn't know.

"May I—may I ask where you live?" Edward said. Asking for her name without being properly introduced seemed too forward, but he had to learn something about her. "I'd like to be sure that you arrive home safely."

"I'll be fine, but thank you for your concern." She hurried off with her load, the basket hanging from one arm as she made her way with careful, quick steps along the tree-lined road.

Edward watched her go, wishing she wouldn't leave, wouldn't go around the bend. Just as she reached it, but before he lost sight of her, he called out once more. "Miss?"

Again, she stopped walking. She looked and turned toward him expectantly, but at that distance, her face was in shadow from her bonnet. How to keep her here for a moment longer? He spoke the first thought that came to his mind. "Do you read?"

Stupid, stupid mind. That is the best you can do? Of course she can read.

"Rather," he said, suddenly nervous, "do you *enjoy* reading?"

Not much better. Fool.

Fortunately, the question had the hoped-for effect: she smiled. He still could not make out the rest of her features, but that sight alone pierced his chest in both a pleasant and painful way.

"I love reading," she called back. "Very much."

"Wordsworth." The name fell out of his mouth of its own accord. How was it that he, Edward Blakemoore, had become tongue-tied? Around a *woman*? This was as far unlike him as an Indian elephant.

Perhaps these woods truly are enchanted, and they have me under their spell, like in Shakespeare's play.

"Wordsworth is a favorite of mine," the young woman said. "One of our most talented poets."

"And Lord Byron?" Most young women he was acquainted with swooned at the very sound of his name. "Or Shelley?"

"Both, naturally," she said, but she brushed them off as obvious talents rather than Egyptian idols to be worshiped.

Refreshing.

"And Shakespeare," she went on. "I adore his sonnets

and many of his plays. Have you ever seen *A Midsummer Night's Dream* performed? I've read it many times, but I've never seen it. I hear it's delightful."

The very play I was thinking of. Almost as if we are of one mind.

"I have seen it, and I enjoyed it very much," Edward said. "Does your mother approve of at least reading Shakespeare, then?"

She laughed so hard that she leaned forward, and hand to her face as she caught her breath. Her laughter sounded like music; it ended all too soon.

I had a small part in making her laugh. It felt like an accomplishment.

"Mother would be appalled if she knew her daughter spent her time reading anything but the Bible or *Pilgrim's Progress*," she said, dabbing at her eyes, likely at tears of laughter. "That is another secret I must beg you to keep."

"Of course." He wished to lessen the distance between them but sensed she'd retreat altogether were he to try.

"In that case, I'll confess something far worse than Shakespeare: I have a private fascination with the work of Shelley's wife, Mary. Mother wouldn't dare sleep under the same roof as a daughter who regularly rereads a frightening tale. She'd cast me onto the streets and then pray for my soul." Her smile widened, and she chuckled again. "Can I trust that you'll never speak a word of my *sinful* reading habits?"

With as much solemnity as he could muster, Edward put a hand over his heart and bowed his head. "You have my word that I shall never tell a soul of how you have read—"

"How I often *reread*," she corrected.

He nodded at the clarification, then added a bow at the waist. "That you have read *and* often reread—and enjoy—a book such as Mary Shelley's *Frankenstein*." He held his bow, but after a few seconds of silence, he straightened only to find that she'd vanished.

She'd left when he wasn't looking. And right when he'd been on the cusp of having the opportunity to draw closer, to see her features clearly and ask her name, or at least her family's name, or the name of their home. *Something* so that he could find her again.

But she was gone.

And he was still utterly lost in the woods. *I should have asked her where to find Dunstead Manor. I could certainly catch up to her on horseback,* he thought, eying the bend. But no. She'd left quickly for a reason, and he would not be so ungentlemanly as to cause her anxiety by following her.

Besides, he didn't want to shatter the illusion that he'd stepped into a dream world and met one of the enchanted creatures living there.

Better to let fairies remain at peace where they belong, he reasoned, half convincing himself that if he were to make chase on the back of his horse that he wouldn't find her after all—only a mist showing where she'd once stood.

No matter. He'd find his way back to Dunstead Manor somehow. Plenty of daylight remained for that. As he mounted Topaz, the cold bothered him not a bit, even though he'd been standing in inches of snow and had even knelt in some while helping the young woman with her basket. Rather, he felt as if he'd been sitting by a toasty fire for an hour, reading a good book.

Perhaps, he thought as he brought Topaz to a trot, *that is exactly what I'll do following supper this very evening.*

Edward found himself grinning. *I wonder if James has* Frankenstein *in his library. I must give it a read.*

Six

For Olivia, the next several days consisted of a very different type of waking dream: a continual parade of possible scenes and outcomes of the ball, some good, some bad. Some extraordinarily good or horrifically bad. The result was feeling constantly jumpy and fidgety, something her mother and aunt noticed and commented on at least twice hourly with such unhelpful words such as, "Are you ill?" and "Goodness gracious. Sit still. You're behaving like a three-year-old."

All of her inner excitement made eating impossible. At one meal, she essentially behaved like the child her mother accused her of being. She only pretended to eat supper, spreading the food around to make the plate look emptier. She simply could not be at ease until she knew more of what Andrew and Emma had planned.

Likely not even then—not until I'm out of the house at the ball, and no one at Pine Park is any the wiser.

As she freshened herself before going down for tea, she felt weak and wanted to eat, but her nerves made her stomach uneasy. Good thing the ball was tonight; she doubted she could survive another day with so little food yet so many emotions—curiosity and worry mixed with a drop of guilt for deliberately deceiving her mother.

But only a drop.

She'd always behaved precisely as her family had expected, excepting her trips to feed some of the poorer families in the area, and she had to believe that such disobedience would be something God would look favorably upon. She hoped the same could be said of giving way to her real thoughts and desires for one evening at Dunstead Manor.

Olivia entered the parlor and sat on a sofa, where she looked at the tea spread and hoped she would have the fortitude to eat enough food to sustain her throughout the ball.

Otherwise, I'll faint straight away and cause a commotion. Then again, that might be enjoyable in its own way, she thought as she took a bite of a scone.

"What?" Mother demanded.

"Hm?" Olivia looked at her mother suddenly, but with her mouth full, she couldn't make a proper reply.

Mother waved one hand around as if drawing a circle about Olivia's face. "What was that just now? You had a *look*."

Olivia swallowed and took a sip of tea. "I'm sure I don't know what you mean." But she could feel heat moving through her traitorous cheeks.

"You smiled," Mother said as if such a behavior were sinful.

"Did I?" Olivia asked absently, returning her attention to her plate.

Aunt Matilda humphed. "She looked exactly like a

young Andrew—one could always tell when he was concocting a prank by the mischievous smile—always in silence as his tricky mind tumbled about his dastardly ideas." Her brows went up as she looked directly at Olivia, head tilted in what appeared to be less observation and more accusation.

Olivia forced her breathing to remain even, in spite of the worry sending her pulse racing. What if they believed that Olivia was planning something untoward—and then locked her in her room? They'd done as much as recently as three years prior when she'd had the audacity to ask about the nature of a midwife's duties. Silly her—after finding herself unmarried far past the usual age, she'd wanted to learn a skill and thought that helping women and their babies would be a good thing. But discussing childbirth even among adult women, in the broadest of terms, had been deemed taboo. Besides, Mother considered midwifery to be a trade, something below a gentlewoman. Yet Aunt Matilda had done something similar in her youth; she'd trained with a nurse and learned some medicinal skills. That had been a long time ago—Olivia scarcely remembered her aunt discussing the healing properties of various herbs.

With the prospect of hearing the lock click in her bedchamber door tonight and missing the ball, Olivia couldn't get a full breath. Her heart sped up as if she'd run the full distance from Landerfield at full tilt. Not knowing how to respond to an accusation of smiling, she glanced to her left at the grandfather clock. When would Andrew and Emma return? They'd claimed to go out for visits, but Olivia suspected that they were shopping and otherwise making arrangements for the evening.

"What exactly do you find so amusing?" Aunt Matilda suddenly asked.

"Yes," Mother added. "Please enlighten us."

Apparently, they did want an answer. Olivia forced away any lingering smile and cleared her throat. "Nothing at all, Aunt Matilda." She indicated the cranberry scone in her hand and murmured, "I must be sure to compliment Cook. This scone is delicious." She slipped a bite into her mouth and chewed slowly so she wouldn't be expected to speak again right away.

Aunt Matilda's eyes narrowed across the table with suspicion. Olivia did her best to look relaxed and at ease, something she found to be harder than a prisoner standing at a mark. Her mother tilted her head, matching her sister's gaze, and Olivia had the fleeting worry that they could read her mind and already knew everything.

A chime rang from the front door, and a moment later, Andrew's and Emma's greetings sounded, followed by Pierce's voice welcoming them back to Pine Park and asking if they wished to join the ladies for tea. By that point, the room had quieted. Olivia couldn't make out Andrew's reply, only murmurings. Perhaps he was whispering instructions.

Please don't let Mother suspect anything, whatever he's planning.

She thought of other explanations: maybe he'd fallen ill and lost his voice. In which case, they wouldn't go to the ball after all. Her speculations came to an end when Andrew appeared in the doorway, still wearing coat and gloves, which meant he'd refused Mr. Pierce's attempt to take them at the door.

Odd behavior. Such things raise suspicion. Olivia couldn't help but sit straighter and take a proper sip of tea, but the cup rattled slightly when she returned it to the saucer.

Wearing a coat and gloves indoors may mean nothing, she tried to assure herself. But something told her that the coat's appearance had something to do with the ball—that the day's ruse was about to begin in earnest. Olivia held her teacup against her lap to keep it from rattling. She didn't dare look up to discover whether anyone watched her.

"Mother, Aunt Matilda," her brother said with nods to each lady. "Pardon the coat. I still need to fetch some packages from the carriage, but I had to first bring these flowers to you before they got bruised or battered in the hustle and bustle." He held out a colorful bouquet of carnations surrounded by lush, if unusual, greenery.

Mother eyed the bouquet but didn't take it at first. "Pierce is entirely capable of bringing up your packages. Is the carriage still out front? I'll send Mary to help so the stable hand can unhitch the horses."

"No need," Andrew said, raising one hand in protest. "Pierce and Mary are both doing that precise thing as we speak."

"Very well," Mother said and again lowered to her seat.

"I do have one package I want to be certain is safe, so I'll be fetching it personally before the carriage is brought back to the stable." He pushed the bouquet forward a bit more. "Here you go, Mother. I thought of you when I saw these. Pink carnations for a woman who will forever have the glow of youth and beauty." He nodded into a slight bow as he held them out.

"Very well," Mother said, with a softer tone. Flattery from her only son tended to have that effect. "Let me see the flowers before one of the kitchen maids finds a proper vase for them."

But Andrew drew them back, just out of Mother's reach. "Oh, of course—I should have given them to one of the kitchen maids. I'll do that now." He smiled broadly, which created distinct dimples in each cheek.

If Olivia had had any doubts as to her brother's machinations, the dimples removed them. Apparently, her mother had yet to realize that dimples meant more than simple teasing from her son, as Mother softened further, relaxing into her chair and even smiling. Andrew had always been able to tease Mother, softening her into putty, but for Olivia, seeing it happen before her eyes would always be something akin to a brilliant magic trick.

The dimples told Olivia what she needed to know. She felt another smile coming on—one Mother and Aunt would certainly notice—so she pretended to dab the corners of her mouth with her napkin while watching the exchange.

"Come, come, Andrew." Mother spoke in as close to a playful tone as she had ever managed. "I'd like to admire and smell the flowers my son brought me. After all, flowers are not a common sight this time of year. Were they grown in a greenhouse in the country or imported from somewhere along the Mediterranean?"

"I'm not sure," Andrew said, holding them out again. Mother reached for them. "The vendor said something about Paris—"

His words were cut off abruptly as the flowers and greenery dropped to the floor and a screech ripped from her throat. "My hands! Oh, my hands! What infernal plant did some numskull put into that bouquet?" She nudged the flowers with the toe of her shoe to get them farther from her, all the while waving her hands in the air frantically. "Oh, they hurt. And look! My hands are all red and blotchy. And they're swelling. Oh, they hurt—and itch. Mary! Mary, where are you? I need help in here."

The maid, who had been entering with a basket of rolls, hurried over with a pale face that spoke of bewilderment. "What shall I to do, ma'am?"

"I don't know. Call for the physician!" Mother's eyes looked wild, something Olivia had never seen.

Mary bobbed a quick curtsy and raced out of the room as Andrew dropped to the floor and gathered the mess of flowers and greenery with his gloved hands. Olivia's mouth opened into a silent O of surprise and understanding. Her brother glanced over from the corner of his eye, winked, and mouthed, "Shh."

Olivia no longer worried for her mother. Whatever Andrew had done was minor; he would never have carried out a prank that caused Mother serious harm. But she did need to be tended to, so Olivia turned to her aunt. "Could you help at least until the physician arrives? You are far more knowledgeable about medicines and plants than we are."

Her aunt placed her teacup and saucer on the side table and rose with the regal bearing of one destined to make all things right. She went to Mother, who held out her rash-covered hands. Aunt Matilda placed a pair of spectacles on the tip of her nose and peered at her sister's skin, careful not to touch it. "Hmm."

"What is it?" Mother wailed.

Aunt Matilda straightened and removed her glasses, which she then used to point at the once-bouquet. "If I'm not mistaken, that greenery includes some poison ivy."

Andrew checked the rug for any missed leaves. "I'll discard this straightaway," he said solemnly. "And I'm so sorry, Mother. This is horrible." He looked genuinely contrite, yet his dimples were showing—deeply. He *must* have known that the bouquet would irritate Mother's skin—hence his gloves and coat, which protected him. But Mother's reaction seemed to have been worse than he'd expected.

So distracted was Mother from the itching and pain that she didn't notice Andrew's words. Matilda was busy with a damp cloth, dabbing cool water from the crystal pitcher over Mother's rash.

With the elder women's attention elsewhere, Andrew leaned in toward Olivia and whispered, "Meet Emma in your bedchamber as soon as possible." And he hurried out with the bundle.

"Definitely poison ivy—or perhaps poison oak," Aunt Matilda was saying with disgust. She called Mary over. "Take Mrs. Wallington upstairs and help her change into clean clothing. Take care to wear an apron and gloves and anything else you can find to keep yourself from coming into contact with the poison, or you'll be useless for your work."

"Yes, ma'am," Mary said with another curtsy.

"And see that Mrs. Wallington's dress is washed several times to be sure the poison is out entirely."

No one seemed to be aware of Olivia's existence in the least. She slowly pushed her chair from the table and stood. When no one looked up, she said quietly, "I think I'll go to my bedchamber so I am not in the way. I hope you feel better soon."

Mother looked over briefly. "Thank you, Olivia."

Taking that as permission to leave, Olivia turned for the dining room door, but her mother's voice stopped her.

"Do stay in your chambers for the day," she said.

"I—I will, Mother." Olivia breathed a sigh of relief that the request hadn't included the night. Of course, lies of omission were supposedly dreadful sins, but somehow not *speaking* the lie made the idea of sneaking off to a ball a little easier on her conscience.

As Olivia left the dining room, she heard her aunt giving more orders: a bowl of milk and another of saltwater to be brought to Mother's chambers. Olivia hurried to the base of the stairs, where she paused, a sliver of guilt slipping into her heart. In the distance, Aunt Matilda explained that alternating baths of milk and saltwater should provide some relief until the physician arrived and could do more, but that an apothecary would likely have some type of concoction that would help.

"Are you coming?" Andrew asked from the top of the stairs. He no longer wore coat or gloves, but his dimpled smile was bigger than ever.

"I most certainly am," Olivia said, lifting her skirts with one hand. Andrew came down and met her partway. She grinned at him. "Well done, brother. You've incapacitated both Mother and Aunt for hours in a manner they will both quickly recover from but will also be entirely consumed by for the interim. And all with one simple 'gift.'"

Andrew put a hand to his chest as he led her up the stairs. "Dear sister, I'm shocked by such an accusation."

"At my presumption that this wasn't an accident?"

He paused and took her hand between his, this time his smile one of affection. "I'm shocked you ever doubted that I would ensure your attendance at the ball. Come. See what Emma has planned for you."

Seven

Not until the carriage pulled up to Dunstead Manor did the full import of what Olivia was doing settle on her mind, and when it did, the weight seemed a hundred times heavier than the velvet cloak Emma had insisted on loaning her.

"Perhaps I should go home," she said in almost a whisper. She didn't want to go home—not remotely. Yet deceiving her mother and her aunt suddenly seemed wicked, though her logical mind argued that there was nothing wicked about attending a ball at her age, whether her relations were aware of it or not.

But was it wrong to attend a ball entirely because of a falsehood and a trick, and because one couldn't obtain permission to do otherwise?

"Go home? Nonsense," Andrew said. As the coachman opened the door and lowered the steps, he went on, "You deserve an enjoyable night out as much as anyone. Mother's unwell, though not in any serious jeopardy, and Aunt is caring for her. You know how much they love a good story about suffering. They're having the jolliest time of their lives." There were his dimples again.

His words and smile did comfort Olivia in some measure.

"And," Emma interjected, "we'll be sure you're home early enough that they won't suspect a thing."

"I've already made sure the household servants keep their tongues quiet," Andrew said.

Emma patted Olivia's arm, perhaps to bestow some confidence or encouragement. "Tonight will be grand."

She and Andrew alighted, but Olivia stayed in her seat for a moment and stared through the carriage door at the magnificent mansion before her. Mother and Aunt and falsehoods aside, did she truly want to venture behind those walls and face who knew what types of people, with their pretentious airs and patronizing ways of speaking to her? She'd grown weary of hearing such talk spoken directly at her, as if she were no older than six or seven and needed everything, including the most basic of manners, explained to her—often by girls ten years her junior who happened to have secured a wedding ring and a husband while scarcely old enough to call themselves women, who somehow had become Olivia's superior in all ways. The memory of such girls back home at Landerfield rankled; Olivia remembered those girls as infants in the pews at church, watched them toddling and half bald. Yet because they were married, and she was not, she was somehow inferior?

"Come, Olivia," Andrew said, reaching into the carriage for her hand. "Remember, not a soul in there knows anything about you. Every encounter will begin free of judgment or prejudice, and I will ensure that you are introduced to only the best gentlemen in attendance."

"Think of it, Olivia—a new beginning," Emma said behind him, her voice growing excited. "How many people ever have such an opportunity?"

"A new beginning?" Olivia repeated, letting the words soak in.

She took Andrew's hand and let him help her from the carriage onto the drive. She tilted her head back and wondered about Mr. Clement, the new owner, and who his guests would be—residents of neighboring towns, surely. Andrew was right; no one through those doors knew anything about her save, perhaps, that she'd recently moved into Pine Park with two elderly widows. For all they knew, she, too, was a widow, merely a young one. Or they might think her younger than her years; she'd been told often enough that even at an undesirable marriage age, she could pass for almost ten years her junior.

Perhaps I'll pass as many things tonight. With that thought, Olivia Wallington straightened her back, lifted her chin, and marched forward, following her brother and his wife into Dunstead Manor, where she was determined to have a new beginning.

Granted, if she ever attended another ball, it wouldn't be in deep green velvet, with her hair in ringlets and a string of pearls about her neck. She wouldn't again arrive with the appearance of an eligible young woman, not by half. For any future balls, Mother would be with her, and she would be introduced as the spinster daughter of Mrs. Frederick Wallington. Mother would expect her to remain as quiet as a lamb unless spoken to, and even then, her answers would have to be no longer than necessary—two or three words, ideally, to ensure a life free of Mother's criticisms and patronizing degradations for the following week. If she danced with anyone, it would be with older gentlemen who'd taken pity on her.

In short, she would be right back to living as she had at Landerfield.

No, tonight wouldn't be a new beginning. It would be a one-time experience that would end when she made her exit. For this one night, she had the opportunity to do and say what she pleased. She knew the proper, reasonable bounds of a young lady—the real expectations of society, not the ones her mother had foisted upon her. But within those bounds lay a freedom she'd never known.

A servant opened the door, and their party walked inside. Olivia crossed the threshold with a wide smile on her face and a shivered thrill going down her spine. Tonight would be one she would never forget. She'd capture every detail—every sound and smell and sight—so she could think of them oft throughout the years and relive the happiness contained therein.

Another young woman in similar circumstances might have found such a prospect bitter, but to Olivia Wallington, having beautiful memories to relive with her shadow prince seemed ample reward for a minor falsehood—and a painful rash—given to her mother.

No one in the ballroom will know me as the girl I always pretend to be, she thought. *For once, I will be myself without fear or worry.*

And she would enjoy every moment.

Eight

Standing near the refreshment table, with his back to the throng, Edward slipped his pocket watch from his waistcoat and flipped it open to check the time. After a quick glance, he snapped it shut and slipped it back into its place. How could only an hour and one quarter have passed? He felt as if he'd spent a full night standing in a receiving line, where he was introduced to women he would never remember, then dancing with two of them and promising later dances with three more. Throughout it all, he'd done exceptionally well at keeping a proper smile in place and his voice perfectly respectful. He felt quite confident that no one, save perhaps James himself, would suspect that his back ached from bowing and standing so stiffly, or that the boots he'd borrowed pinched something terrible—he'd have blisters by morning, no doubt. If he'd known his new pair wouldn't arrive from his usual cordwainer in time for the ball, he would have brought a different set with him. Hopefully, no one could tell that his feet hurt or that his cravat seemed to have taken on a life of its own, with the self-appointed mission to choke the very life out of him.

"Come now, old chap. Hiding in the corner already? The night is still young." James had found him all too easily.

Curses. Next time, I'll seek out a less obvious place to hide than the refreshment table.

James had been correct on one count, however; he'd known Edward's current state of mind. He turned around to find James holding two glasses of punch, one extended for Edward. "The night is young, but the room is already quite warm with so many dancers. I imagine you could use some refreshment."

"Thank you, yes." Edward took the glass and drank from it. Ironic that he'd taken cover near this table but had not availed himself of anything on it. He eyed his drink. He would have preferred to drink it all in a single gulp, but not only would that have been unseemly, it would also have made his mouth available for conversation that much sooner. At that moment, he had no desire to talk even to an old friend. So he made the most of every intentionally small sip, nodding and murmuring "Mm-hmm," at appropriate moments as James spoke, unwilling to let on just how much he wasn't enjoying himself. He'd agreed to attend a ball in his honor entirely for James's sake, yet it was something James wanted entirely for Fanny's sake.

The things men will do for the women they love, Edward thought with an ache. He wished he had such a woman for whom he'd hold a grand ball, even if it meant making an old friend uncomfortable and hot. It would mean having a love and companionship in his life that he didn't used to think he wanted, but now felt the absence of acutely—a hole left, oddly, by something he'd never possessed. And the hole ached more the longer he stayed at Dunstead Manor, witnessing the affection and devotion that James and Fanny had for each other. Much longer, and the hole would throb unbearably.

James leaned in and lowered his voice. "Are there not enough pretty young ladies to tempt you to dance, at least? I fully understand not wanting to become better acquainted, as most are far below your station, but that doesn't mean you can't enjoy a few dances with a pretty thing on your arm." He grinned as if daring Edward to disagree, an expression he'd often used at Eton to goad Edward into doing things he otherwise would have rejected out of hand. More often than not, he'd gone along with whatever plan James had concocted, and almost as often, Edward had been glad of it.

He highly doubted that this evening would fall into that category, however.

For Fanny's sake as much as for James's, Edward decided to make the best of the evening. That meant not complaining or criticizing or voicing his desires, even when what he would have preferred to be doing tonight was retiring to his bedchamber, where he could finish reading *Frankenstein* in blessed peace and think on the young woman from the forest. What was *her* position? Even with tailored clothing and an education, she might not be the kind of woman his mother hoped to find in a daughter-in-law. Yet unlike many with such fortune, the young woman was clearly concerned with the well-being of those in lesser circumstances. And she helped them in secret due to difficult relations at home. The entire situation intrigued him more than he truly admitted even to himself.

He became vaguely aware of James talking, so he murmured something along the lines of agreement, hoping it would be enough to keep his friend content. In spite of the many pretty ladies in the room, Edward had no desire to dance with any more young women he did not know, let alone with two or three, as James had suggested.

I already promised three more. These blasted boots will make the night pure misery.

He did have a hankering to interact with one young woman in particular, but only that very specific one. Would the girl from the woods come to the ball? And if she did, would he recognize her, seeing as he'd only had glimpses of her profile and dark eyes—and her smile at a great distance? Edward's gaze slid to James. He would know almost as well as Fanny who had been invited tonight and who was likely to attend. Surely he would know the identity of the mysterious young woman.

Edward chastised himself for not asking about her before. He'd stayed silent, to keep the memory safe from the merciless teasing that informing James about it would have brought about. One did not attend boarding school for years with another person without learning precisely how to make their lives miserable. James enjoyed a good joke at others' expense more than the average gentleman. So as much as Edward loved James as a brother, there could be no sharing of such things as a sudden mysterious meeting with a beautiful woman in the snow-covered wood. More, James would have laughed, and for good reason; Edward had long poked fun at anyone swooning over the poetry of Lord Byron or the love sonnets of Shakespeare.

The young lady admitted to enjoying Byron, but she seemed far more enthusiastic about Mary Shelley, he remembered with satisfaction. She wasn't one of the silly girls taken by the notion of heroic, romantic tales, which Lord Byron was responsible for getting into the heads of the day's young women. Yet Edward now understood the fervor of the flames Byron had fanned; every time Edward mentally relived the scene from the woods, he knew why men stood before crowds and recited Byron's poetry, declaring their love for one woman alone.

"My goodness," James said suddenly, looking across the room.

"What?" Edward asked, shifting his gaze in the same general direction but seeing nothing unusual.

"Unless my eyes deceive me, Wallington has arrived, and with him, two young ladies."

"Wallington?" Edward repeated. "You mean Andrew from Eton?"

"One and the same."

"Where?"

"By the second vase on the right. His father died last year, and his mother's dowry house was in the area, so I sent him an invitation to visit any time he wished, along with one to the ball. But I had no idea he would come, or that he'd bring guests." He turned toward the entrance of the ballroom again. "I'd wager that one of the ladies is his wife."

"I believe he did marry not long ago. Who is the other lady, do you think—his mother?" Edward ventured. He still couldn't spot their former classmate or his guests.

"Most definitely *not* his mother," James said with a chuckle. "A younger woman, perhaps a relation. Quite pretty."

"You don't know her?" A simple question to the casual observer, but saying the words made Edward's heart speed up. He had a feeling that he knew precisely who this mystery woman was, even without laying eyes on her.

"Come," James said, reaching for Edward's glass. "As host, I must greet them." He set the glasses on a servant's tray, then peered through the crowd again, stretching to see better. "It appears that Fanny has already reached them, but we must make certain to be next." He tsked and added, "Fanny was right; we should have kept the reception line a bit longer."

Without waiting for Edward to respond in the affirmative, or even to see whether he'd follow at all, James walked away. Edward tarried behind with indecision for but a moment, wherein he pondered whether meeting a fairyland creature outside the mystic woods would shatter the image he'd created in his mind, something he wasn't sure he would be able to endure. But before James's light-brown hair disappeared into the crowd entirely, Edward hurried after him.

Perhaps this night wouldn't be so dull after all.

Nine

Edward followed James through the crowd until it parted to reveal, sure enough, their old Eton friend Andrew Wallington with two young ladies at his side. One had her hand through his arm—Andrew's wife, no doubt. Beautiful in her own way, no question, but blonde and fair, not the type of beauty Edward found himself drawn to. The other woman, however, was strikingly beautiful—not in a classical way with the usual lines and features touted as beauty. In fact, taken individually, her features weren't much to look at, but put together, they created an impression of uniqueness, quiet strength, and a beauty he would be hard-pressed to forget. Her dark hair seemed to have red tints where the candlelight reflected off curls. She appeared content, if not entirely at home, as she looked about the room, taking in the sight of guests, decorations, stringed quartet—but not him.

Why not me?

James greeted Andrew with a hearty handshake and was quickly introduced to the new Mrs. Wallington. Before Andrew introduced James to the second woman, however, he spied Edward standing a few feet back.

"Edward Blakemoore, is that you?" Andrew stepped forward, tugging his bride along and making James step to the side. "James said you might be here, and I certainly hoped such would be the case."

"I did not expect to see you here," Edward said with a firm handshake. "What has it been, five years since the house party at Breckenridge?"

"At least," Andrew said. He clapped the side of Edward's arm and addressed his wife. "Between Mr. Blakemoore and Mr. Clement, my time at Eton was made bearable—and often featured colorful mischief the likes of which only the two of them could dream up."

"Rather, the likes of which one Mr. James Clement could dream up," Edward said, nodding toward James, who had always been the brains behind their school-year pranks. "He had a way of ensuring that his friends came along, even if it did mean we got close to expulsion more times than I have fingers."

"Or toes," Andrew added, grinning at James, who raised a hand in surrender.

"My days of mischief are over, gentlemen." He placed his free hand over Fanny's and gazed into her eyes. "I've found a far better diversion than stealing uniforms or hiding rotten eggs in professors' desks."

"Indeed," Andrew said, copying the gesture and gazing into his own wife's eyes. "I understand completely."

Both men seemed so taken with their wives that the world itself had fallen out of their consciousness, leaving Edward standing there alone. *I might have done that too, had*

I a wife, he thought, granting them a moment of thoughtlessness. *Very well, I* would *have done that very thing.*

A few minutes in the woods with what might have been something he'd elevated so high in his mind that no woman could meet such expectations, but if he ever met her again, he, too, might forget about everything and everyone else.

Andrew returned to his senses first, as he stepped back and opened his arm to the second young lady. "This, my dear friends, is Miss Olivia Wallington, my elder sister." To her, he said, "Olivia, may I introduce Mr. James Clement, whose wife you met moments ago, and another dear friend of ours from Eton, Mr. Edward Blakemoore."

Olivia Wallington gave him a curtsy. "How do you do?" The two men responded with proper bows and responses.

James gave Edward less-than-subtle gestures hinting that Miss Wallington should be asked to dance. Just Edward's luck, the previous dance ended right then, and couples were gathering on the floor for the next set. For someone who had recently decided he didn't enjoy the ball, the timing couldn't have been worse, yet considering the company, the timing suddenly seemed perfect. Dancing with the unusual beauty that was Andrew's sister might be enjoyable, or at least different from the other women he'd met tonight. As a relation of Andrew's, she would probably be a lively conversationalist, something that would certainly brighten the evening.

"Miss Wallington," he said with a bow, "would you do me the honor of being my partner for the next dance?" He straightened, and her attention, which had previously been focused on the room only now fully landed on him. She took him in and paled, her eyes widening.

Not precisely the reaction a gentleman hopes to elicit from a young woman.

"Unless you're unwell," he added quickly. "I wouldn't want—"

"No, I'm quite well. Thank you, Mr. Blakemoore," she said, dipping into a small curtsy. "I would be pleased to accompany you." As quickly as she'd paled, a smile returned to her lips and her posture straightened. Her head came up as well, and as they walked onto the floor, she looked as if she belonged at Dunstead Manor as much as any other lady present.

Whatever had caused her unease—if that was indeed what he'd seen—appeared to have passed. He certainly hoped so, though he worried about the need to catch her if she fainted. As the music started, Edward noticed a couple of young women in the set giving him disapproving looks. At first, he had no inkling why, and then remembered that he'd promised them dances, and here he was dancing with a new arrival.

Moments into the dance, Olivia Wallington's face lit up as bright as a summer's day. Her clear enjoyment radiated so much that Edward found himself diverted more by this dance than any other in memory. Her form was very good, although on occasion she seemed to forget what came next, as if she hadn't attended a ball in some time. On such occasions, Edward simply led her into the next formation as if he hadn't noticed her hesitation. She always sent him a grateful look, her brown eyes sparkling.

Another attractive woman with brown eyes, Edward mused as they went under the arched arms of the other couples. *What is so appealing about brown eyes?*

Her smile stood out to him as well and, at moments, seemed to be the twin to that of the woman from the forest. Unlike the face of his mystery wood nymph, his had not been obscured or covered that day. Were they to meet again, she would most certainly know him, but he would be unlikely to know her. Yet at their introduction, this woman had given no sign of recognizing him. Therefore, he had to assume that his dryad had a name other than Miss Olivia Wallington.

Fairy, nymph, now dryad. I've been reading too many fantastical works, Edward thought, and stifled a chuckle. No more mythology for him any time soon, or he'd be liable to believe in such ethereal creatures. And he most sincerely wanted to believe that intelligent, kind, strong women like the one from the woods existed in corporeal form rather than as the figment of one's imagination.

"Pray tell, what do you find so amusing, Mr. Blakemoore?" Miss Wallington asked as he led her about a circle.

"Am I so transparent?" He reminded himself to think of her not as Andrew's sister, but as Miss Wallington—though he'd already started to think of her as Olivia, as improper as that might be. If Andrew knew that he'd been taking such license, even in his mind . . .

He'd have my hide in ten seconds flat.

"I wouldn't call you transparent," Miss Wallington said. She lifted one eyebrow and seemed to choose her words. "You carry yourself quite . . . nobly. That is not meant as a criticism. But when your oh-so-serious, noble expression falters to make way for a smile, one can't help but notice it, and then it's a simple matter of deduction to know that the earlier expression was little more than a mask."

"One must be exceptionally observant to notice such a thing." Edward took her other hand and led her into the next step. "I find that to be a bold statement, considering the fact that we've only just met." She was both bold and intriguing. He admired a woman who spoke her mind without fear of repercussions—something all too rare.

"Mmm."

Now what did she intend to communicate with that? The sound seemed weighty enough to carry a meaning, but of what, he couldn't fathom.

Taking a page from her own book, he paid special attention to her face and noted twin pink circles slowly blooming on her cheeks. They could indicate embarrassment, but the sparkle remained in her mesmerizing eyes, and her smile only widened. He suddenly didn't care what she'd meant by the enigmatic *mmm*. He cared about one thing: making her smile again, and broader, maybe to the point of laughter. He wanted to spend time looking into those eyes, which were downright intoxicating with their browns and golds, like a warm chocolate drink with maple syrup and a bit of melted butter drizzled on the top, then swirled by an artist's hand.

Would that I'd have gotten a better look at the nymph's dark eyes. I wonder if they have a similar mixture.

At the thought, he suddenly found *himself* blushing, as if he'd been caught thinking about another woman in the presence of a lady. Best to introduce another topic of conversation, and quickly, for the sake of his flushing skin and ever-tightening cravat.

"How long will you and your brother be visiting Glenworth?"

Olivia's—rather, Miss Wallington's—eyes briefly flicked to his, and she hesitated before saying, "I believe that Andrew plans to return to Landerfield within the week."

A simple statement, yet Edward sensed she'd withheld a piece of the truth.

"A week," he said. "So soon."

His well-intentioned attempt at conversation ended there, as they lapsed into silence for the rest of the set. When the violin's final note trailed off and the dancers clapped their approval, he was loath to step off the dance floor. To his surprise, the feeling had nothing to do with facing the other ladies waiting for him—or, rather, ladies waiting to dance with a wealthy landed gentleman. He knew better than to think that they cared one whit for him, because they did not know him as anything other than Mr. Blakemoore.

He wanted to stay at Olivia's side, not escort her back to her brother and sister-in-law. To prolong their time together, Edward pretended to look about for Andrew, giving the task minimal effort, before saying, "Shall we take a turn in the gardens? I understand that a path has been cleared of snow, and that candles are lit throughout so guests may take a walk to get some fresh air after the heat of the ballroom."

"I would enjoy that very much," Olivia said. "I'll fetch my cloak."

Minutes later, with a beautiful cloak of green velvet draped about Olivia's shoulders, they walked through the doors leading outside. Two couples passed them on their way in, leaving only Edward and Olivia on the flagstone terrace atop a staircase leading to the gardens. They were alone, save for two servants at the doors. The cold came over Edward like a wave, surprising him with its intensity. Of course it would be chilly out. It was nighttime in the middle of winter.

Daft idea if you ever had one, Blakemoore, he thought, then thought of Olivia's feet in their thin slippers, and worry came over him for her well-being. The chill would go right through them to her feet, and the moisture would likely ruin her slippers completely. He didn't know much about women or fashion, but many a time he'd heard his mother complain about rain, snow, and ruined slippers. The terrace was dry, however, and it was illuminated by candles, sconces, and the nearly full moon. This would do, especially seeing as how the area had recently been vacated save for the servants. At least, it would do for a time; if the lowering clouds in the distance were any indication, a dreadful storm would arrive soon. One more reason to not venture too far.

"Perhaps we should stay up here?" he suggested. "I'd hate to see you fall ill on account of walking through snow in silk slippers, and a storm looks to be on its way."

She lifted her skirts enough to poke one slippered foot out. "I suppose you're right," she said. "Though I do so enjoy the outdoors."

They walked to the edge of the flagstones and took in the view. Below them, he could make out several dwellings, where windows were lit by lamps or candles. Groupings of lights were clustered together, with large swaths of darkness between them. In the distance, the storm clouds darkened the horizon.

And right before them, straight below, in the center of their view, a large area had no lights at all—the woods. With every passing hour, the details of the scene he'd played a part in grew blurrier, until he'd started to wonder how much of it had been real. Perhaps he'd been nigh unto freezing and had hallucinated the entire episode.

"Everything looks so different from up here," Olivia said. "It's nothing like being in the valley." She spoke softly, almost reverently. One hand held her cloak together under her chin.

"Indeed," he said. "Though I haven't visited much of the valley."

"It's so beautiful from here." Her voice seemed to hang in the air before dissipating like their white breaths.

"It is," Edward said.

How could he enjoy the company of one woman so thoroughly while at the same time longing for another he'd scarcely laid eyes on? Yet that's what this moment was, and he could make no sense of it. Perhaps he'd fallen so in love with the *idea* of finding what his friends had. Perhaps he wished so much for as perfect a match for him as Fanny was for James, and as Emma appeared to be for Andrew, so much that he now found beauty and—dare he think the word?—*romance* at every turn. First the dryad, now Olivia Wallington.

He'd lost the dryad, and he had no reason to believe he would find such a love with Olivia. Such a future would likely remain nothing but a dream. That's all the country seemed to be of late: one long taunt of fate showing him an ethereal happiness he lacked and could only yearn to find.

Perhaps I should go back to London, he thought, *so I'll no longer see the happiness I lack.*

"Look at those clouds," Olivia murmured suddenly, stepping forward and gazing into the distance.

In spite of himself, Edward felt drawn to her; he moved closer to her side and looked at the angry clouds too. *Not the most romantic scene,* he thought with a hint of levity. *Probably a good thing. I've had enough of romance in the country.*

Yet he didn't retreat from Olivia's side; he couldn't. In spite of how often his mind argued that a woman to love would never be in reach, he wanted to stay with Olivia and never leave her side. He found himself sidling closer to her, to the point that their arms touched. He held his breath, wondering if she'd take a step away. When she didn't—just smiled wider as she continued to gaze across the valley—he could breathe again. Perhaps even a stormy sky had the makings of romance, of a sort. And perhaps he could enjoy a little of that romance, for a moment. He could leave for London in the morning with a pleasant memory of spending time at the edge of the flagstones with Olivia Wallington.

"Remarkable clouds," he said, unable to think clearly

enough to conjure a better response. She *had* been talking about the clouds, hadn't she?

At Eton, I excelled in debate and oratory, yet a beautiful, intelligent woman has made me unable to form a coherent sentence.

"I know it really happened during that dreary, cold summer of '16, but I like to think that a powerful winter storm like that one was the real inspiration for *Frankenstein*."

She suddenly sucked in a breath and lowered her head so he couldn't see her face—a movement precisely like one he'd seen elsewhere a few days before. All he could see was the tip of her nose

As before.

This *was* his nymph, his dryad. The kindhearted, clever, well-read woman he'd been thinking of for days.

Olivia quickly turned away and spoke, her words tumbling about in starts and stops. "I'm sorry—that's not what—never mind. I—Ex-excuse me. It was a pleasure to meet you, Mr. Blakemoore." She lifted her skirts and made a move to run into the house, but Edward hurriedly grasped her arm to prevent such flight. By necessity, Olivia stopped her forward motion but didn't turn to face him. A blush crept up her neck in spite of the cold, and she closed her eyes tightly, sending a tear down the one cheek he could see.

"Miss Wallington," he said softly. "Please don't go." Oh, how he wanted to wipe that tear away.

"I must." She pulled her arm, and he released it, suddenly ashamed for restraining a woman for any purpose. Fortunately, she didn't flee. Her head tilted his direction, but only by a fraction, and as it had that day in the woods, her gaze remained on the ground. "Mr. Blakemoore, I apologize—"

"There is no need for an apology, least of all from you,"

Edward said. "I'd no idea you were the woman I came across in the woods, or I would have . . ."

What *would* he have done, exactly, beyond trying to win her good graces, beyond ridding himself of any guilt connected to being drawn to two different women, who were, in fact, one and the same? He found his capacity for speech severely hindered yet again. How could he tell her any of that?

She must have sensed rejection in his hesitation, because she lowered her chin further and said, "People often say I look younger than my years, but the truth is that I am far too old to tempt the most modest of gentlemen. Andrew is correct that I am the elder sibling, so you can quite easily deduce my years. I have a meager dowry left by my father, and a mother unlikely to approve of any match. I appreciate your kindnesses, but you certainly have no obligation to continue them. I shall take no more of your valuable time, and instead take my leave so that you may be free to dance with far more eligible ladies."

That was quite likely the longest stream of words he'd heard from her. He tried to find the correct way to convey the smallest part of his thoughts and feelings since he'd first seen her in the wood. All he could manage was the simple, "Please. Don't go. I've thought of you every hour since the woods."

She lifted her chin a fraction. "You—you have?"

"Yes," Edward said, his confidence returning. "You are the reason I've read *Frankenstein* three times in as many days."

"Really," she said, seemingly intrigued. "I wouldn't have suspected you to be the rebellious type."

"Oh, my mother has no qualms about my reading Mary Shelley or Shakespeare," Edward said, enjoying every moment of his time with Olivia and wondering at his fortune. "She might, however, be disappointed to learn that in my Bible reading, I read only the interesting parts."

"Leviticus?" she suggested with a teasing tone.

"Merciful heavens, no," Edward said with a faux grimace. "Song of Solomon, rather."

Fool. You went too far, he thought, his neck growing hot.

But she didn't look shocked or offended. Instead, she put a hand on his arm. "Thank you for making me laugh, Mr. Blakemoore. I haven't smiled so much in years. My cheeks are starting to ache."

"My pleasure." A phrase he'd never meant more sincerely in his life. The slight weight of her hand on his arm felt warm. He reached up and took her hand in his, remembering the moment when their hands had touched briefly in the wood, remembering again the ache in his chest when he heard about her mother and aunt's treatment. "I've kept your secrets," he said. "All of them." He hoped she'd know that he meant not only the authors she'd read but also the words she'd spoken about her family.

"Thank you." Her fingers gave the barest squeeze of gratitude.

"I've done more than read *Frankenstein* these last days," Edward said, measuring his words. "I've pondered your mother and aunt. Has Andrew ever . . ." He struggled to voice his worry, which felt somehow disloyal to his friend.

"No," she assured him. "My brother's tongue has not the slightest barb."

"I am relieved to hear that." Edward felt his shoulders drop as the worry did. "And yet . . ." As his voice trailed off, he studied her face, and she gazed back into his eyes.

"Yes?"

"I cannot bear to think of you living in such conditions.

Perhaps I could be a means of freeing you from an undesirable—"

She lifted her chin with a sharp movement, cutting him off. Her eyes were suddenly pained. "You wish to *rescue* me?"

Why did she sound so disappointed, so hurt? "I—"

"You *pity* me?" she said, her voice growing increasingly tense.

How could anyone pity a woman of such fortitude? "No, of course not," Edward tried to say, but she wouldn't hear him.

"I thank you for the consideration, Mr. Blakemoore," she said with a cold formality, "but I shall save you from such an odious obligation. Good night." She hurried inside, her eyes again on the ground—oh, how he hated seeing that, and knowing he'd caused it.

He wanted instead to be the one who could create the spark he'd seen in her eyes, to lift her chin forevermore, to see that smile always. *That* was what he'd meant by his offer, not that he pitied her. How could he feel pity for someone so strong, capable, and clearly making the best of a difficult situation?

He did wish better for her, and the time he'd spent with her—brief as it had been—had given him the hope of finding the very love he'd wished for since coming to Glenwood.

He wanted a better life for Olivia, and he wanted to be in it—if she'd let him. He ached to take her into his arms, kiss her soundly, and whisk her away from a life where she was mocked and treated poorly by her own relations.

With equal intensity, he wanted to scream into the night to let out his frustration over losing the one woman he'd ever wanted to pursue. His feet might as well have been cemented to the flagstones; he couldn't chase after her knowing that she wanted to go.

She had to have known who he was at their introduction; he knew that now. That was why she'd paled. But then she'd recovered so quickly and had seemed to enjoy his presence. Had she enjoyed dancing with him and talking with him? Or had she merely placated him by pretending she did?

With nothing else he could do, Edward sat on a bench and raked his fingers through his hair. Every time he closed his eyes, there she was—his nymph turned flesh, Olivia Wallington, the perfect woman for him, who remained just out of reach.

Ten

The morning after the ball, Olivia went through her usual toilette and preparations in silence, not having the heart to engage in idle conversation with Mary while the latter helped her get dressed and did her hair. Olivia's enjoyment of the evening, including the rare opportunity to think nothing and care nothing about what her mother and aunt would think, her chance to speak whatever she thought, had been cut short. Mary brushed through Olivia's hair, then put it up in a simple twist, but Olivia asked her to please make it looser than usual. Even if Mother thought a softer silhouette to be vain, Olivia could not bear to have her hair pulled tightly any longer. Not after she'd seen how pretty it could look when done in a manner other than one expected of a spinster. Still sitting at her dressing table, Olivia dismissed Mary, then studied her reflection.

She looked different, somehow. The softer lines of her

hair contributed, certainly—something she'd hear an earful about later, no doubt. But the change consisted of more than that. Her eyes lacked the light and excitement of the previous night, surely. *Maybe that's all it is*, she thought as she stood and moved to her bedchamber door to go down to breakfast. But as she walked the hallway and descended the staircase to the dining room, she knew there was more to the change than lapsed excitement and hair that didn't pull at her scalp to the point of a headache.

When she reached the bottom of the stairs, she paused with her hand on the newel post, thinking about the one dance partner she'd had before fleeing to ballroom of Dunstead Manor, waiting out the ball in a dark corner where Mr. Blakemoore didn't find her. She would have preferred going straight home, of course, but she couldn't justify ordering the horse hitched up again, taking her home to Landerfield, and the resulting unhitching upon returning to Dunstead Manor, followed by hitching again when Andrew and Emma were ready to leave and yet a final unhitching back at home. That would mean extra work for the driver and the stable hands at both Dunstead Manor and Landerfield entirely on her account.

She'd sat on a wingback chair in the dark and thought of handsome, rich, kind, funny, *good* Edward Blakemoore. Of how he'd felt *pity* for her. He needed a wife; Andrew had said that quite clearly. When she first met Edward in the wood, she hadn't known who he was, of course. She'd been eager to deliver the food to the Wilby family and return home quickly so Mother wouldn't question her absence or order her to stop helping the poor, who, in her estimation, must deserve to be poor or they wouldn't *be* poor.

Edward had looked and acted just as she'd long dreamed her shadow man to be. She'd found herself giddy and flushed and hadn't been able to think of anything else after he'd helped her in the wood. She'd headed home with broken bread and spilled soup, but half forgot that she never made it to the Wilby residence, caught up as she was in thoughts of the man on the forest road. On her subsequent morning walks, as she followed Mother and Aunt, she hadn't flown away to her regular fanciful dreams of her shadow man. Her mind instead had held fast to the memory of the man in the woods—a man who turned out to be Edward Blakemoore. He'd completely replaced her shadow man, something she now regretted.

She'd gone to the ball in hopes of creating real memories to relive, only to return without her fancies to escape to. She'd never again be able to think of her shadow man as he once was; Edward Blakemoore's face—and his pity—would forever occupy that place in her mind.

If only she could have kept her identity a secret. Before mentioning the book, she'd enjoyed the ball in ways she'd only dreamed of. Everything had been perfect—an adept dancing partner who enjoyed conversation and whose gaze could melt ice, a gaze trained on *her*. A walk onto the terrace with an unparalleled view. Perfection to such a degree that she'd grown entirely comfortable with Edward—then ruined everything by mentioning the one subject he'd remember her for, thereby connecting the oppressed life she led with the woman before him.

The facade had crumbled. She'd felt it collapsing about her the moment she'd spoken the title; she'd sensed a shift in Edward. He'd seemed on the verge of offering his hand in marriage, which on the outside sounded like a dream, if he'd done it from love. But he hadn't. He'd done it from pity.

Many a woman would jump at such a man, eager to take a hand offered from pity if it meant having a handsome, rich husband and getting free from Mother's thumb. Oh, were I that woman, but I am not.

Her hand gripped the newel post harder until the carvings in the wood bit into her palm. She let go and smoothed her skirts, wishing she had as simple a way to smooth her rumpled spirits. She lifted her chin, straightened her shoulders, and moved again toward the dining room. No one would ever suspect a thing.

Upon entering, Olivia noted the absence of Andrew and Emma. They were probably sleeping late after the festivities and having breakfast brought up to them. That meant facing the two elder ladies alone, as usual. Having her brother and his wife present was something she'd looked forward to during their visit; having them at meals deflected some of the criticism and attention.

She stepped through the door. "Good morning, Mother, Aunt—" Her greeting to Matilda stuck in her throat upon seeing her mother's face and hands covered in patches of something white smeared on them.

Some remedy for the poison ivy, most likely. She'd forgotten about her mother's rash. How was that possible, when it was the very thing that had gotten her to the ball in the first place?

She rounded the table and took her seat. "How are you feeling this morning?"

"Quite unwell, if you must know," Mother said with far less enthusiasm than she usually gave such statements. "Although Matilda's ointment has helped significantly."

"Thank you for caring for Mother," Olivia said to her aunt. "No one else knew what to do." With her knife, she sliced the top off her boiled egg, which sat upright in its stand.

"One does one's duty," Aunt Matilda said with a sniff. "I

couldn't sit idly by, watching my sister suffer while I had the means to ease her pain, now could I?"

"No," Olivia said quickly. "Of course not. No one would ever question your devotion to Mother." But as she reached for her egg spoon, she surreptitiously searched her aunt's face. Did she think Olivia shirked her duties toward Mother? Before scooping a bite of egg into her mouth, she took a breath, ready to lavish further praise on her aunt and assure both women that she herself would never, ever abandon her filial obligations, especially with such good examples of proper devotion in the two of them.

But before a single word escaped, she reconsidered. No more saying what they wanted to hear simply to avoid their disapproval. She took a bite of egg after all.

I did nothing wrong, she thought. *I shirked no duty.*

Besides, she knew nothing of poison ivy or medicinal aids. Had she stayed by her mother's side instead of going to the ball, she would have only been in the way, helping no one. A proper daughter wouldn't have attended a ball in secret, but other than that, Olivia had always been loyal and true, sacrificing her own comforts for the sake of her mother's and aunt's well-being, even when such sacrifices weren't necessary. Pushing her desires to the wayside had been her way of attempting to make peace under a roof where peace rarely reigned. Turmoil of one kind of another erupted in some form at least once a day, whether in the form of criticizing others or a complaint of some physical ailment that did not actually exist.

As Olivia sat at the table, spoon poised in the air above the egg, understanding dawned on her. Nothing she'd done to make her mother or aunt happy worked any better than surrendering to the tantrum of a child who only grew more spoiled as a result.

Perhaps I shouldn't have left my true self in my dreamland so entirely over the years, she thought, slowly scooping out another bite of egg. *Would life with Mother and Aunt be easier today if I'd spoken my mind all this time?* She'd never know what might have been, but she could begin such a life now—a more honest one, where she didn't have to hide her true thoughts and character away from her family.

Odd that she'd felt guilty hiding the ball from her family, even though she'd spent years hiding her true self. Hadn't she been living a lie with them every day?

The very idea of saying her true thoughts and feelings to her mother and aunt seemed as unattainable as the golden goose from the fairy tale, but she wanted to try. And as she imagined what life would be like speaking as herself, she couldn't help but reflect on the almost magical time she'd spent with Edward. Talking with him, dancing with him, walking with her arm through his, looking over the valley—throughout it all, she'd felt more alive, more genuinely herself, than at any other time in her life.

And then he'd ruined it all with his pity.

What if she could leave this house on the arm of Edward Blakemoore, or someone like him, someone who cared for her instead? She studiously salted her egg while trying to hide a sigh. The chances of falling in love with a man who truly wanted her aging hand were so low as to be almost laughable. That was why she'd made the best of her situation. With Andrew as her brother, she'd never want for food or shelter, which was more than many unmarried women could say. She should be content with her lot. She'd had a few moments of magic with Edward, moments she could relive again and again, should she so desire.

Maybe one day she could think of him without pain, and her dream world would again satisfy her, although she doubted it ever would. Not after experiencing a taste of what real life could be like.

Throughout the rest of the breakfast, remaining properly silent became a simple task; Olivia had nothing she wanted to offer up in conversation to those at the table. If Edward had sat opposite her, they would no doubt never run out of enjoyable topics. Unlike many men of her acquaintance, Edward hadn't seemed intimidated by an educated and well-read woman. Oh, why couldn't he have cared for her instead of seeing her a potential recipient of his charity?

I could never live in such a marriage, forever in debt to my husband, as I feel forever indebted to Mother and Aunt. That life would be too similar to what I already have.

She tried to assure herself as she ate egg and sipped tea. Edward's money would make life for someone like her far more comfortable in temporal matters, and that was not something to brush off as inconsequential.

In spite of herself, her mind kept wandering back to Edward's rugged features, his broad shoulders, wide smile, warm eyes, strong hands . . .

Her breath stilled as realization shot through her: She'd fallen in love, quickly and intensely. How did one control the heart? She had no ideas on that count and certainly couldn't talk to Andrew or Emma about it. All she could do was hope that Edward Blakemoore's stay with Mr. Clement would be brief—that he would leave for London soon and never return. That would be for the best.

But if that was so, why did tears swim in her vision at the thought of never seeing Edward again?

"I do wish Andrew and Emma had come down for breakfast," Mother said, picking at her food with the tines of her fork. "But I suppose that's to be expected after returning late from the ball."

"Indeed," Aunt Matilda replied. "I anticipate hearing all about Dunstead House, its new owner, and his new wife."

Olivia looked from her mother to her aunt, her heart rate picking up and her eyes drying in an instant from sudden nerves. She felt as if she stood on a precipice, as if her actions, or lack thereof, in the next moment would determine her destiny. She could remain silent and continue as she had for years, or she could speak boldly for once in her adult life. She clasped her hands in her lap to stop them from shaking, then enunciated as clearly as she could, "*I* could give you as good a report as either of them, seeing as how I also attended the ball at Dunstead Manor."

Matilda gasped, leading to a coughing fit. Mother seemed oblivious to her sister; her fork dropped to her plate and her jaw hung open as she gaped at Olivia. "You . . . you *what*?"

No more pretense.

"You heard correctly," she said. "Emma was kind enough to lend me one of her gowns, and I rode in their carriage." She looked about the table, which had grown eerily silent. Even Aunt Matilda's coughing had ceased, and her mouth hung open as well. The two elder women looked as if they'd seen the very monster of Frankenstein.

Olivia refused to recant her words, though every nerve in her body demanded it. The consequences of such an admission would be dire. With equal intensity, her heart refused to surrender. *If my experience at the ball is to not go to waste, I must press on.*

She swallowed, gripping her hands even more tightly in hopes of keeping the rest of her body from trembling. "That's right. I attended the ball. After we arrived, Andrew was kind enough to make introductions to both Mr. Clement and to his guest, Mr. Blakemoore, with whom I enjoyed a dance. He is quite accomplished on the dance floor."

And he's intelligent and well read and kind and . . .

When silence continued from the others, Olivia went on. "Dunstead Manor is magnificent. The ballroom is the largest I've seen, with a beautiful inlaid floor and sparkling chandeliers. Gorgeous tapestries. I believe even you would be impressed with the size and elegant decor." She wasn't entirely sure which woman she meant with the latter comment, but it fit either.

"Well, I—" Matilda began.

"No daughter of mine—" Mother tried.

But Olivia refused to listen. She pushed away from the table, stood, and said, "I won't be accompanying you on the morning walk today. I'm quite fatigued from the ball, you see. I shall retire to the library to *read*."

Heart pounding like a drum, Olivia walked out of the dining room, head up and shoulders back, much as she'd walked into Dunstead Manor. She'd only just gotten out of their line of sight when her knees refused to carry her farther, and she had to lean against the wall for support. In her middle, the old dread fought against a delicious thrill and excitement—and the thrill won. Olivia grinned, looking back at the dining room door.

Mother will likely call a doctor to find something wrong with my head.

The thought should have been only a shade away from horrifying. Instead, Olivia laughed, feeling the weight of a lifetime of pretense exiting her body and making way for the real Olivia to live. She took a deep breath and, as promised, retired to the library to read in peace instead of turning her toes to ice while walking behind her relations. She slipped a volume of Shakespeare's sonnets from one of her many hiding places. Forcing thoughts of Edward out of her mind, even though he was the reason behind the selection, she settled on the window seat, reading by the light of the morning sun.

Eleven

The last thing Edward expected from knocking on the front door of Pine Park was a dismissal. He held his top hat in both hands and cocked his head to one side. "Pardon?"

"Mrs. Wallington and her sister are not available at the moment," a middle-aged and somewhat irritable-looking serving woman said, holding the door open only six inches or so.

"Is Miss Wallington in?" Edward pressed.

The woman blinked as if bored, something Edward wasn't used to. "I believe she's home, but—"

"May I speak with her? It's about a most urgent matter." He had to use effort to not bend the brim of his hat and to sound firm yet polite. He had to see Olivia. Had to. He knew little of the ways of women's minds and hearts, but he felt in his bones that any delay in seeing her would cost him the opportunity to be with her—a price he was entirely unwilling to pay.

The servant woman raised her brow, creating rows of wrinkles on her forehead. "Alone?"

"No," he said. "I mean, technically alone, yes, but—"

If only the winter had passed; then they could take a turn about the gardens, with chaperones walking ahead, and then he could speak from his heart. He hadn't thought about what such a conversation would entail indoors, or that her mother, aunt or both—heaven forbid—would be present for the sake of propriety.

"Please, may I come in? I'm willing to wait."

The woman tilted her head and seemed to consider, which made hope flare briefly in Edward's chest. She opened the door a bit wider too. But then she seemed to reconsider. "Sir, I regret to inform you that—"

"Why, Edward, is that you?"

"Andrew!" Edward called with relief. Of course. Why hadn't he thought of asking for him first?

The servant woman released the door and turned to Andrew. "You know this gentleman, sir?"

"I most certainly do," Andrew said, ushering Edward inside. "This is Mr. Blakemoore, whom I've known since I was a boy. Come in, old chap. Let's go to the library for drinks."

"Mr. Wallington, sir," the woman called apologetically.

Andrew turned about expectantly. "What is it, Betty?"

The maid's eyes darted between the men, and she wrung her hands as if worried that the lady of the house would dismiss her for letting a stranger inside. "Miss Wallington is already in the library, sir." She took a nervous step forward. "Shall I bring you tea in the parlor instead?"

With a nod, Andrew began to reply, but Edward raised a hand to interrupt. He spoke in a hushed tone directly to Andrew. "The library. Please."

For a few seconds, not a word passed between the friends; the only sound in the hall was Betty's shoes shifting nervously, accompanied by her shallow breathing. Edward silently pled with every ounce of his soul, praying that Andrew would either understand his desires or agree to the library purely on the grounds of friendship.

"V-very well," Andrew finally said, drawing out each word. "Shall we . . . inform Miss Wallington of our impending arrival so she may vacate the library if she wishes?"

The only answer Edward gave was the shake of his head. He wanted to say more, to explain, but that would have to wait until the listening ears of servants weren't around.

Andrew looked past Edward to Betty. "Tea in the library, Betty. For three?" He eyed Edward, who nodded again. "For three," Andrew confirmed. "I'll escort Mr. Blakewood myself."

Betty curtsied. "Yes, sir," she said and hurried down the hall.

When she was gone, Andrew turned to face Edward full on. "What was that all about? If I didn't know better, I'd think you'd been hit in the head. Is my mother's library so extraordinary that you must see it this morning?" He turned toward a corridor off the foyer, gesturing Edward to follow and speaking over his shoulder as he walked. "If I didn't know better, I'd think you were—" His step came up short, and Edward nearly ran into him.

The two stared at each other. Edward's heartbeat thudded in his ears as Andrew's gaze seemed to rake him over. Edward stood as tall as he could; he had at least two inches over Andrew. "You'd think I was what?" He wasn't sure whether he wanted Andrew to guess the truth or remain ignorant.

"That you were hoping to see a lady in the library—alone." Andrew chuckled and shook his head. "But that's stuff and nonsense. It's only Oli—" This time, understanding broke over his face as if someone had suddenly shone a lamp there.

"Shh," Edward said, putting a finger to his lips. He stepped to the side of the hall, taking his friend with him. "I must speak with her, and you may be chaperone, but you *mustn't* listen."

Andrew folded his arms and leaned against the wallpapered hall. "And if I do?" he asked, grinning mischievously.

"Stop that," Edward said. "That face belongs to a young James laying tacks on the headmaster's chair."

"You didn't answer my question." Apparently, Andrew wouldn't be dissuaded.

"Very well." Edward sighed and pinched the bridge of his nose and let out a breath before launching into the truth. "I hold your sister in high regard. We haven't been acquainted for long, but we did meet before the ball, quite accidentally, and she's been on my mind ever since. As her brother, you're likely unaware of how remarkable and beautiful—"

"My sister," Andrew said. "You speak of Miss Wallington?"

"Yes."

"Miss *Olivia* Wallington?"

"Yes. Of course I mean Olivia." Edward sighed, raked his fingers through his hair, then turned his back to the wall and leaned against it, feeling the weight of defeat. "As her brother, you are likely unaware of her many admirable qualities, but I assure you, I am not so ignorant."

"What qualities do you mean?" Andrew said, his voice no longer teasing.

"She is . . . *beautiful*. Breathtaking." Edward knew his voice must sound like a fool's, but he didn't care. He could see Olivia in his mind's eye and, at the moment, wanted nothing more than to dance with her again, walk the terrace with her again—and then attempt to change how they'd parted. "She is remarkable, Andrew. Intelligent. Funny. Clever. Kind. Intriguing. And I simply cannot get her out of my mind." He rested his head against the wall and closed his eyes. "But I'm afraid I said something last night that wounded her—entirely without intention, you can be assured—and she left, hurt and upset nonetheless."

Edward stared at the rose pattern on the rug at his feet. "I cannot bear to think that I am the cause of her pain. Whether she will forgive me or send me away, I don't know, but I must apologize. And then I hope that she'll give me another chance. Surely you understand, Andrew. As a newly married man, I imagine James would too."

"Understand what, precisely?" Andrew said.

"What it feels like to have fallen in love." He stood there, leaning against the wall, one leg bent at the knee, hat in hand, his heart sinking further and further.

After what felt like a near eternity, with no answer from his friend, Edward turned his gaze from the rug toward Andrew, but he no longer stood there. Olivia had taken his place, and Andrew had retreated at least two yards down the hall. He, too, leaned against the wall in a similar stance, and he wore a grin wider than the Channel itself. Edward looked at Olivia, who stood only an arm's length away. She had a book clasped in one arm and wore an expression of hope rather than of hurt or anger. Edward glanced in Andrew's direction again.

"I'll be in the library if anyone needs me," Andrew said, and ducked into the room.

Alone at last, Edward stepped forward and took Olivia's free hand. "Did you hear what I told your brother?"

Olivia shook her head, looking flushed and bewildered. Edward screwed up his courage and said what he'd come to say. "I have been utterly wretched since last night. Please accept my deepest apologies."

"It is quite all right, Mister—"

"No, it isn't," Edward said, stepping a hair closer.

"It isn't?" Olivia said a tad breathlessly. He took that as a good sign.

Shaking his head, he said, "No, it isn't all right. I must explain myself and hope I do a far better job than I did last night. You are a strong, wonderful woman—one who, quite simply, needs neither pity nor rescuing, as I believe my foolish tongue implied last night." He lifted her hand to his lips and pressed a kiss to her fingers, then stroked them with his thumb. He had no desire to ever release her hand. "The truth is, Miss Wallington—"

"Olivia."

He smiled at that. "The truth is, *Olivia*, that I've come to care for you—and far deeper and more quickly than I ever thought possible. I want to come to know everything about you, to hear you talk about books and anything else you learn and discover and think."

"Why didn't you say those things last night?"

"Because I'm a fool," he said simply. "And because I didn't yet have the words. I spent all night trying to find the right ones."

"So you don't see me as a damsel to rescue?"

"No." How did one put this next part into words without offending her family? "I want you to be happy, to feel safe and content, to be able to express yourself. If being with me enables those things to happen—and prevents some measure of hurt from coming upon the woman I love—then that is what I want for her. What I want for you. I want you to be happy."

"You . . . love me?"

He stepped even closer and gazed into her eyes. "In spite of my long-declared status of a bachelor, I do—very much."

Now it was her turn to step closer; he could smell her fragrance. "What would you have done if I'd sent you away?"

Still holding her hand, he reached up with his other and stroked her cheek. "I would have cried out, 'Oh! Stars and clouds and winds, ye are all about to mock me; if ye really pity me, crush sensation and memory; let me become as naught; but if not, depart, depart, and leave me in darkness.' I would have no longer desired to exist."

She bit her lower lip, her cheeks turning pink in the way he'd come to love as she looked into his eyes. "You really did read the book."

He nodded. "Poor Victor," he said, then leaned forward and brushed a kiss against her cheek. "Delightfully terrifying story."

"Most definitely," she murmured.

He kissed her jawline once, and then a second time, then paused for a moment to take in her beauty before closing his eyes and kissing the sweetness of her lips. She kissed him back, then pulled away, looked into his eyes, and gently ran a finger across his lower lip. "A real kiss is much sweeter than any dream."

"Good heavens," came a deep voice from inside the library. "How much longer must I abide such talk?"

The two stepped apart as Andrew came into the hall. Edward felt his ears turning red but couldn't find it in his heart to mind, not when Olivia looked every bit as pink as he felt, and not when she'd accepted his kiss and forgiven him.

"What a delightful turn of events," Andrew said, clapping once. "Who should tell Mother?"

Olivia laughed, the sound free and delightfully loud. "Not I, dear brother," she said, pulling Edward along behind her and into the library. "Edward, neither. I've done enough of handling Mother and Aunt with kid gloves. It's your turn."

"I suppose I deserve that," Andrew said, grinning through the doorway as his sister and friend settled side by side on a couch to read her book—a volume of Shakespeare's sonnets.

"Mother will take the news far better from you anyway," Olivia said, looking up.

"Although," Edward said suddenly, "let's be clear on one point: you are not announcing a courtship. This, my friend, is an engagement." He looked at Olivia hopefully.

Olivia threaded her arm around his, and, without looking at the text of the book, quoted, "'Doubt that the stars are fire, Doubt that the sun doth move, Doubt truth to be a liar, But never doubt I love.'"

Edward raised her hand to his lips and kissed it, relieved beyond measure.

From the door, however, Andrew apparently couldn't resist adding to the moment. "That's not one of Shakespeare's sonnets, dear sister."

"No," Edward said, not moving his gaze from Olivia's beautiful face. "It's from *Hamlet*. But I echo the sentiment heartily." He glanced at Andrew for but a moment and grinned at how the latter was rolling his eyes. "If our heartfelt poetry is so unbearable, I suggest you leave and inform your mother of our impending nuptials. We intend to read through every lovesick word the Bard ever wrote, regardless of how long it takes. Isn't that right, Olivia?"

"Of course," she said. "'Doubt that the stars are fire,' but never doubt that I'll sit for hours reading a good book with you."

"'Twould take a lifetime to read half of them."

"Then we'll need at least that much time together, won't we?" Olivia leaned against Edward. He wrapped his arm about her, and she fit perfectly in the hollow, as if she'd been born to belong at his side.

"Undoubtedly, we will need at least a lifetime," Edward said, and leaned in to kiss her forehead.

Andrew muttered something but left them alone at last, just Edward, Olivia, the fire, and pages and pages to read together.

ABOUT ANNETTE LYON

Annette Lyon is a Whitney Award winner, a three-time recipient of Utah's Best of State medal for fiction, and a four-time publication award winner from the League of Utah Writers, including the Silver Quill Award in 2013 for *Paige*. She's the author of more than a dozen novels, almost as many novellas, several nonfiction books, and over one hundred twenty magazine articles. Annette is a cum laude graduate from BYU with a degree in English. When she's not writing, knitting, or eating chocolate, she can be found mothering and avoiding the spots on the kitchen floor.

Sign up for her newsletter at AnnetteLyon.com/contact
Website: AnnetteLyon.com
Blog: Blog.AnnetteLyon.com
Twitter: @AnnetteLyon
Facebook: Facebook.com/AnnetteLyon
Pinterest: http://Pinterest.com/AnnetteLyon

Michele Paige Holmes

OTHER WORKS BY MICHELE PAIGE HOLMES

Counting Stars
All the Stars in Heaven
My Lucky Stars
Captive Heart
A Timeless Romance Anthology: European Collection
Timeless Regency Collection: A Midwinter Ball
Between Heaven and Earth (Power of the Matchmaker series)

Hearthfire Romance Series:
Saving Grace
Loving Helen
Marrying Christopher

One

Bishopbourne, England, October 1819

Eleanora Whitticomb half walked, half ran across the meadow leading from the stables to her father's stately country manor. The riding crop dangling from her hand swung jauntily as she breathed in the crisp autumn air and enjoyed the season's splendor, bursting all around her in burnished gold and the brilliant reds of Goresley Wood. She loved this time of year; she loved her home. And on glorious mornings like this, she loved life.

If only Mother and Father were here to enjoy it with me.

As quick as it had come, she pushed the melancholy thought from her mind. It was too beautiful a day to feel sad. She would not allow it. Pulling the ribbon from her hair, she shook her tousled curls loose and forced a smile to her face. Her mother likely *was* enjoying the changing season, watching over her from heaven.

And Father . . . Ella sighed. Father was enjoying other grandeur right now. Perhaps even this very minute standing in the stirrups of his camel—

Do camels have stirrups? Perhaps not.

She amended the picture in her mind and imagined her father leaning forward on his camel to better view the pyramids rising in the distance.

Someday she would view those pyramids too, as well as the other wonders Father traveled to see. She was twenty now—just last week—and surely her gift from Father would be arriving any day. Soon he would keep his promise to send for her so she might accompany him on his adventures.

Though I shall miss the horses.

As she crossed the drive, her stomach growled, so she took the steps leading to the double doors two at a time and arrived not breathless, but with cheeks rosy with cold from her early morning ride, and with an appetite most young ladies would be ashamed of.

The front door swung open, and Peters welcomed her. "Pleasant morning, Lady Ella. I trust your ride was satisfactory."

"Far more than that." She removed her gloves and placed them in his outstretched hand. "Chance is coming along so well with his jumping, and the hillside is awash in color. You really must get up there to see it."

"Perhaps some afternoon, if my duties allow," Peters said formally as he closed the door behind her.

"*I* shall see to it that someone else attends to the door and the silver and whatever else it is keeping you indoors during such a marvelous season." Ella reiterated the promise she made almost daily. That the butler never availed her of it did not surprise her, but neither did she understand his refusal to leave his post or the house. It wasn't as if they ever had any visitors.

"A gentleman is here to see you," Peters said, as if he'd

discerned her thoughts and was eager to point out how imperative it was that he maintain his duties.

"A man? Here?" Ella's brow furrowed, and her stomach growled again, reminding her of the scones waiting on the sideboard in the other room.

"A *gentleman*," Peters corrected. "He comes bearing a letter for you and insists he is to give it to you personally. He has been waiting in the drawing room nearly an hour."

"It must be from Papa!" Thoughts of breakfast fled as Ella raced across the foyer, slowed to a brisk, purposeful walk just before the doors, and entered her least favorite and the most seldom used room in the house. She walked directly to the stranger, rising from a stiff-backed chair near the empty fireplace.

"He sent you to bring my birthday present, personally, didn't he?" She beamed at the messenger as she held her hand outstretched, her fingers practically itching to snatch the envelope held in the hand at his side. "Did he tell you where he's going next? Where *we're* going?"

The man did not return her smile, but appraised her most solemnly. "If by *he*, you are referring to Lord Benton—"

"Who?" She paused. The name was vaguely familiar. *One of father's friends?* For the first time she considered that this messenger might be delivering something other than birthday greetings, something other than a ticket for her passage and the long-awaited invitation to join her father. But if not that, then—

"Has something happened?" That would account for the messenger's aura of gloom. "Has Papa fallen off of his camel or had some other mishap?" Her chest squeezed with anxiety, though she told herself all was well. If he *was* hurt, it wouldn't be the first time. Fortunately, nothing too serious had happened before. *Only serious enough that he felt it too risky for me to accompany him.* But Papa was getting older now and, in the years since her mother's passing, reckless as well. *If he is hurt—*

"I am not aware of your father's well-being at present. We are not acquainted," the man said.

Ella felt further frustration—more with herself and Papa than the stranger. She should never have supposed that the man would know her father, as fine and fashionably as this gentleman was dressed. From his smartly tied silk cravat to the polished buttons on his double-breasted waistcoat to the tips of his shiny top boots, he looked as if he might have come straight from the social pages of London, something Father avoided at all costs. *What sort of messenger dresses so fine?*

"You *are* Lady Eleanora Theodosia Whitticomb?" The stranger tilted his head slightly to peer at the writing on the envelope still clutched stiffly in his hand.

She cringed at all twelve syllables of her name pronounced so distinctly. "Lady Ella, if you please." Such pomp had been all her mother's doing. Ella hadn't even been able to pronounce her entire name until she was four, much less spell it. Now that she was grown, she could hardly stand it.

His brow furrowed, and his look turned quizzical as he studied her again, as if he were not entirely convinced of the truthfulness of her answer.

She felt a twinge of embarrassment and regret over her lack of manners. At the very least, they should have had a moment of introductions, but his identity seemed of less importance than the contents of the correspondence in his possession. *It still might be from Papa.* "Peters said you have a letter for me." She glanced at his hand and noted that it remained at his side, slightly behind him, so as to be out of her reach. *Does he intend to give the letter to me or not?* "May I read it, please, to reassure myself that my father is well."

"I know very little of your father, save his name and that he is given to wandering the Continent and beyond." The man paused long enough to peer down his nose at her, as if he were accusing her of being the reason for Papa's absence. "The message I bring is not from him, neither has it anything to do with him."

"Oh." Ella sagged in both relief and disappointment and let out a long breath. She dropped her hand to her side, no longer concerned with whatever the packet held. Though it did seem rather odd that he had not given it to her yet. For a messenger, he was not very efficient. "Why ever did you not say so earlier? And here I was imagining the worst."

"I am doing more than imagining it," the man muttered. Ella's head jerked up at this, and she caught his baleful expression as he finished a more thorough perusal of her.

"Who are you, and what is it you want?" she demanded, pulling herself up to her full height and gripping the crop firmly. Gentlemen never called upon her—nor did ladies for that matter—and this one was a reminder of how very little she cared about that lack of attention.

"Mr. Alexander Darling." He gave a slight bow.

Another ridiculous name. Nothing darling *about him,* she thought as he righted himself and his blue eyes fixed her with a piercing stare.

"I have been charged with personally delivering this letter to you. It is from a longtime and dear family friend, Lord Henry Benton—your affianced," he added at her blank look.

"Lord Benton is *dead.*" *Though I ought to have recognized his name.* Ella narrowed her eyes, appraising the man as he had done her a moment earlier. "He died five years ago. I shall ever recall that I was forced to wear black during one of the hottest summers of record. Because Lord Benton foolishly challenged a man and got himself killed."

"It is unwise to judge something you have no knowledge of," Mr. Darling said, a hint of menace in his voice. "And unfortunate you feel so *inconvenienced* by your fiancé's death."

She'd barely felt that at the time. "Lord Benton and I were not well acquainted. We met only once, and I was quite young. But that is neither here nor there, as we both agree he *is* deceased . . ." She waved toward the parchment in Mr. Darling's hand. "It would seem—"

"I agreed to nothing, except that I would deliver this letter, written by Lord Benton. Mr. Darling took a step toward her, swung his arm forward, and rather awkwardly thrust the envelope at her.

Ella snatched it from him, lest he change his mind. "It appears the dead have powers from the grave." She dropped into the nearest chair, then broke the seal and tore the envelope open.

Bold, masculine handwriting sprawled across the page.

Dearest Eleanora,

Ella felt her face redden at being addressed thus, and moreover, by a man unknown to her.

If you are reading this letter, then you have arrived at your twentieth birthday and are yet unmarried. As your betrothed, I must apologize for this, as it is likely my fault you remain unwed. I beg of you to forgive me my folly. The rashness of my youth has not served me well. Perhaps you will understand; I seem to recall that you were of a similar temperament—at least as a child. It was one of the things, so many years ago, that gave me hope we might someday suit each other well.

Or be an absolute disaster together, Ella thought, then immediately felt absurd for thinking of this at all. Lord Benton was deceased and had been so for a quarter of her lifetime. *So how is it I am in possession of his letter now?* Hoping to discover why, she continued reading.

I recall visiting you when I was sixteen and you were seven. Your father returned from a trip and brought you a doll. You were quite vexed with him when he gave you the doll and then gave a fishing rod to the servant boy. You said you wanted to trade, and when your father would not allow it, you accused him of loving the servants more than his own child. I decided then that we might just get along famously when you grew up. I very much hope you still enjoy fishing in the pond near your home. You took me there once, and it is a memory I cherish to this day.

Unexpectedly, Ella felt her eyes smarting. She blinked, then briefly closed them. She hadn't thought of that fishing trip for years, had barely remembered it until just now, and even then it was only the vaguest of images that played in her mind. She certainly hadn't remembered that her companion that day was Lord Benton, but she recalled catching fish after fish, while the older boy she was with couldn't seem to catch anything. That he, Lord Benton, should remember that day somehow touched her.

She glanced up and found Mr. Darling watching her.

Annoyed at his intrusion in what felt like a private moment, she turned sideways on the chair, facing away from him, and continued reading.

> *Any young lady with that much skill has no doubt grown into an extraordinary woman—one who ought to be happily married.*

I am happily un*married,* Ella thought.

> *And so it is that I request your presence in London, for the Duke of Salisbury's November ball. If fate is willing, we shall be reacquainted there, and I shall at last discover if you dance as well as you fish.*
> *With much affection,*
> *Lord Henry Benton*

Ella stared at the paper in her lap for several seconds while her normally placid emotions churned out of control. *He remembers me. I am still betrothed. Impossible. He* is *dead!* At last, with what she hoped was a composed expression, she turned in her chair and faced Mr. Darling once more.

"This letter is obviously a hoax. My father attended Lord Benton's funeral. I was in mourning for an entire year." Or she'd worn black at least. At fifteen, the news of her fiancé's death had not caused sorrow. She'd not known anything of the man—their forgotten fishing excursion having been many years before.

Mother had told her not to fret, that she would find another to marry when she had her coming out. But when Mother had died the very next year, it became apparent there would be no Season. Father no longer had any use for London, and Ella had not felt much need for it either. She'd not mourned the loss of fancy gowns or balls. But along with no trips to the city, there had been no trips for her at all these past five years. Only lonely nights at home, while Father drowned his grief in traveling the world.

"I assure you, Lady Ella, it is no hoax." Mr. Darling considered her a moment before continuing, "Furthermore, I am charged with escorting you to London Monday next."

Ella rose from her seat. "You may uncharge yourself then, because I have no intention of going to London or any place else with you." *If only he'd been a messenger Father had sent.* She took a step back, then walked swiftly toward the open doors. "If Lord Benton desires my company, he can remove himself from his resting place long enough to come visit me himself." The image of a corpse rising from the grave sent an involuntary shiver down her spine.

As she opened her mouth to summon Peters to fetch Mr. Darling's coat and hat, he brushed past her. Their arms touched for the briefest second, but long enough that she felt the heat radiating from him and caught the scent of whatever cologne he used.

He paused just outside the drawing room. "I will see myself out, and I will see you Monday morning. I assume you have a lady's maid to travel with you as chaperone. Have yourself and your maid ready to depart by eight o'clock." He turned away, walking toward the front doors, but continued talking to her as he went, much as she had done to him the moment before.

"I'll be at the Woolpack Inn near Canterbury until then. Should you need assistance arranging for another chaperone, you may reach me there." Mr. Darling collected his hat and coat from Peters without stopping, though he paused at the threshold and looked toward her once more.

"Lord Benton and I have been friends since childhood, and the bonds of that friendship compel me to do whatsoever he requests—including abducting his fiancée if need be."

Two

Lord Gregory Benton removed his greatcoat and topper, placed them on the chair beside him, and sat down across from his brother-in-law at a table in the Woolpack Inn. "Tell me, Alexander, was your errand thus far as awkward as you feared it would be? How did the young lady receive your news?"

"She didn't." Alex sipped slowly from his mug of ale. "Eleanora Whitticomb is young, and her absentee father is a marquis, but going so far as to afford her the title of a lady is another matter entirely. She smelled like a horse." *And her wild mane of hair rather resembled one too.*

"I should think that would have endeared her to you immediately," Lord Benton said with a chuckle.

Alex sent him a sharp look. "It did not." He wasn't certain what he had been expecting Lady Eleanora to be like—a demure shut-in, shy and quiet perhaps. A young woman long forgotten and neglected and with only a life of spinsterhood to look forward to. At the very least he had believed that as the daughter of a marquis she would be a well-bred, polite young lady.

The bold, vibrant female who had marched up to him and practically demanded that he surrender Henry's letter had quite taken him by surprise, as had her ensemble. Women simply did not wear their hair in such disarray. And the top several buttons of her riding habit had been undone, revealing the white shirt beneath, while her skirt came well above her ankle and exposed a pair of *breeches*. He'd felt at once uncomfortable with her state of undress, and it caused him no little concern about the nature of her character.

"Did you explain to her why you'd come?" Gregory asked, sounding nonplussed. "It is difficult to imagine that a young lady so long in isolation would not be both grateful and excited for the opportunity of a trip to London— especially one whose cost is to be entirely sponsored by a benefactor."

"Think again," Alex said. "Lady Eleanora expressed nothing but displeasure at the idea."

"I am astounded." Gregory accepted a drink from the innkeeper, but instead of availing himself of it, leaned forward, apparently eager to hear details of the visit. "How did she react to my brother's letter?"

"She did not believe it was from him," Alex said, omitting the small detail of the reaction he had observed in her as she read the letter. For a woman who had claimed no attachment, she had been quite moved by something that Henry had written. Alex wondered if her reaction had surprised her as much as it had him. "I regret to tell you this, but she suffered no sorrow at his passing."

Gregory nodded. "I suppose that is to be expected as they knew very little of each other. I once asked Henry if he regretted being bound to a marriage from such a young age."

"Did he?" Alex asked. *Might there yet be some hope of ending this excursion?*

"Oddly enough, he said the opposite. He told me he trusted Father's judgment, and that Lady Eleanora was not just any marquis's daughter; he found her to be singular—extraordinary."

Alex snorted at this just as he'd begun to sip his ale again and inhaled instead of swallowing. This resulted in a loud coughing spell that lasted several seconds and drew the attention of the others in the tavern.

Looking somewhat amused, Lord Benton raised his eyebrows. "I take it you disagree."

"You'll see for yourself soon enough," Alex managed.

But Lord Benton's curiosity did not appear to be satisfied. "So she felt little regard for my brother and did not express any sort of gratitude at the opportunity for a Season?"

Alex shrugged and tried to shove off the guilt he felt regarding the way his visit with Lady Eleanora had concluded. "We didn't really discuss that she would be coming to London with the intent to prepare for the Season. Henry's letter mentioned only the Duke of Salisbury's ball."

"You didn't tell her?" Gregory set his tankard on the table rather harder than necessary. "She has no idea she's to be gone for the next several months? That beyond this initial stay in London, she is to join us for the holiday and then return for the Season she never had?"

"She hardly let me get a word in edgewise," Alex said, hating the defensive tone in his voice. He hadn't asked for this assignment. "When I did have opportunity to speak, I had to be brief—and blunt."

Gregory cringed. "Knowing how sharp your tongue can be, I pity Lady Eleanora already."

"You should," Alex said, a wry smile twisting his lips. "I predict that it will take someone who pities her a great deal for her to secure any sort of offer by the end of the Season. Her lineage is well enough—at least on her mother's side; there are rumors about her father's mental state at present. If your solicitor Mr. Hobbs is correct, he cares little for her, as evidenced by his gallivanting about the world. Her manners are severely lacking, and little wonder, given that she has had no guidance these many years."

"Regardless of her current circumstance, we must do right by her," Lord Benton said, fixing Alex with a look that said all too clearly that there would be no backing out of this arrangement. "We owe it to Henry."

"I know." Alex frowned into his cup. *It should have been me who challenged Sir Crayton,* he thought for at least the thousandth time. But Henry had gone in his place, and nothing could be done to call that disastrous night back. The best he could do was to follow his friend's wishes.

Alex looked up to find Lord Benton studying him with a curious expression.

"No one is to say we cannot have a bit of sport while we are helping launch Lady Eleanora Whitticomb into society. Perhaps that will make this situation more palatable to you."

"Why do I get the feeling you are up to no good?" But Alex smiled. *A bit of sport* was exactly the thing Henry would have proposed in a situation such as this.

"Would you care to wager on Lady Eleanora's success in the marriage mart? Clearly, you do not believe she shall be able to procure a husband. While I—with her sight unseen, I remind you—am willing to wager that she shall find herself betrothed by the first of May." Gregory leaned forward, his hand outstretched, ready to make the bet.

"Six and a half months is a long time," Alex said. "Anything could happen."

"So you are not confident in your initial assessment?" Lord Benton withdrew his hand and leaned back in his chair. "Perhaps the lady does have some virtues."

She has pretty eyes. But that is not enough to make up for her other faults. "I am confident," Alex said, recalling again the moment Lady Eleanora had burst into the room in complete dishevel. "What is it you wish to wager for?"

"Stoutheart."

"My *horse!* Are you mad?" Alex pushed his chair back and stood so abruptly that he startled the older man at the table beside theirs, causing him to leap from his stool as well.

"Pardon me, mate," Alex apologized. The man appeared to be well into his cups. Noting his spilled drink and generally poor state of dress, Alex fumbled in his coat pocket, then withdrew a coin, leaned over, and set it on the man's table.

Returning his attention to Lord Benton, Alex lowered his voice. "A man in my position has very little to recommend him and hardly anything that satisfies, but at least I have and am able to ride my own horse—an animal you'll recall I saved long and searched far for. Not to mention the amount of time I spent in training Stoutheart to my specific circumstance. Would you have me lose that as well?"

"I thought you said you were confident in Lady Eleanora's failure." Lord Benton smirked, then at once held up his hand when Alex made to speak again. "But you did not hear me out. I would like to *borrow* Stoutheart, particular-ly to mate with the mare I bought last year. It would not be for long, and no doubt your horse would be returned to you in good health and fine spirits."

"No doubt," Alex said, his tone surly. These days everyone seemed to be in good spirits but him. Many of his peers had married in recent years, and by and far marriage had agreed with all of them, changing each—for the better. Lord Benton was no exception.

While I continue on in this miserable, guilt-ridden existence. From the corner of his eye, he noted that the older man at the nearby table was leaving the pub without procuring a drink to replace the spilled one. Alex watched his shuffling gait until he had exited the room.

Is that to be me with time? Would his discontent with life and his inability to fit into society as he once had lead him to drowning his sorrows, alone in a sorry tavern? *No. One night of drink has already cost me—and others—dearly.*

"No wager is needed for you to be able to make use of Stoutheart," Alex said to Gregory, feeling contrite. His temper was ever short lately; he must learn to control it.

"Ah, but a wager makes it more amusing," Lord Benton said. "If *I* win, you must bring Stoutheart to my estate. If you win, I will bring my mares to visit at yours. Either way, you shall be the recipient of one of the foals sired."

"A generous offer," Alex acknowledged, feeling worse by the minute for his behavior. He leaned forward, his left hand extended. "To Lady Eleanora's prospects this Season."

"Lady Eleanora's prospects," Gregory agreed, the smile still upon his face as he clasped Alex's hand firmly.

"There's to be no meddling," Alex said, wishing he had specified that before agreeing to their wager. Though, in truth, losing would not be bad. He never minded an excuse to visit his sister and her husband. In the last five years, since the duel that had cost them all so much, he and Gregory had become close friends. *Nearly as close as Henry and I used to be.*

"I give you my word that I shall not do a single thing to invite the attention of any male member of the ton toward Lady Eleanora."

"Good," Alex said. "And see that you keep my sister from playing matchmaker too."

"Easier said than done, my man," Gregory said as he shrugged on his coat. "Someday you shall see for yourself that women have minds of their own, and there is very little that can actually be done to curb them."

Alex said nothing, but knew Lord Benton's words to be true. He suspected he would discover just how true, sooner rather than later, as he escorted Lady Eleanora to London.

Three

"Lord Benton's letter is the most romantic thing that I have ever heard." By lantern light, Lucy removed another gown from the dressing room and laid it across the bed. "Most girls go to London with the intent of *finding* a husband. But you shall have an entirely different experience. You merely have to discover *where* yours is." She and the other maid assisting her exchanged a look, and the latter burst into a fit of giggles.

Ella took no offense. As the servants were her only company, she was used to such conversations and even encouraged them. Her mother would have disapproved, but Ella thought it the better path than insanity—a point she was sure to have arrived at by now, if not for the friendship of Lucy and the others working at her father's estate these past four years. *Conversing with the servants is surely better than talking to oneself.*

"I know where my fiancé is." Ella selected a string of pearls from her jewelry box, thinking how odd it felt to be up so early and not dressing to go riding. "Unfortunately, Lord Benton is far removed from London, from this world." *He is dead, isn't he?* The past four days she'd had frightening dreams in which a faceless man rose from his grave and chased her through a ballroom.

Ella scowled at the letter upon her dressing table. Mr. Darling would soon be here to collect her. After nearly four days of debating the course she should take, she'd risen before the sun was up so she would be *prepared to leave* as he had suggested—not because she feared his threat of abduction, but because she'd grown angry and impatient with her father. Instead of a ticket for her passage, yesterday she had received a letter detailing his visit to Cairo and the excursion down the Nile he was planning next. It seemed he had forgotten all about her birthday and his promise.

He has forgotten me.

A trip to London then, a little adventure of her own, seemed just the thing. Perhaps, when Papa realized she had gone, he would both regret his neglectfulness and see that she was old enough to be his traveling companion.

"Will you be wanting this gown as well, milady?" Lucy held up a white Grecian ball gown, silk with an organza overlay and a ruffle of gold and lace trailing from the shoulders to the low bustline. Gold beading and lace edged the puffed sleeves, crossed beneath the bodice, and continued down the front of the gown. It had been a gift from Papa this past spring. He had sent it to her while on one of his many trips to Paris.

When Eleanora had first seen it, she'd felt much like her seven-year-old self receiving an unwanted doll. Simpler dresses were more to her liking, and this one seemed particularly impractical.

"Have you ever seen anything so ridiculous?" She

crossed the room to Lucy and fingered the gold ruffle along the shoulder. "Itchy. It would seem impossible to wear a gown such as this and not scratch oneself half to death during dinner."

"Leave it then?" Lucy asked.

Ella sighed. "Bring it. It is the nicest gown I own, and perhaps I shall have to endure an evening of itching if I am to be properly attired. I've not the faintest notion what current fashions are. Mother's subscriptions to Ackerman's Repository ceased long ago."

"Very well." Lucy gave a quick curtsy and hurried off with the gown to have it wrapped. Ella stared at the empty dressing room. It hadn't been very full to begin with—what did she need many clothes for way out here on her own? Before Mother died, Ella had owned plenty of gowns, all very fine and fashionable. But that had been four years ago, and most of that wardrobe no longer fit. Father's neglect of all things at home had included her clothing, and she had not minded—too much. But as close to empty as her dressing room had been, seeing it entirely vacant felt strange—a little exhilarating and the tiniest bit frightening as well.

I am really leaving. Going somewhere at last. Even if it was only London for a week or two. She did not know exactly when the Duke of Salisbury's ball was, and it was possible she might even find herself home again before the week was out.

"Funny thing how your father sent you that gown," Lucy said upon her return to the room.

"Yes, isn't it?" Ella quite agreed. "Did he expect I should wear it to church?" She laughed at the ridiculous thought. Their parish was largely made up of farmers and townsfolk. Only a few estates dotted the landscape this far from Canterbury. To appear in such a dress at church would feel positively sinful.

"It's almost as if your father knew you would be attending a ball." Lucy began packing the meager contents of Ella's dressing table.

As if he knew . . . Ella whirled to face her maid. "You don't think my father *planned* this? He wouldn't have sent Mr. Darling to fetch me to London as some sort of surprise—or test?"

Lucy's eyes had grown large. "I wouldn't be knowing. I didn't mean to suggest such a thing. Though Mr. Darling *did* arrive just after your birthday, and your father had said he would send for you then."

"Yes." Ella began pacing back and forth in front of the bed. "He said he would, and then he didn't, unless he really did and my conduct with Mr. Darling is just a test to see how I'll fare in polite society, with new people and new experiences." She snapped her fingers. "It's just like Papa to do something unconventional like that." In the next second, her face fell. "And then I went and behaved so dreadfully to Mr. Darling." She groaned and flung herself back on the bed.

"Your hair," Lucy cried. "You'll muss it." She grabbed Ella's arms and pulled her to a sitting position. "It will be all right. You'll see," Lucy said reassuringly. "If your father did arrange this, all the better. It may be that he *is* waiting to surprise you. Now all you've got to do is go to London and prove yourself."

"How shall I?" Ella felt suddenly forlorn. Perhaps it was the early hour, the dark still covering the grounds outside. But she could not entirely blame her discomfort on that. She had acted badly—childishly—when Mr. Darling had called on her. *And if Papa somehow learns of that* . . . She should never be allowed to join him on his travels.

Lady Eleanora Whitticomb was consistent in her eagerness, at least. At their first meeting, she had bounded up to him almost as a puppy might, when greeting its master. This morning, as Alex arrived in the Benton carriage that was to convey them to London, Lady Eleanora and her maid were seated together on a trunk at the top of the drive.

"We are ready as you requested," Lady Eleanora called out, rising from the trunk and walking toward the coach before he'd even fully alighted from it.

"Thank you," he said sincerely. At the end of their previous visit, he'd been uncertain whether or not he would even find her at home today. That she was ready to go and seemed to bear him no malice seemed as good a start as any.

She came forward and held her hand out to him. This was much more than he had expected, but after a brief hesitation, he took her hand, leaned over, and kissed it—an action which earned him the oddest of stares.

"Will you help me up, please?" she asked. "It *is* customary for a gentleman to help a lady into a carriage, is it not?"

He was more accustomed to having the servants do such, but Lord Benton's had not yet descended their perch and none of Lady Eleanora's household appeared available. *It is fortunate I am on this side,* he thought and kept hold of her hand, turned toward the carriage, and helped her inside—without appearing too awkward, he hoped. He assisted her maid as well, then glanced over at Lady Eleanora's trunk, quite small by most standards, and felt a pang of unease. Leaning into the carriage, he spoke again.

"Where might we find the remainder of your luggage, Lady Eleanora?"

"Oh, that is all there is." She blushed as if embarrassed. "I assure you I've everything I require for the duke's ball.

Lucy's belongings are there as well." She glanced at her maid.

"Very well." Alex nodded to the coachmen—standing behind him now—to load the trunk. He wasn't entirely certain, but it seemed most women traveled with a great deal more than Lady Eleanora, even when their visits were quite short. What would she do when she discovered she was to stay longer?

He leaned into the carriage once more. "It is possible . . . that your stay in London may be extended. Parliament is to convene this week, and there will be many in town for the special session. Often one's attendance at one ball leads to an invitation to attend another, or a dinner party, or . . ." His voice trailed off. She was not looking at him with alarm, but with what appeared to be keen interest, even hope perhaps.

Is this the same woman I spoke with a few days ago?

"And, of course, it is considered impolite to turn down invitations, so it may well be that you could remain in London for quite some time."

"I see," she said. "Thank you for telling me. I shall write to my father and advise him of that possibility."

She did not seem at all upset by this, which puzzled Alex further. *What changed her mind?* "Would you not like to take a few minutes more, another half hour even, to pack additional gowns and underclothes." *Underclothes?* Now he was the one blushing. What kind of idiot would she take him for, discussing such matters with a lady?

"Nearly all that I have, I have brought with me," Lady Eleanora looked at the carriage floor as she spoke, no doubt embarrassed over such a delicate subject matter. "If I require additional garments, I shall simply have to purchase them in London. I will advise my father of that as well."

"It will not be necessary." Alex climbed into the carriage, and the door was shut behind him as he took the seat across from the ladies. "Lord Benton wishes to purchase and provide anything that you may be lacking or even desiring."

Lady Eleanora looked up at him. "I could not allow that."

"Did your fiancé ever buy you anything previously?"

"Yes." She tilted her chin up, and a wistful smile lit her face. "He sent me a fishing rod once."

Alex could tell she was serious, and he had no response. Whoever heard of a man sending a woman a fishing rod? Were not jewelry, love letters, or forget-me-nots the sort of things that women desired?

"And did you like this gift?" he couldn't help asking.

"Oh, yes." Lady Eleanora's smile reached her eyes. "I still have it."

She is singular indeed, Alex thought, finding himself suddenly intrigued by his traveling companion. He had dreaded the hours ahead of them today, but possibly they would not be so unendurable as he'd believed.

"I am glad of it," he said. "But you will find that such an article will do you little good in London. And it still stands that Lord Benton will provide for you anything you find yourself in need of for the Season." He added the term casually at the end of the sentence, as if assuming she would be in the city come spring. But if Lady Eleanora took note of his not-so-subtle hint, she did not reveal herself.

"My father is capable of providing for me," she said politely, but with a tone that suggested their conversation on the subject was closed.

Alex recalled Gregory's advice about women having minds of their own and decided he was not wont to press the issue of who should purchase the many items Lady Eleanora would, no doubt, require for a successful Season.

It is not my concern, Alex told himself and settled in for a long ride as the carriage lurched forward and started down the drive. Both Lady Eleanora and her maid turned their faces to the glass on either side. Alex watched as Lady Eleanora's gaze remained not on the house but strayed to the woods surrounding it.

"Have you ever been far from home?" he thought to ask, worried that he might soon be seated across from a pair of overly emotional females.

"Not since my mother died," Lady Eleanora said, offering no further explanation.

"Never, sir," her maid added forlornly, further surprising Alex, as he had not been addressing her.

"It will be all right, Lucy." Lady Eleanora reached for her maid's hand. "Just think of the grand adventure you'll have to tell the others of when we return."

Alex watched this exchange with growing discomfort. Surely Lady Eleanora knew that a lady did not treat her servants as equals. Doing so would only draw unwanted attention and gossip to herself. He would have to speak with his sister about this. She would know what to do.

Still, another part of him felt a twinge of admiration for Lady Eleanora. *She has not become accustomed to the snobbish ways of the ton. Not yet at least.* He wondered how a few months in London would change her and found himself hoping they did not—too much. The idea of a woman who preferred fishing rods over flowers as a gift rather intrigued him.

The carriage reached the end of the drive and turned onto the lane. Lady Eleanora hadn't ceased staring from the window, craning her neck in what had to be a most uncomfortable position. Alex decided now was the opportune time to put on the appearance of napping, so as to avoid having to converse with either female—especially if either was inclined to be sad.

He leaned back into the seat, closed his eyes, and carefully crossed his arms before him, holding the right on his lap by placing the left over it, in what he hoped to be a casual manner. He'd become good at disguising his deficiency in the previous years, though it was not often that he found himself seated in a coach across from a lady, and her nearness made him more conscious of all he lacked.

I am here. Henry is not. I should feel grateful. But as always, he could not summon gratitude to the forefront of his mind. The layers of guilt and anger burying it ran too deep.

"Please stop the carriage. I must look back at home once more and make a last wish." Lady Eleanora leaned forward, as if to grasp the door handle. Only his hand on hers stopped her, but his other hand, left unsupported, slid from his lap and hung awkwardly at his side. Alex turned his body quickly, angling his leg to hide the abnormality. It was fortunate that Lady Eleanora's attention was focused out the window. Her maid's, however, was not, and Alex caught her questioning stare before she looked away.

"Please stop the carriage," Lady Eleanora pled.

"We are going over a bridge," Alex said exasperatedly, having not the faintest notion what she was talking about. "Can you wait but a moment?"

"This bridge is the spot I must wish from." Her cheeks grew flush as she withdrew her hand from beneath his, but he did not think the color had anything to do with embarrassment. Clearly, she was excited about something.

"I must smell autumn once more and have a last look upon home. If I am to be in London for weeks, possibly, then winter will be here before I return."

Spring will be here before you return, he ought to have

amended but did not. *First wishes and now smells.* Nothing she said made any sense. He'd never thought of the seasons as having a particular scent, and he didn't imagine that he was the only one who had missed this. Rather, she was possibly the only individual who discovered or believed they did. Nevertheless, Alex banged on the top of the carriage and called for the driver to halt just the other side of the bridge.

The second the wheels had stopped rolling, he jumped up and hurried ahead of her outside, worried that her timely appearance and seeming good humor at their departure had been nothing but a ruse. He did not trust her to be outside by herself. Who knew but that she had planned this all along and would make her escape and cause him to make good on his promise to abduct her if necessary?

She clambered down behind him, the skirt of her gown scrunched carelessly in her hand as she marched toward the bridge they'd barely crossed. He followed close behind, never allowing her to get more than an arm's length away.

At the center of the bridge, Lady Eleanora stopped, braced her hands on the rail, and leaned forward, tilting her face back, and drew in a deep breath. This she did twice before her shoulders relaxed, and she released a blissful sigh.

"Isn't it glorious? All clean and crisp and fresh." She continued on without giving him a chance to speak, which was well enough, as Alex had no response. "Pine and earth and rain, with a hint of wood smoke." She stared down at the water rushing over the rocks below them. "The river flows quickly here, but just a mile or so farther down, it becomes much slower."

The perfect place for fishing, he wondered, recalling Henry's unusual gift. But he didn't ask. He didn't want to be here all day.

"And there, if you look between the trees, you can see Father's estate."

He followed her gaze and saw that her home did make a pretty picture, framed as it was by the golden leaves with the colorful hills sloping upward behind. For a moment, he allowed himself to simply look and enjoy the serenity the view offered.

For the first time, he felt badly for taking her from it. But then he reminded himself that he and Lord Benton were about to do Lady Eleanora Whitticomb a very good turn—or so they hoped. Surely marrying well would be better than continuing to dwell here in isolation—no matter how beautiful a spot it was.

"Lady Eleanora." He spoke quietly, almost hating to break the silence and peace surrounding them.

"Ella," she reminded him. "Please."

"Lady Ella." *What does it matter?* he wanted to ask but didn't. Ella did suit her better. It sounded far less fussy, and in the short time of their acquaintance he had already realized she was a woman less fussy than most. "We should be going. As it is, we shall already be arriving after dark."

"Let me make a leaf wish, and then we may go." She leaned her head back and studied the trees over the river. "That one, I think." She pointed to a field maple and stared at it intently.

"A leaf wish?" He regretted his question immediately. Its answer would only delay them further.

She turned to him, wide-eyed. "Surely you've made a leaf wish before."

Certainly I haven't. "I'm afraid not," he said stiffly, with a hint of irritation.

"It's quite simple," she said, her attention on the great tree once more. "You've only to watch for a leaf to begin to fall then follow its progress downward. Just before it touches the river, you make your wish. The leaf will carry your wish with it downstream."

Absurd. Alex wondered if all women believed such ridiculous nonsense. The next thing, she'd be telling him she believed in fairies.

"And what good does that do?" He'd done it again. *Why, he wondered, is it so difficult to refrain from engaging in conversation with this woman?*

"The leaves continue downstream until they reach the still water where the fairies go to admire their reflections." She spoke as if this were a fact she'd learned in a school book.

"If a leaf is blocking a fairy's view," Lady Ella continued, "she'll pick it up to move it. And if she touches a leaf with a wish upon it, she is obligated to use her magic to make that wish come true."

"Ahh . . ." He nodded his head as if a great mystery had just been revealed. In a way, it had. *Her mind is addled.* Little wonder Lady Eleanora's father kept her at home instead of taking her with him on his travels.

"It is all right if you don't believe me," she said without a trace of reproach in her voice. "Fortunately for you, you do not have to believe to have your wish come true."

"I only have to have a fairy discover it." Alex rolled his eyes at such nonsense.

"That is why you should choose a large leaf—like that one." Of their own volition, his eyes followed her outstretched hand, pointing to an oversized crimson leaf as it relinquished its grasp on the tree branch and began to float downward, toward the rushing river below.

"Quickly, make your wish before it touches the water," she urged.

I wish to be done with this errand. That was no good.

They might well be halfway to London before the leaf made its way downstream.

I wish I could go back in time to the night Henry faced Sir Crayton. Another impossibility. Simple wishes might come true—only through coincidence, of course—but no power on earth could turn back time.

The leaf had nearly reached the water.

I wish I could do all that a man should.

"I wish Papa would come home, and I wouldn't be alone anymore." Lady Eleanora whispered her wish at the same instant he thought his.

The leaf seemed to pause midair, as if caught on some invisible breeze. It twirled once, then touched the water where it was quickly swept beneath the bridge and on its way downstream.

"Was that not *my* leaf?" he asked, exasperated that she had spoken over his wish, after encouraging him to participate in such nonsense.

"No one owns the leaves." She spoke as if he were daft. "So of course two people can wish on one together."

Of course. She was like a child, making up the rules of a game as she went along. "May I suggest that the same two people also make use of the same carriage." He held out his good arm to her.

She accepted, placing her hand gently upon it, and they left the scenic bridge. At the carriage, they paused, and she removed her hand from his arm to gather her skirt. Alex stepped aside, to allow her to enter first. But he was unable to assist her, standing to her left as he was. She looked at him expectantly.

"Must I beseech you for assistance every time?" she asked after a few seconds had passed in awkward silence.

"Must you make a continued mockery of my arm that is

lame?" She had to have noted his awkwardness and inability the day he delivered her letter. Did she continue to taunt him about it in the hope he would leave her behind? *Would that I might.*

"You have *two* hands and arms, do you not?" Lady Ella asked, meeting his gaze directly instead of staring down at the useless limb. "And you are a gentleman, are you not? I am not mocking anything but would greatly appreciate your assistance. This gown and my cloak are rather cumbersome and more than I am used to wearing."

Considering her state of undress at their previous meeting, Alex could not argue with her statement. Silently, he walked around to the other side of her and offered his hand.

"Thank you, sir." He heard only sincerity in her tone and felt strange comfort in the pressure of her hand on his as she climbed into the carriage. It was a simple thing, helping a woman into a carriage, but he felt oddly better for having done it.

He climbed in himself, gripping the side with his left hand while the right hung uselessly. Lady Ella's attention was focused outside once more, and her maid sleeping. His embarrassment ebbed slightly, and he felt grateful for Lady Ella's casual dismissal of his condition. But that did not change it, or the difficulties such a circumstance continued to present.

What a fool he was, wishing on a leaf for a miracle. There had been and would be none. And forevermore he would find himself in awkward situations such as this, save for the time he spent at home by himself. *Forever alone.*

Perhaps the only similarity he and Lady Eleanora Whitticomb shared.

Four

"Lord Benton has invited you to lodge at his townhome during your stay," Mr. Darling explained as the coach drew to a stop before the steps of the appointed home.

Ella raised her head from where she had been resting it against the side of the coach and peered through the window and the dark at the tall, imposing grey building.

The carriage door opened, and Mr. Darling indicated that she should alight first. Ella rose from her seat and stepped forward, ducking as she exited the carriage and took the hand of the servant waiting outside. Lucy followed close behind, and Mr. Darling came last. Though it was full dark, a half dozen servants, their faces shining pale in the lamplight, stood on the steps to greet them.

A matronly woman with grey hair and a no-nonsense expression on her face stepped forward. "Welcome to London, Lady Eleanora, Mr. Darling." She inclined her head toward each of them, then turned her full attention on Ella. "I am Mrs. Prichard, Lord Benton's housekeeper. Lord Benton will not be arriving until next week, but he has been expecting you and has asked that I help you get all in readiness for the Duke of Salisbury's ball. Follow me please, and I will show you to your room."

No one had said anything to Lucy, and Ella floundered a moment, wondering where she should direct her maid, when another servant came forward and indicated that Lucy was to come with her.

Ella felt both relieved and panicked at the thought of being alone, but obediently she followed Mrs. Prichard up the steps and into the marble foyer. They paused just inside the doors, and Ella had a moment to appreciate the striking decor. Outside may have appeared drab, but the inside was completely opposite. A colorful stained glass sunburst headed the doorway of whatever room lay to her left. Gilded tables lined the hall, with vases on each, some overflowing with late autumn cuttings, while others stood empty but were no less pretty of their own accord. Jeweled boxes and other trinkets—each of which she would have liked to stop and examine—stood beside the vases, and elegantly framed portraits and paintings lined the walls.

Treasure. She had a brief vision of the items Father must see on his travels and wondered what it would be like if he ever brought even one or two of them home. It would have been a pleasure to display such things of beauty and interest in their home as well. Most of the items her mother had collected had disappeared in recent years. Seeing them made her father sad. And so they had been packed away.

Like me. What reminded her father most of his loss could not be wrapped in paper and shut up in a box in the attic. And so he had taken to traveling far and wide, where he did not have to look upon the daughter who reminded him of the woman he had loved.

"The drawing room is to your left," Mrs. Prichard said, pulling Ella from her unhappy thoughts. "The dining room is behind it." She walked swiftly, and Ella hurried to keep up. "The library is farther down the hall to the right, as is the music room."

Ella longed to go in each of these, to see what wonders lay behind the doors.

"And there is the ballroom." Mrs. Prichard indicated a far set of doors, also topped with a stained glass header.

Without waiting to be invited, Ella continued past her to the double doors and then boldly turned the handle on one and peered inside at the elegant, but empty ballroom. A shiver passed over her. *A premonition?* She had not allowed herself to think overmuch on Lord Benton. Yet here she truly was, a guest at his house in London. What was she to think? Was she somehow mistaken about his death, and he would arrive and take her in his arms to dance in this very ballroom? If so, would she find him the same as his letter described?

"Your room is above, on the third floor." Mrs. Prichard pulled Ella from her fantasy.

Something about the housekeeper's tone seemed to suggest that this arrangement put Ella firmly in her place. A girl from Bishopbourne did not merit a second floor bedroom but should be placed farther upstairs, perhaps near the nursery.

I am no child, Ella thought as she squared her shoulders and followed Mrs. Prichard across the foyer.

With a last glance behind her at Mr. Darling, still standing in the open doorway, his outline silhouetted in the light from the gas lamp shining outside, Ella began ascending the stairs of Lord Benton's townhouse. Halfway up, they turned and went the other direction. She took this opportunity to search for either Lucy or Mr. Darling below, but both had disappeared—Lucy to the servants' quarters and Mr. Darling to his own residence, she supposed. She was surprised at the twinge of regret and discomfort she felt knowing that he was gone and wished she hadn't been so entranced by her surroundings that she had neglected to thank him for accompanying her.

While she had not been overly fond of Mr. Darling at their first meeting, she had found him more amiable today and had found herself more curious about him during the long hours of their drive. More curious and sympathetic when she'd realized that what she had supposed was a great reluctance to hand her the letter last week had been inability. She had not noted, until today, that his right arm did not function as it should.

Upon realizing that, when they stood together at the bridge, she had done what she supposed any lady would—she had expected him to act the gentleman, regardless of the state of his arm. To assume any less would have seemed as if she were treating him as less than any other man, which she did not believe he was.

They reached the third floor. "This is to be your room." Mrs. Prichard opened the door ahead of her, and Ella followed her inside. The chamber was lovely by any standard, but she felt especially warmed and welcomed by the tones of green in the bedding, wallpaper, and curtains. It was as close to home as she was likely to get in London, and it did her heart good.

"Thank you," she said appreciatively. "It will do nicely." She recalled her mother telling her that one could not be too personable with servants. It seemed an absurd rule to Ella, but Mrs. Prichard seemed to approve of and perhaps even prefer this, as she inclined her head in acknowledgment and a brief flash of admiration shown in her eyes.

"I've arranged for your dinner to be brought up tonight. Breakfast tomorrow will be in the dining room, unless you wish otherwise."

"The dining room will be fine," Ella said, eager for any excuse to come downstairs and explore the house.

Mrs. Prichard left, and when the door had closed softly behind her, Ella hugged herself in a state of disbelief.

"I've done it," she whispered triumphantly. "I am in *London.*" It wasn't Paris or the Taj Mahal, but it was a start. Either Father had summoned her here, or he would soon realize she had gone without him. Both possibilities held promise for her wish to come true. Soon she would be with her father, and she would not be alone anymore.

Five

London, November 1819

Ella flopped backward on the bed, disturbing the deep green coverlet and the mountain of pillows the maid who'd left had just finished straightening for the third time today.

"Your hair!" Lucy wailed, leaving the gown she'd been about to hang in the clothes press and running around to the other side of the bed. "You'll muss it, and I've no time to redo it before supper."

"It's already mussed," Ella said crossly, "after having had no fewer than two dozen hats placed upon it at the milliners this morning."

"Those'll be arriving soon too, I suppose," Lucy said, a note of frustration in her own voice. "Being a lady's maid in London is a far sight more work than in the country. I'm going to be in the basket if Mrs. Prichard finds this room a mess again. But all this changing of clothes three or more times a day is wearying."

"Don't I know it." Ella rolled onto her stomach, braced

her chin on her hands, and watched Lucy. "If this is Papa's idea of a splendid birthday present, then he is even less aware of me than I believed. For all the money that has been spent on new clothes, he could have bought me another horse."

"Have you not written and told him as much?" Lucy asked, sounding hopeful.

Ella shook her head. "No. If he is behind all this, it must be so I will be prepared for whatever voyage we are to take next. This time in London is merely to make me ready." *Unless it truly is Lord Benton who has summoned me here.* She pushed the thought aside, both because it frightened and excited her. "A short while here and I will have full trunks and adequate practice with society for wherever it is Papa and I are off to."

Lucy peeked around the door of the clothes press. "And will I be going with you?"

"That depends," Ella said, "on whether you wish to or not."

"Mmm." Lucy pressed her lips together and said no more. Had they been at home, Ella would have asked her feelings. And she would have helped with the work as well. Of course, had they been at home, Lucy would not be overwhelmed with the volume of clothing—stays and shifts, morning gowns and day frocks, stockings and shoes and bonnets—that had been arriving all week. But, of course, she must behave differently here than at home.

Ella scowled. There was nothing for a lady to do in London as far as she could tell—no horses to ride, it was not considered acceptable for her to go out walking alone, and she was not even free to roam about the house and visit with the servants as she had done at home. If anything, she felt lonelier in London than she had, isolated as she'd been, in the country.

A scratch sounded upon the door, and Ella sat up quickly as Mrs. Prichard entered.

"Mr. Darling has arrived and inquired after you. Shall I tell him you are at home?"

"Yes, please." Ella scooted from the bed, stood, and smoothed the front of her gown as she recalled her mother doing before greeting visitors.

"He is in the parlor. I will let him know you are at home."

After nearly a week in this house, Ella knew that *letting him know* she was here entailed Mrs. Prichard telling one of the maids to summon the butler who would then take it upon himself to let Mr. Darling know that Ella would receive him. It would seem much simpler for her to greet him herself, but she had learned—through an unfortunate experience with a caller earlier in the week—that simply was not the way of things.

As quickly as was acceptable, Ella hurried down the stairs. It seemed odd that Mr. Darling had been shown into the parlor when the other guests she'd received this week had waited in the drawing room. She wondered if it was being cleaned at present and when she reached the main floor, she peeked her head inside to find out. The drawing room sat as it always did—a perfect masterpiece of lovely, ornate furnishings and rugs, with interesting objects and fine art to admire.

The parlor, on the other hand, was a smaller, more comfortable room—one she was told that Lord Benton frequented. She actually preferred it over the drawing room, but it seemed odd that a guest would not be shown to the finer of the two.

"Good afternoon, Mr. Darling." Ella curtseyed slightly before crossing the room to him. He looked much as she remembered—far too solemn, giving the appearance of a man much older than he likely was.

"Good afternoon, Lady Ella. I came to see if London is treating you well."

"London is boring me to tears," she said, then seated herself on the opposite end of the sofa he had just risen from. "Please sit, and I'll ring for some tea."

He looked suddenly uncomfortable, and his good hand rose, as if to stop her. "That won't be necessary. Nothing for me, please."

She recalled how he had not eaten supper with her and Lucy at the inn the day they'd traveled to London. *Does he never eat in the company of others?* she wondered. The thought saddened her.

"I would be a terrible hostess indeed not to offer you some refreshment," she said, leaning back to the bell pull before he could object again. "As I have already played the part of a terrible hostess to you once, I feel I must do better this time."

The skin around his mouth seemed to tighten, but he said no more on the subject and retook his seat upon the sofa. "I see you have been relearning the ways of society."

"I have." Ella nodded. "It is my hope that I am not entirely hopeless. After all, I was sixteen when my mother died. Up to that point in life, I had been taught the decorum expected of young ladies who are the daughters of a marquis. I cannot believe that a mere four years has wiped the previous sixteen away entirely."

"It has not," Mr. Darling assured her. He leaned back against the sofa, seeming to relax a bit. "Only the more tedious parts have fled."

"My thoughts exactly." She smiled at him and felt suddenly grateful for his visit. *Did Lord Benton send him?*

"I hear you have had a visit to the modiste," Mr. Darling remarked. "Has that not agreed with you?"

"It has not," Ella said. "And when I next speak to Papa, he is going to hear of it. He could have bought me a horse for all that has been spent on clothing since I arrived."

A corner of Mr. Darling's mouth quirked up, and he gave a slight laugh. "Am I to understand that you would prefer a horse over having new gowns?"

Ella considered a moment before answering. "Not entirely," she said. "I think I would have preferred to have one new gown for the ball *and* a horse."

He laughed outright at that. "Spoken like a true woman."

"We do have a reputation for wanting it all." She fluttered her fingers in the air as if she too were one of those vain, vapid women London was so reputed to promote.

"Something tells me that your definition of *all* would not be what your peers would choose." He spoke warmly, as if he appreciated her differences.

"Perhaps not," Ella said thoughtfully. *All* to her would be her family intact as it used to be. She'd had what she wanted for so many years and never fully appreciated it. She could not be the first person to have made that mistake, to have taken that which was precious for granted. "Perhaps that is because most people like us already have it all, and they do not stop to realize it. I believe that too often we presuppose what is given us, until it is no longer ours."

"An astute observation." Mr. Darling's ponderous look turned suddenly dark as a maid entered carrying the tea service. This was set upon the table, and Ella began to pour out.

"May I ask you something direct?" she asked, looking up from her task.

He visibly tensed, and his answer was slow in coming. "If you must."

"I do feel so." She set the teapot down and caught his eye. "Where is Lord Benton? Is my fiancé living—or not?"

Mr. Darling's mouth opened, then closed as a flicker of relief crossed his face. This was followed almost immediately by what Ella would have sworn was a look of shame.

That was not the question he was expecting. But neither does he wish to answer it.

Mr. Darling leaned back against the sofa cushion and drew in a great breath, as if summoning courage before revealing something of importance. "Lord *Gregory* Benton is even at this very minute on his way to London with his wife, my sister Ann."

"Gregory is Lord Benton's—Henry's—younger brother," Ella stated the genealogy as a matter of fact, but could not deny the disappointment she felt at gaining this knowledge. To hide her feelings, she looked down at the tray and busied herself arranging a plate of biscuits for her guest.

If the title had passed to Gregory, there was no need for Mr. Darling to say anymore. *Lord Benton—my Lord Benton—is dead.* She had found herself hoping that he was not, that in spite of her memories of that long, hot summer spent wearing black and receiving callers bearing their condolences, there had somehow been a terrible mistake and he was very much alive and in fact even cared for her and they would soon be reunited.

"You seem to know the Benton family history rather well, considering you claimed to have had little recollection of your fiancé." Mr. Darling's tone was not complimentary.

"There is a family tree in the library here." Ella handed him the plate of biscuits. "But it did not provide any death dates, so I was not certain about—Henry." She swallowed thickly and tucked away her regret in a far corner of her heart. With her emotions firmly in check once more, she raised her head and met Mr. Darling's eyes. "Will you please explain the letter you brought? Why am I here?" She held her hand in front of her, indicating the fine room, and all of London, for that matter.

Mr. Darling balanced the plate upon his knee and took up a cookie in his left hand. "The letter was discovered recently by Lord Benton. He believes Henry wrote it the night he died, before he faced Sir Crayton in the duel that killed him."

"I see," Ella said, though really he had not clarified as much as she wished. "Why did you lead me to believe otherwise?" She searched his gaze, knowing full well that evidence of hurt was still traceable in hers, but there was little that could be done about that. He had brought her hope, then dashed it almost as quickly.

Mr. Darling shifted uncomfortably on the sofa, then leaned forward and set his plate on the table.

"You may not leave without explaining yourself," Ella said, assuming he was about to do just that.

"I have no intention of running out of here like a coward." His brows rose. "Unlike a certain young lady I called upon last week, who fled the room as soon as her discomfort became apparent."

"I did not flee the room," Ella said defensively, then realized she had scooted to the edge of the sofa, as if preparing to do that very thing again. "You were a strange man in my house, and I was somewhat afraid of you." Even to her ears, it sounded a poor excuse for her behavior.

Mr. Darling rolled his eyes. "I very much doubt that you are a lady who *ever* finds herself afraid of anything at all."

You're wrong. She was afraid of being alone—not frightened of the dark or the quiet house or anything of that sort, but she was afraid that Papa would never come home, afraid that a lifetime of loneliness, and the continued pain it brought, awaited her. But, of course, she could not tell Mr. Darling that. It was not something a man like him would understand.

"I am sorry I treated you so poorly upon our first acquaintance." She was not above apologizing when she knew she had been in the wrong.

Something about his look softened. The blue of his eyes seemed to brighten as they gazed at her with approval. "Apology accepted. I too regret my actions at our first meeting. I did, deliberately, deceive you, and for that I am sorry."

"Accepted," Ella said, but she was not about to let him get out of an explanation. "Why did you lead me to believe my fiancé might yet be alive?"

"Because I did not think you would agree to accompany me to London under any other circumstance."

"What other circumstance might there be? Under what pretense *am* I here? Did my father . . ."

Mr. Darling took another long, deep breath. "You are here so that Lord Benton—Gregory," he clarified, "and I might fulfill one of Henry's last wishes: that you be both provided for and happily married to another in his stead."

"*Married!*" Ella stood abruptly, her knee knocking the table in front of her and causing the tea in her full cup to spill over the edge. "I do not want to be married—to anyone. Why should Lord Benton's wish be fulfilled? What about mine? I am the one yet alive."

"And what kind of life are you living?" Mr. Darling asked carefully. With equal care, he reached for his cup, took it in his left hand, and drank slowly.

Ella walked around the table and began pacing the room, feeling very much trapped. But she dared not leave, not after his earlier accusations.

"I have a very lovely life," she said. "Papa has left me in charge of the estate, which I manage to run quite smoothly," she added. "The days are mine to do with as I wish. I choose to spend much of them riding and grooming the horses I love. I am able to roam the countryside as I please—whereas here, I am not even allowed to venture past the front door without a chaperone. My life in Bishopbourne is pleasant. I am content there. I did not ask for this—had no yearning or desire to come to London and be paraded about in search of a husband."

She stopped before the fireplace, folded her arms across her middle, and glared at him, daring him to come up with a rebuttal.

"If all you say is true, then why *did* you agree to come with me? You seemed almost eager to depart Monday morning."

"I—" She hesitated, uncertain what to say but incapable of being anything less than honest. "I hoped my father was behind your invitation and might meet me here, that he had sent for me on my birthday as he had promised. And then there was Lord Benton's letter . . ." She shrugged, pretending it had meant little to her.

"What about his letter?" Mr. Darling's voice was soft and encouraging, as if that might somehow make her wish to admit her folly.

"It was very kind," Ella said. "It made me feel—wanted." She looked past him, wondering if she ought to have told Mr. Darling something other than the truth. "It caused me to hope, and I had to see if he . . ."

"—was yet living as I had implied." Mr. Darling set his

cup in its saucer on the table and rose. He walked toward her, his good hand upon his chin in thoughtful consideration, while his other hung awkwardly at his side. "It is my turn to apologize. I have done you a poor turn."

Ella forced a smile. "You coaxed me here to London, for a short while at least. That is something, though I would very much like to return home now. I've hardly worn any of the items that have been purchased. Most should be able to be returned without trouble. Those that are being sewn for me, I shall be sure to reimburse Lord Benton for. Had I believed it was he who was paying for them, I should never have agreed to any shopping at all."

"Of course we cannot keep you here," Mr. Darling said. "But it also seems a shame for you to have traveled so far without enjoying all that London has to offer."

"What has it to offer?" Ella asked, wondering that he had not agreed to return her at once. "Aside from stuffy air and people, ridiculous rules and—"

"An honest young lady—I like her already!" Another gentlemen entered the room, his grin spread nearly as wide as the arms he held outstretched. "Alex, you failed to mention that the woman who was almost my sister-in-law is refreshingly unspoiled by the ways of this city." He took Ella's hand and kissed it briefly. "Lady Eleanora. It is a pleasure to see you again. On our two previous visits, you were quite young and likely do not remember me. I hope the staff has made you feel welcome here."

"They have," Ella said, dropping into a proper curtsy. Ella liked Lord Benton already. He dressed as a gentleman, but did not seem one given to pretense.

"Glad to see you've finally managed to arrive at your own party," Mr. Darling said, a hint of annoyance in his voice.

"I told you we'd be here by the ball, and so we are," Lord

Benton said. "Ann is just giving instructions to the cook and shall be along shortly." He glanced at Ella, then back to Mr. Darling. "It appears we came just in time. What have you done to make Lady Eleanora wish to return home so soon?"

"She prefers to be called Lady Ella," Mr. Darling informed him, pleasing her. "I was but remedying my earlier error of not fully explaining to Lady Ella how, exactly, she came to be your guest." Mr. Darling shifted his weight from one foot to another as he looked at the floor, bringing to mind a child who had been caught and scolded. "I deceived her in the worst way," he said. "Leading her to believe that Henry was yet alive. Without the promise of seeing him, or her father, she finds little else compelling her to London."

"In all fairness, I was somewhat stubborn upon our first acquaintance." Ella was not certain why she felt the need to defend Mr. Darling, when clearly he had tricked her into being here. But a man who admitted wrongdoing seemed a rarity, and she wished to reward this virtue.

"Not well begun then," Lord Benton said. "But no matter. You've months in which to improve upon a friendship, and as you are both my guests, I expect that will be accomplished shortly."

Months? We are both his guests? Ella wondered why Mr. Darling did not reside at his own residence. She told herself it did not matter because she would soon be gone. "I was just explaining to Mr. Darling that I am certain the purchases made on my behalf can be returned," Ella said. "I had believed—falsely—that my father was behind this expedition and it was his money I was spending. Your generosity is overwhelming, but it would not be right to have you pay for my gowns or other articles of clothing."

"A woman who is honest *and* does not wish to spend a

man's every last cent." Lord Benton's smiled deepened. "No wonder my brother was smitten with you, Lady Ella."

She supposed he was plying her with compliments purposely and told herself she must resist both his charms and generosity. "I was not old enough for him to be smitten with me," she reminded them. "Unfortunately, we had very little interaction together before his passing."

"That is unfortunate," Lord Benton agreed. He swept his hand in an arc before the chairs and sofa. "Why do we not sit and enjoy the refreshment I see has already been brought?"

A few minutes ago, Ella had been ready to leave but now found herself drawn once again into the center of the room, this time seated across from Lord Benton and once more beside Mr. Darling.

"There you are, Darling." A woman swept into the room, her pale yellow gown a pretty contrast to the chestnut curls topping her head. She was tugging off gloves as she came, and instead of walking up to Lord Benton as Eleanora had supposed she would, she went straight to Mr. Darling and gave him a hug.

"It is good to see you," she said when at last they had pulled back and she studied him at arm's length. "You look rather tired, though. Have you been keeping late hours at Whites?"

"That is a poor jest, sister." Mr. Darling's expression returned to its near customary scowl. "You know I should rather be caught dead than to make a fool of myself there." He gave a short, harsh laugh. "Of course, there is a very good chance that if I did frequent Whites, I *would* be dead quite soon. Perhaps I shall consider such a course."

"Enough of that," Lady Benton said abruptly, a tone of reprimand in her voice. Ella noted with fascination that her scowl almost perfectly matched her brother's.

An Invitation to Dance

"Crayton has been blackballed from White's anyhow," Lord Benton said. "Had something to do with the Duke of Salisbury's recently discovered granddaughter, I believe. The duke may be old, but he's not to be trifled with."

"Lady Ella, may I introduce you to my sister Ann?" Mr. Darling said, rather cleverly changing the topic of conversation, Ella noted. "Ann at times feels that her position as Lord Benton's wife elevates her to knowing what is best for me," Mr. Darling added.

"I do know what is best for you." A smile replaced Lady Benton's frown as she turned to Ella. "It is so lovely to finally meet you. Ever since we discovered Henry's letter, we have been all agog wondering about you."

"Oh?" Ella said, her discomfort growing. "I am certain Mr. Darling can tell you there is not so much to wonder about at all. I am a simple country girl and happy to stay that way. In fact, before your arrival we were discussing my wish to return home."

"But you've only just arrived," Lady Benton exclaimed.

"You cannot leave us yet," Lord Benton agreed. "You might be a bit of a green girl to the ways of London, but Ann shall see you through."

"Please," Lady Benton implored, seating herself in the chair closest to Ella's end of the sofa. "You must agree to stay for a short while at least. You've no idea how thrilled I've been at the prospect of another woman in the house. It will be so much better than enduring life with these two." She rolled her eyes at her husband and brother.

Mr. Darling really does reside here?

"So much for your warm greeting," Mr. Darling said good-naturedly, while Lord Benton appeared to ignore his wife's comment altogether.

"I saw Stoutheart out back by the carriage house.

Decided to bring him to London, did you?" Lord Benton took up a plate of biscuits as he waited for Mr. Darling to answer.

"I went back for him, yes. I only just returned today." Mr. Darling glanced in Ella's direction, as if to see if she was listening. She was, though also trying to answer Lady Benton's questions about the gown she was to wear to tomorrow evening's ball.

Ella faced Lady Benton and attempted polite small talk, while keeping her ear attuned to the men's discussion of horses—in particular, one called Stoutheart.

"I think you ought to reconsider entering him in the races," Lord Benton was saying. "I've never seen a faster horse."

"Nor one more dependable," Mr. Darling said. "I won't risk injuring him. I'd prefer not to spend another three years training a different horse to neck rein. Not to mention what I paid for Stoutheart."

Ella's interest was greatly piqued. She was unfamiliar with the term he'd used but interested in all things having to do with training horses. While Lady Benton expounded upon the possible hairpieces that might match her gown, Ella reached for her teacup on the table, as a pretense for leaning closer to better hear Mr. Darling.

"Well, with any luck, you'll have a Stoutheart the second to train next year," Lord Benton said.

"And were any of your new hats made with *horse*hair?" Lady Benton asked, flashing Ella a knowing smile over the rim of her teacup.

"Pardon?" Ella asked, wondering when the discussion had changed to bonnets.

"I take it you enjoy horses, or riding," Lady Benton said, the twinkle in her eye matching her grin. She'd spoken loud enough that the men ceased their conversation and once more engaged with the women.

"Both," Ella said, returning Lady Benton's smile, while feeling grateful to her for providing an entry into the men's topic. "At home, I ride for two hours every morning. And I often ride in the afternoons and evenings as well."

"Mr. Darling must take you out while you are here then," Lady Benton said, with a pointed look at her brother. "There is no finer rider than he in all of London."

"I would like that very much," Ella said, then shifted her gaze to her teacup when Mr. Darling did not say that he would enjoy that too. He had probably already endured more of her company than he wished.

"Where do you go riding in London?" she asked, attempting to mask her discomfort.

"Hyde Park, of course," Lady Benton said, sounding somewhat surprised. "Have you not been there?"

"I have not seen much of London at all," Ella confessed. "Excepting Bond Street—which I have seen enough of."

"Lady Ella, you have only to utter such sentiment once at the upcoming ball, and you shall be a favorite among many there—or the men at least," Lord Benton predicted. "Is it not every man's dream to have a wife who does not live to bankrupt him with her clothing purchases?"

"Surely I have done significant damage already," Ella said, "with the garments ordered since I arrived. To have someone other than my father pay for them seems unjust at best."

"It is perfectly just," Lady Benton said. "Did Mr. Darling not explain to you the money discovered with Henry's letter?"

Ella shook her head.

"A £400 was sealed in the envelope with the letter, which

I discovered inside an obscure volume in our library. A book about fishing, oddly." Lord Benton shrugged. "I'd never noticed it until a few weeks ago, when it nearly fell from the shelf. Maids must have moved it when dusting. Inside were your letter, the money, and instructions to me—which I have followed in bringing you here."

"So, you see, it is *your* money," Lady Benton said. "Henry was wise enough to leave it discreetly, so as not to complicate matters."

"He used to talk of you quite frequently, you know," Lord Benton said. "At the time of his death, he was anticipating eagerly the day you would come of age to marry. I daresay you would have had a child or two at least by now."

Beyond a blush, Ella felt her face catch fire.

"What are you thinking of, talking to her of such things?" Lady Benton scolded her husband.

"Makes me look better at least,"—Mr. Darling coughed into his hand—"considering I spoke to her of undergarments the day we traveled."

"You're both hopeless," Lady Benton scolded. "You see why you must remain here with me, Lady Ella?"

Ella nodded. It seemed equally hopeless that the conversation would return to horses and the possibility of accompanying Mr. Darling to Hyde Park, but she found herself enjoying their company just the same. The afternoon waned to evening as they visited until it was time to change for dinner. She did, going upstairs after promising that she would remain in London.

Until the week's end at least. She would attend the Duke of Salisbury's ball, and then she would return home and perhaps ready herself for another trip. This one to join her father.

Six

"Was that not the second dance for which Lord Dersingham requested your hand?" Lady Benton asked, as Ella rejoined her after a most enjoyable cotillion.

"It was." Ella watched her partner walk away and realized several pairs of eyes were still directed at her, as they had been during their dance. She clasped her hands in front of her to keep from self-consciously smoothing the skirt of her pale pink gown or fussing with the beading in her hair.

"He has already been predicted to be the catch of the Season," Lady Benton whispered behind her fan. "Newly titled, deliciously rich, dashingly handsome . . ."

"He knows a fair amount about horses as well," Ella said, adding her own thoughts of approval. No matter what they said, she was *not* here in search of a husband.

But if I had been . . . Lord Dersingham would not have been a bad choice.

"Have you set your cap for him then?" Lady Benton asked, her fan beating quicker with her excitement.

"Heavens no," Ella exclaimed, then found herself wanting to giggle at the absurdity of it all. "He is far from my reach, even had I wanted him."

Lady Benton shook her head and took Ella's arm, pulling her closer even as her head bent low. "You are the daughter of a marquis, and Lord Dersingham is an earl. It would be a good match for you both."

Ella sighed and knew it was of no use to explain to Lady Benton her feelings on this subject. Titles were all well and good, and she knew society revolved around them. But simply because one had one—or one's parents were of the peerage, as was her circumstance—did not necessarily elevate him or her to a certain status. Ella knew she could never be content to live in the city, hanging on her husband's arm at dinner parties and leading a life of social calls and teas. A marquis's daughter or not, she felt more comfortable on a horse or walking a lone country path, a fishing rod slung over her shoulder—something she very much doubted that any gentleman in this room would approve of.

"I am not as polished as Lord Dersingham," Ella said in an attempt to explain.

"Never mind him then," Lady Benton whispered. "Your next partner approaches."

Ella turned from her as a gentleman stopped before them.

"Good evening, ladies. Lady Benton." He bowed. "I do not believe I have the pleasure of knowing your companion." Dark eyes full of interest and speculation focused on Ella.

"Mr. Woodward, may I present to you *Lady* Eleanora Whitticomb. She is a guest of ours this month and will be returning with us for the Season as well."

Ella smiled at him while inside she writhed. Lady Benton's introduction had no doubt alerted Mr. Woodward that Ella was on the marriage mart. *How I detest this game. No wonder Papa never wants to come to London.* She determined to be kind to Mr. Woodward, without giving him false hope of her interest.

"A pleasure." He bowed once more. "Whitticomb?" His overly large brows drew together. "By chance, was your father a member of the House of Lords?"

"He was," Ella said, careful not to let her smile falter.

"But he abdicated his position, did he not?" Mr. Woodward asked.

Ella nodded. She had been through this same discussion twice already this week, with visitors who had come to call. "After my mother died, Papa's grief was such that he took a season off. During that time, he traveled and found it agreed with him so much that he resigned from his seat permanently."

"How peculiar," Mr. Woodward said. "How very interesting."

Ella did not particularly find it so but had learned many others did. Apparently, what her father had done was unheard of. *It is as if he has turned his back on society,* one of her visitors had commented.

It is as if he has turned his back on a life that was both tedious and boring, Ella thought, though dared not voice that opinion.

"They are forming for another set," Lady Benton said, as if Ella and Mr. Woodward could not see the same for themselves.

"Would you care to dance, Lady Eleanora?" he asked quickly.

Falling too easily for Lady Benton's scheme. "I should be

delighted," Ella said, eager indeed for another of the formation dances that kept her far from her partner and left little time or room for conversation. She accepted Mr. Woodward's arm.

"I must tell you that I admire your father's gumption," Mr. Woodward said as they made their way to the center of the ballroom. "I daresay there are many men sitting in parliament who would like to do as he has but haven't the courage."

"On his behalf, I thank you for your kind words," Ella said, her initial opinion of Mr. Woodward altering somewhat.

"I find myself wondering if you take after your father," Mr. Woodward said. "Doing as you please without overly caring what your peers think of you?"

"I hope to," Ella answered. "In truth, I have little thought of my peers as I am not often among them. This trip to London is my first in many years."

"Then come with me for a stroll on the balcony after this dance," Mr. Woodward invited. "It is far more pleasant in the cool night air than in this stuffy room."

"All right," Ella said, though Lady Benton's earlier caution about going outside with any gentleman rang through her mind.

The dance passed pleasantly enough with their continued light conversation and the enticement of what she was about to do. When the last steps were taken and the orchestra ceased, she once again took Mr. Woodward's arm and allowed him to lead her outside through one of the sets of double doors off the east side of the ballroom.

The balcony was not as deserted as she would have supposed, and Ella felt a little of the tension leave her as they strolled amid other couples. They reached the edge of the balcony overlooking the gardens, and she released her hold on Mr. Woodward and stepped to the side, placing her hands on the low stone wall and putting a bit more distance between them, though the night was chill.

"Did your chaperone warn you not to come outside with anyone?" he asked, looking down at her with a mischievous smile.

"Yes," Ella answered honestly. "But I am my father's daughter." She attempted a careless laugh.

"Beware of that then," Mr. Woodward said, sounding quite serious of a sudden. "Rumor has already circulated that you are here as a guest of Lord Benton and are in search of a husband."

"Are not many young ladies here in search of one?" Ella asked, feeling humiliated and wishing that the night was over and she might leave.

"Of course. That is the game of the Season each year, is it not?" Mr. Woodward said. "But most young ladies have parents to look out for them. You do not, and while Lord and Lady Benton are well respected, it is not the same as having a father and mother with you, to whom any suitor would be accountable. Furthermore, there is the mystery surrounding your father's position. I tell you all this, Lady Eleanora, because I find myself—like many others in attendance this night—rather taken with you. And I should hate to see any take unfair advantage."

"As you have in leading me out on this balcony?" She ignored his comment about being taken with her, believing it to be untrue.

"Perhaps." Mr. Woodward's grin broadened. "Though I daresay that Lord Dersingham has done the same, asking you to dance twice in succession."

"We had a bit of refreshment in between," Ella said in her defense.

"Ah, but the point is that you remained in *his* company for nearly an hour."

"You seem to know quite a bit about the goings-on at tonight's ball," Ella said, feeling that she ought to be suspicious of Mr. Woodward but instead appreciating him for his candor.

"As you should learn to be as well," Mr. Woodward advised. "It is the only way one survives the ton. For example, I am quite aware that another gentleman has been watching you this entire night. He followed us outside and is even now spying on us from a bush behind you."

Ella started to turn her head, but Mr. Woodward's hand over hers on the wall stopped her. "Better not to let him know you are aware. I'll keep an eye on him for you."

"Will you now?" Ella drawled. "And what reason have I to trust you?"

"This one." He moved away from her. "It is time to return inside before you are missed. Do not take my arm. Go through the far door—alone—and I will take the opposite. Good evening, Lady Eleanora. It has been a pleasure to make your acquaintance, and I hope to enjoy your company again soon."

With that, he was gone, leaving Ella with somewhat confused feelings regarding him. She followed him inside a moment later, only just resisting the urge to look behind her and see if she was, indeed, being followed. She found Lady Benton almost frantic.

"Where have you been? I must have you in my sight throughout the evening."

Ella took Lady Benton's gloved hand and squeezed it gently. "All is well. Though I am a little tired. How much longer must we stay?"

"Until the end, of course. This is your first ball, and to be a guest of the Duke's is no trifle."

She was, quite suddenly, very tired. Perhaps the night air had not been good for her. Good or not, she'd no time to dwell on it as she soon made the acquaintance of one Lord Lewes. He seemed closer to her age and less stuffy than many of the others in attendance. Mr. Woodward did not ask her to dance again, nor did she discover the mysterious man who had been spying upon her—if there really was such a person.

Seven

"Lady Ella, wake up." A cold hand touched Ella's shoulder and she rolled away from it. "Lady *Eleanora*, please."

"I wish to be called Ella." She pulled the pillow over her head. It couldn't be time to rise already. It seemed she'd scarcely gone to bed.

"Do you also wish for a morning ride?" an exasperated voice demanded. "If so, you must get up. Mr. Darling is downstairs, waiting to take you to Hyde Park."

It took only a second for the words to register before Ella flung off the covers and bounded from the bed, startling Lucy so that she jumped back.

"Mr. Darling said he would take me for a ride—on a horse?"

"Unless they've camels here too," Lucy said, shaking her head as she walked to the clothespress. "I didn't know you were going riding or I'd have readied your outfit."

"I didn't know either." Ella hurried behind the screen,

An Invitation to Dance

already pulling her nightgown over her head as she went. "I said that I wanted to go riding, but he never said a word about taking me." She tossed the gown over the side of the screen and hopped about, freezing and impatient. "What time is it, anyway?"

"A little after seven." Lucy appeared with Ella's riding habit. "I fear this made-over garment is not at all fashionable enough for London."

"Fashion does not help one to stay seated upon a horse." Ella waited for Lucy to finish lacing her stays, then thrust her shivering arms through the sleeves of her blouse as quickly as she could. She wasn't certain if it was the cold or the excitement of being able to go riding causing her gooseflesh. "Mr. Darling knows I am coming? He is still waiting?" she asked, impatient with the time it took to don her skirt and jacket and put on her stockings and shoes.

At last, she was dressed and practically flew across the room toward the door.

"Your hair," Lucy wailed.

"Why must you always fuss over it?" Ella ran her hand down the back of her hair, still plaited from the previous night. "I slept but a few hours. It can't be that messy."

"Let me brush it and tie it in a ribbon, at least," Lucy said.

"Hurry then." Ella didn't bother returning to the dressing table, but quickly undid the plaiting herself while Lucy fetched the brush and ribbon. Two strokes of the brush and Ella pronounced it satisfactory and snatched up the ribbon to tie it herself. She was still finishing as she ran down the stairs.

Mr. Darling watched her approach, an unreadable expression on his face.

"I'm sorry you had to wait," Ella said, breathless with

excitement. "I would have been ready had I known you were going to take me."

"You did say you wished to ride." Mr. Darling lifted his head to stare at some point past her, as if to avoid looking at her directly. "And you also said you would be leaving after last night's ball, so I thought it best to take you today—before you return home."

"Thank you." Ella finished with the ribbon and clasped her hands together in front of her. "I am ready now."

"Yes, well . . ." Mr. Darling bit his lip.

"Is there a problem?" Ella looked longingly toward the front doors.

"Only with your jacket." He stared the opposite direction.

Ella frowned and placed her hands on her hips, annoyed and slightly hurt at his criticism. "I know it is not stylish in the least, but I've not had a new riding habit made since before my mother died four years ago."

"I am not speaking of the style, but of the *buttons*." Mr. Darling's voice was quiet, terse—and embarrassed.

Ella glanced down and at once realized the problem. The top two buttons were undone already, creating a swell of gaping fabric at her chest, revealing the shirt beneath. "Oh." *Bother.* Annoyed at the delay, she fixed the buttons, then stood straight and tall—the only way she could stand in the overly snug garment. "*Now* I am ready."

Without looking at her to see if she was indeed put together this time, Mr. Darling offered her his left arm, and they exited the back way. He led her through the carriage house out to the small stable, where the most magnificent horse she had ever seen was waiting.

"Oh, but he's gorgeous." She took a step toward the

majestic black stallion, then paused, glancing back at Mr. Darling for permission.

"Go ahead," he urged, nodding his head toward the open stall. "Stoutheart will let you know if he wants you to touch him or not."

Ella didn't need a second invitation. She walked forward, her hand outstretched, palm up. Stoutheart sniffed it, then nickered softly. Ella reached up, stroking her fingers down the sleek hairs of his nose. "What is he, sixteen hands? It must feel grand to sit atop him."

"Nearly seventeen, and it does feel rather grand to seat him." Mr. Darling offered her a smile at last.

"Quite large for a blood horse, is he not?" Ella asked. "Was he bred from a Turkoman or an Arabian?"

"Arabian."

"I thought so," she said, secretly pleased at the surprise and respect in his voice. "Arabians are better known for their ability to form a cooperative relationship with humans." *And if this one is specially trained . . .* She recalled the conversation between Lord Benton and Mr. Darling, during which they had discussed Stoutheart. "You're friendly, aren't you?" she said, petting his nose once again.

Stoutheart must have understood and approved of her praise as well, for he lowered his head to her. She rested her cheek against it for a second and sighed blissfully. "And I hear you are equally smart and fast too."

"If you wish to ride—truly ride, not just promenade around the park—then we had best be off." Mr. Darling stepped forward to lead Stoutheart from the stall. "The early morning hours in the park are reserved for the grooms to exercise the animals, and for those who wish to ride at a pace above a trot."

"How one can ride here is even dictated?" Ella said,

indignant at such an idea. She followed him from the stable.

"*Everything* in London is dictated," Mr. Darling said. "I should think you would have discovered that at last night's ball. Did any gentleman ask you to dance more than twice? Were you ever allowed out of my sister's sight? If you longed for a drink or a bit of fresh air, were you able to serve yourself punch or walk out on the balcony?"

Instead of answering, Ella made a pretense of examining the sidesaddle of the horse waiting for her in the yard. It was a fine Irish Hunter of perhaps fifteen hands, beautiful as well, though not nearly the animal Stoutheart was.

"Silly rules," she said, not mentioning the fact that she had broken some of them last night. *Who would have thought it a faux pas to ladle your own punch?* There had been no servants at the table, and no gentleman had recently offered, and she had been thirsty. Lady Benton had been appalled. "And an impractical society." With the groom's assistance, she mounted, settled her right leg over the pommel, and took up the reins.

"You do not look the least silly seated thus," Mr. Darling observed, the glow of approval in his gaze.

"Thank you." Ella smiled as she appreciated his good form as well. She watched as he mounted, using only his left hand to pull himself up. When he was seated, his left hand lifted his right and placed it carefully in a strap connected to his jacket. She caught the almost imperceptible movement of his legs, and Stoutheart started forward. The longer reins lay slack in the palm of Mr. Darling's left hand, giving Ella the impression that he did not need them at all to guide his horse.

They rode in silence until they reached the corner of the park and the beginning of Rotten Row, a somewhat narrow sand covered thoroughfare, with a low fence on either side.

An Invitation to Dance

For someone used to the freedom of hills to roam, the path held little promise. Disappointment must have shown on her face, for Mr. Darling sought to console her.

"Many of the grooms will have finished by now, so there should be ample room to run, and the row continues for over a mile. Do your best to ignore the fence and enjoy the trees and the Serpentine River running along beside. Who knows—you might even be able to make another leaf wish."

Stoutheart took off at a gallop before Ella could decipher whether or not Mr. Darling had been serious or mocking her. But it mattered little. Her only wish at the moment was to keep up with him—a tall order. But she leaned forward, pressed her leg and the crop into her horse's side and commanded him to go.

The fence was soon forgotten, as was the ribbon in her hair that fluttered free behind, loosing her curls. Ella raced on, always a full length behind Mr. Darling, yet happy with the wind at her face and the familiar feeling of a horse beneath her. They covered the distance quickly, and London's limitations were soon forgotten, left behind in the joy of riding. When they reached the end of the row, Mr. Darling slowed, turned Stoutheart, and found Ella right behind him.

"Well done," he said, and this time she was certain of the admiration in his voice.

"It is I who should be saying that." She inclined her head toward the reins, still slack in his hands. "How do you do it? How do you direct your horse without the use of your hands?"

"I have the use of one if I need it," Mr. Darling reminded her. "But Stoutheart has been specially trained. In addition to forming relationships with their humans, Arabians are quick to learn and like to please. He responds to cues from my body, a slight pressure from my knee, the movement of each finger—every nuance of motion means something to him. It requires great care and focus when riding. If I were to become casual with my movements, I might find myself thrown over the fence and into the river."

Ella laughed at the picture that brought to mind. "You are too fine a rider to ever allow that to happen," she predicted. "I see now why Lord Benton named you the best."

"Yes, well—" Mr. Darling cleared his throat. "I suppose it is good to be best at *something*. Shall we make our way back—slower now. I'm afraid the hour for racing is over." Without waiting for her to answer, he started Stoutheart forward again, this time at an easy trot.

Ella followed and considered Mr. Darling's choice of words and the way he had received—or not received—her compliment.

"I think there is nothing I would rather be best at than riding," she declared.

"You are quite good at it," Mr. Darling conceded. "In fact, I have never met a woman so adept."

"Thank you," Ella said, hoping to exemplify to him the way one ought to receive a compliment. "And you are extraordinarily skilled at riding as well, doing—I daresay—what no other man in all of London can."

"No other man in London *has* to ride the way that I do," he said, with more than a tinge of bitterness in his voice.

Ella guided her horse closer to his. "This bothers you? Your hand bothers you?"

His head snapped around to look at her. "Of course it does. It would trouble you too, if you had only one hand with which to do things. You cannot deny noticing my inability."

"Today, I have noted only your *ability*," Ella said. "I imagine that riding was important enough to you that you figured out a way to accomplish it. I should similarly imagine that if other activities were equally important, you would also discover a way to participate in those."

He gave a short, harsh laugh. "You don't think that I've tried? It has taken me the better part of five years to learn to function at this level of normalcy."

Ella pulled on the reins and stopped abruptly. "Five years? Do you mean that you were not born with this condition?"

Mr. Darling guided Stoutheart to a stop as well and turned him so that he faced Ella and took up much of the path. "Of course I was not born this way. Had I been, my mother probably would have left me for dead."

"I should hope not," Ella said, horrified at the idea of a mother abandoning her child simply because one of his arms was malformed. But she knew it happened, as she also guessed that society must unfairly judge a man different from most, as Mr. Darling was. "How did your arm become as it is?"

Mr. Darling closed his eyes as if pained. "I expected you to ask me sooner—in the carriage, or the other night in the parlor."

"I did not think there was anything to ask," Ella said, nonplussed that he had worried over his condition and what she might think of it. "I assumed it was something you were born with—as I was born with brown eyes instead of the lovely shade of blue yours are. We are none of us perfect, you know."

"Do not attempt to compare eye color with a limb that does not function."

"I'm not," Ella said defensively. "I wasn't."

"And there is nothing at all wrong with brown eyes," Mr. Darling said. "Yours are quite expressive."

A compliment? "Will you tell me how it happened?" Ella

asked, softer this time. "Your arm does not bother me in the least, but it is apparent that it troubles you. Perhaps if you talk about—"

"Speaking of it will not make it better," Mr. Darling said. "I know. I have spoken of it to countless physicians. I have even spoken *to* it—to my arm itself—in an attempt to command it to move. And just last week, I was foolish enough to wish on a leaf for its recovery."

"Leaf wishes are not foolish," Ella insisted. At least one had come true recently. She had wished for company and had wished to travel. And here she was, out riding in London with a fine gentleman. No matter that she had been imagining her father and the pyramids when she made that wish.

"We should go." Mr. Darling tilted his hand ever so slightly, and Stoutheart turned around once more. "There will be gossip enough already."

"Who is to gossip?" Ella asked. "No one is awake at this hour. And if they were, what is there to say? That we were out riding together?"

"They will say that Lady Eleanora Whitticomb was seen in the presence of a cripple."

"Or," she countered, glancing down at her jacket that had come undone once more, "they may say that Mr. Darling was seen in the presence of a woman whose riding habit hasn't fit properly in three years."

A corner of his mouth quirked. "A scandal for sure."

"Of the worst kind." The subtle shift of his mood relieved her. She would not ask him again the circumstance relating to his arm, but neither would she feel sorry for him.

From the corner of her eye, she studied Mr. Darling as they rode. Anyone who could ride so well was not in need of pity.

Eight

When they reached the stables, the groom came out to help Ella dismount, but she waved him back inside with her hand, a quick shake of her head, and a finger to her lips. He retreated, leaving her to watch Mr. Darling dismount and hand Stoutheart off to the groom who had come to attend him.

Mr. Darling started toward the house, then paused as he realized that Ella was still seated upon her horse. "Was there not a man come out to attend you?" he asked, glancing toward the stable doors.

Ella shrugged. "I sent him away. I would prefer to have you help me."

Mr. Darling frowned. "Lest you have forgotten in the last half hour, I have not two hands with which to catch you."

"You have one." Ella delicately swung her leg over the pommel so she sat completely sideways. "And one shall do just fine. In case *you* have forgotten in the last half hour, I have quite good balance."

Mr. Darling gave an audible sigh, then stepped forward and held his left hand up to her. "If I drop you or you fall, it is not my fault."

Ella took his hand, gripping it securely, then leaned forward and slid from the horse. She landed perhaps a little harder than usual, but certainly on her feet and with no harm done.

"Thank you, sir."

Mr. Darling did not release her at once, and the pressure of his warm fingers upon her chilled ones felt unexpectedly pleasant. He looked down upon her, a questioning vulnerability in his gaze that made her wonder at his thoughts while hers felt suddenly peculiar.

"I lost the use of my arm five years ago," he said quietly. "I was second for Henry the night of the duel. It was my sister's honor he was defending, and I should have been the one out front. But he made sure to get me foxed enough that I didn't overly protest when he left me behind in the woods." Mr. Darling lowered their hands but still kept hold of Ella's. If anything, it seemed his grip tightened, as if he were holding on to her for support as he shared his tale. She gave it, covering his hand with her other.

"Go on," she coaxed.

"Sir Crayton—the infamous, knighted pirate—had somehow gained admittance to Almack's. And he had taken a fancy to my sister and lured her to another room. I was dancing, and Gregory as well, though he was only biding his time until he could ask Ann to dance again. But Henry saw Crayton forcing Ann to come with him. Henry followed and stopped Crayton before any real harm was done. Then he called him out for his actions."

"Why was it not Lord Benton—Gregory—Henry's brother, who defended your sister's honor? If it was she whom he cared for?"

"He intended to, but Henry gave him the wrong time and place of meeting. As the oldest, Henry felt it his responsibility to go. We all knew Crayton's reputation, knew that the chance of anyone coming out of a duel with him alive wasn't good."

"Then why did he do it?" Ella asked, saddened at the image of the young man who had taken her fishing going willingly to meet his death.

"Because he'd called Crayton out, and rash though that might have been, Henry wasn't one to back down. He felt he had to go. He and I never agreed on that." Mr. Darling squeezed her hand in a gesture of comfort, and Ella glanced down, startled to discover that sometime during their conversation he had become the one attempting to soothe.

"And your arm?" Her gaze slid to the motionless limb.

"When I came to and realized what Henry had done, I hurried to find him. I arrived in time to see him fall from Crayton's shot. I picked up his pistol, intending to finish what he'd started, but Crayton fired before I'd even taken aim. I don't know if he meant to kill me or simply to disarm—no pun intended." Mr. Darling's expression was grim. "But he injured me enough that I was unable to get Henry help in time, and he died as a result. My arm became so infected I nearly lost it. Only Gregory's insistence that the doctors not amputate allowed me to keep it. Instead of amputating, they removed as much of the infected areas as they could—much of the innards of my arm. It was a torturous, bloody surgery and no little miracle I didn't die from it. For a long time I wished that I had."

Ella worried that there were times he still did. "Does it pain you now?" she asked, her brow wrinkling with concern.

"Only in the sense of inconvenience. It pains me that I cannot do the things I once did—that I cannot accept an invitation to dine among friends, cannot dance at a ball, cannot help a young lady from her horse."

"You just did." Ella tugged her hand free and looked away, hoping to hide the swell of emotion engulfing her. Struggling with a constricted throat and stinging eyes, she tried to make sense of her tender feelings. Were they due to learning more about Henry Benton, or were they more from the compassion she felt for Mr. Darling—compassion she feared he would interpret as pity and therefore shut her out, as it seemed he had most everyone else? He had not even taken supper with them the previous night, and Lady Benton had confirmed what Ella had previously suspected—that Mr. Darling chose to be alone, rather than risk embarrassing himself or causing those around him discomfort.

"Our ride has left me quite famished," Ella said, when she trusted herself to speak once more. "Shall we join Lord and Lady Benton for breakfast?"

"Thank you, but I have dined already," Mr. Darling said.

"At least come for conversation then," Ella insisted and waited for him to step up beside her. "Lord Benton shall surely be appreciative of another gentleman to sway the conversation away from the fashions of last night's ball."

"My sister does like to talk of clothing, doesn't she?" Mr. Darling said, and Ella sensed his indecision. Taking adventage, she placed her hand upon his good arm.

"But *I* should prefer to talk of horses. Please say you'll join us."

"Very well," he said at last.

Progress. Ella supposed she should put on a morning gown but feared that taking the time to do so might be time enough for Mr. Darling to change his mind. So, conscious of the buttons on her jacket, she instead pulled him along toward the breakfast room where they found Lord and Lady Benton already seated and eating.

Each looked up as Mr. Darling entered, with Ella on his arm. And while Lord Benton managed to cover his surprise, Lady Benton appeared so astonished that she nearly dropped her glass. Her gaze slid from her brother to Ella, upon whom she bestowed a look of warm appreciation.

Ella smiled as she exchanged their silent corresponddence.

"And how was Stoutheart this morning?" Lord Benton asked.

"Perfectly marvelous," Ella answered before Mr. Darling could. The astonished expression returned to Lord Benton's face.

"You allowed her near Stoutheart? I had to wait months for that privilege, and we are practically brothers."

Mr. Darling handed a plate to Ella. "Lady Ella has both considerable experience with and knowledge of horses. She was not the least frightened or intimidated, but took to Stoutheart and he to her quite easily.

"Your horse must prefer women," Lord Benton mumbled as he returned to eating. Though his words were grumpy, Ella caught the jest in them as well.

She filled her plate alone, conscious of Mr. Darling standing a short ways off. *Has he really eaten already?* She had never before considered the difficulties involved in serving oneself breakfast from a sideboard if only one hand was available. It would be impossible to both hold one's dish and serve at the same time. And most sideboards allowed no extra space where a plate might rest while being filled. *But could not such a design be constructed?* Easier yet, could not the dishes be placed on the table within easy reach for those eating to serve themselves? She found herself irritated that no one had thought of that.

Mr. Darling stood waiting at the chair beside his sister. This he pulled out for Ella when she had finished serving herself. Then he took the chair on her other side.

"I almost forgot," Lady Benton said, her hand flying to her chest in sudden excitement. "A letter for Lady Ella arrived this morning. Do give it to her, Gregory," she instructed her husband.

Lord Benton withdrew an envelope from his jacket and handed it to her.

"From my father, perhaps," she said excitedly as she tore the letter open. "*Dear Lady Eleanora.*" She paused and tried to mask her disappointment. "Or perhaps not." She smiled bravely and bent her head to continue reading in silence.

> *It was lovely to see you at last night's ball. You showed definite pluck and the ability to think and act for yourself. It is my hope we will have the opportunity to see each other again soon and become better acquainted.*
>
> *Yours,*
> *An admirer*

"How peculiar." Ella glanced up from the paper to find all three studying her.

"Who is it from?" Lady Benton asked.

"I haven't any idea." Ella pushed the paper closer to Lady Benton so she might read it.

"Pluck? The ability to think for yourself? What odd compliments—if that is what they are intended to be."

"May I see the letter?" Lord Benton asked. Ella nodded, and Lady Benton handed it across the table for him to read.

"Very odd," he agreed upon finishing. "What do you make of it, Alex?"

Mr. Darling leaned across the table and took the letter in his good hand. He too read it, then shrugged. "It does not seem so odd to me that Lady Ella should garner an admirer. Is that not what she is aiming for when the Season begins? Generally, a man must admire a woman before he proposes marriage to her."

"Generally, a man admires a woman's form—or her gown or hair or manners or *something* feminine," Lady Benton said.

"Obviously *this* man,"—Mr. Darling allowed the letter to fall to the table—"cares about more than how fashionably a woman is dressed."

"Who do you think wrote it?" Lord Benton asked Ella. "Aside from Lord Dersingham, were there any other gentlemen who paid you special attention last night?"

"As her chaperones, shouldn't you know?" Mr. Darling sent reprimanding looks at both his sister and Lord Benton.

"Lord Lewes enjoyed your company as well, did he not?" Lady Benton said to Ella.

"I believe so," Ella said. "We danced." And then there had been the mysterious Mr. Woodword, daring her to go out to the balcony as he had. Of any who might express admiration of her pluck, she guessed it would be him.

"I suppose we shall have to wait and see if your admirer reveals himself at tomorrow's ball," Lady Benton said.

"But I am going home today," Ella said, feeling slightly panicked at the idea of being away even longer. *What if Papa returns home for me and I am gone?*

"We have already been invited," Lord Benton said. "*All of us.*" This time it was he sending a pointed look at Mr. Darling.

"You know I cannot attend balls," Mr. Darling said.

"Cannot or will not?" Ella asked without thinking.

"Both." Mr. Darling pushed back his chair. "It is not a subject up for discussion."

"I apologize." Ella turned in her chair to face him. "What you do or do not do is none of my concern." *I shouldn't have pushed him.* But she could not seem to help thinking that his life could and ought to be better than it was.

"Apology accepted," he said, some of the frost vanished from his tone. "I do, however, think that you should attend tomorrow's ball, Lady Ella. It would behoove us to discover just who this admirer is."

"I do not know if I can stay in this city another day." Her hands fidgeted in her lap, and she noticed her topmost button had come undone again.

"Would it help if I promised to take you riding again tomorrow?" Mr. Darling asked. "I know it is not the same as riding in the hills you are used to, but—"

"It would help immensely." Ella sent him a smile of gratitude.

"In that case,"— He stood and addressed Ann—"may I suggest, dear sister, that you spend today making use of your fashionable sensibilities and connections and secure for Lady Ella a riding habit that fits."

Nine

London, December 1819

Dear Lady Eleanora,
 Your cleverness and skill last night at whist quite impressed me. Little wonder that so many were vying to be your partner. It is my hope that I may have that honor sometime soon.
Yours,
An admirer

"His letters do not seem to get any longer," Alex remarked as he reached across Stoutheart to return Lady Ella's most recent note from her as yet unknown beau.

"But clearly he is someone with whom I am acquainted, and who frequents the same events as I." She folded the paper and tucked it in the pocket of her new riding habit.

"It would seem so." Alex stroked his chin thoughtfully as he noted how the dark green fabric of her jacket complemented her dark hair and eyes. "Yet he continues to remain vague. He never actually admits to dancing with you, being your partner, escorting you into dinner. It is almost as if he wishes to do all those things, but cannot. That he is the bystander looking on with desire."

So close to the truth were the words to *his* feelings that Alex urged Stoutheart to a quickened trot, lest Lady Ella think he was confessing to being her admirer.

"I had not considered that." She kept pace and had the further advantage of looking at him as they rode, seated sidesaddle as she was.

Alex worked to hide his growing feelings for her, a task that had become increasingly difficult over the past weeks. "I see no rush to discover this gentleman's identity. You've callers aplenty as it is." Hardly a day had passed since the Duke of Salisbury's ball that she did not receive callers— many of them gentlemen whom she had danced with at balls the previous evenings and who expressed interest in becoming better acquainted with her.

"I am not after more visitors." Lady Ella laughed. "I am hoping for *less*. When my admirer makes himself known to me, I shall be free to dismiss the others who call and spend my time going driving with the man who is so eloquent and complimentary."

"I do believe his words are starting to go to your head." Alex twisted his mouth in mock disgust, while feeling just that about himself. *I can never take her driving.* Controlling Stoutheart with a single hand was one thing. He could never risk harming Lady Ella by attempting to drive a buggy and team with only his left hand.

"Better that I love a man's words than his money," she said. "Ann keeps encouraging me to go after Lord Lewes, as he is particularly flush in the pockets. But that is not at all why I care for him."

"What do you see in him?" Alex asked, having found Lewes particularly annoying as of late.

"He makes me laugh," Lady Ella said, a wistful smile on her face, "and forget my troubles."

"I thought riding made you forget your troubles," Alex said.

"It does," she agreed. "But only when I ride so fast that it feels as if I am flying."

"Why didn't you say so?" With a signal to Stoutheart, Alex was off, Lady Ella following so close they were nearly neck and neck. He knew the second her ribbon tore free; he noticed when her concentration was taken over by habit, as she ceased biting her lip and a smile broke out across her face.

How he loved that smile and these mornings with her. Who would have believed, just eight short weeks ago, that he would be enjoying this time in London? That he would have found friendship in the most unlikely of places—with Henry's fiancée? For the first time in many years, he had something to look forward to each day.

Thank you. Alex sent his silent gratitude heavenward and tried to feel content with this time he had—more than Henry had been granted.

Once Lady Ella's admirer was revealed, Alex knew everything would change. But for now, for two joyous hours every morning, he was with her and that was enough.

Ten

January 1820, Eve of the midwinter ball

"Wherever did this come from, and why have you not worn it?" Lady Benton exclaimed as she watched Lucy remove the white gown from Ella's trunk.

"Paris. It was a gift from my father. And the lace itches terribly." Ella winced as Lucy pulled a curling paper from her hair. The holiday at the Benton's country home had been lovely, but now they were returned to London for the Season, and Ella was not at all certain that she should have allowed them to talk her into coming.

"How do you know it itches? Have you ever worn it?" Lady Benton took the gown from Lucy and laid it across the bed.

"No," Ella admitted. "But just feel it." She watched in the glass as Lady Benton did just that.

"It is exquisite. How perfect that you have saved your loveliest gown for the ball we are to host. You *must* wear it tonight. You'll be all the rage, and heads will be turning everywhere."

Ella grimaced. "I should prefer everyone's heads to stay on straight, thank you."

Lady Benton laughed. "Oh, Ella, you have spoiled me so with your humor these past weeks. I fear that I shall never again be able to endure London without it."

"You may have to soon," Ella said. "For I really *must* go home before the end of the month. My father said he would be returning to England soon." She hadn't gone home for Christmas because the thought of spending it by herself—after enjoying the companionship of Lord and Lady Benton and Mr. Darling—had been too disheartening. And now she had returned to London not because of the balls or dinner parties, not because of the continued shopping trips with Lady Benton, and certainly not because of the gentlemen who called upon her. The one thing she would miss, the thing she felt holding her here was not a thing at all, but rather an extraordinary man and his horse.

Riding with Mr. Darling each morning had become the highlight of her day. At first, she had felt that way simply because of the opportunity to ride, and to ride alongside such a magnificent creature as Stoutheart. But gradually her reasons for cherishing that time had changed, and of late she found herself looking forward to Mr. Darling's company more than anything or anyone else. The thought of parting from him brought her much sorrow—more even than she had felt at leaving home. And so she had delayed her departure, using her as yet undiscovered suitor as an excuse. That he had known her whereabouts over the holiday and continued to send correspondence was both intriguing and concerning. But mostly, at present, it provided a convenient excuse.

Lady Benton called admittance to Mrs. Prichard, and she entered the room. "Another letter has arrived for Lady Eleanora." Mrs. Prichard handed Ella the envelope.

"Thank you." Ella broke the seal and unfolded the parchment, knowing it was of no use to put off reading the letter, as Lady Benton's curiosity surpassed her own in the matter.

"What does he say this time?" Lady Benton left the gown and came to stand behind Ella.

With reluctance, she began to read.

> *Dear Lady Eleanora,*
>
> *These past weeks have been sweet torture as I have missed being in your presence. As the new year has arrived, let us therefore usher out the old and welcome in the new with the midnight waltz at the midwinter ball.*
>
> *If my words have at all touched your heart, please say yes when—just before midnight—a gentleman requests your hand for our dance.*
>
> *Yours affectionately,*
> *An admirer*

"Oh my." Lady Benton placed her hands over her heart. "You will discover your devoted this very night!"

"Yes." Ella stared at her forlorn reflection in the glass. After tonight, she would no longer have an excuse for remaining in London. And worse, after tonight she would have to decide if her admirer was someone she wished to have as an ardent suitor. *What if he requests my hand for more than a dance?* She'd professed that she did not wish to find a husband, and she meant it. Though if she ever were to marry, her best chance to do so was now.

An Invitation to Dance

So why does the prospect of discovering my suitor make me sad? The answer was both obvious and disturbing. *I am happy with life as it is right now, with Mr. Darling as my friend.* And it could not be he who had written the letters. He would never invite her to dance. He rarely attended any of the evening events, preferring to stay home alone.

Ella wished fervently that she might stay in her room tonight also. For in all probability, everything was about to change.

Eleven

Alex tugged on his watch fob and withdrew his watch from his vest pocket, checking the time once again. *Eleven forty-three.* On the far side of the Benton's ballroom, Lady Ella stood on the outskirts of a group of women clustered around his sister.

Discussing who is wearing the best and worst gowns tonight, no doubt. Personally, he thought Lady Ella's outdid them all. Or perhaps it was simply that she outshone all of the other ladies in attendance—regardless of what she wore. At least one other man here shared his opinion, and Alex both desired and dreaded to know who it was.

He scanned the room once more. Lord Dersingham was, at the moment, conversing with Miss Ashworth, daughter of the prominent Earl of Pendelton, who was known to frequent and have excellent luck at the races. Alex had spoken with Pendelton a time or two, before purchasing Stoutheart. Miss Ashworth and Lord Dersingham made a handsome couple, and silently Alex wished Lord Dersingham to take note of that, instead of allowing his gaze to continually stray in Lady Ella's direction.

Not too far from Dersingham and Miss Ashworth, Lord Lewes stood with a group of men, in apparent deep conversation. Alex took comfort that, for the moment at least, Lewes did not appear to be searching out Lady Ella.

Only Mr. Woodword remained unaccounted for, and based upon his conversations with Lady Ella, Alex feared it was him she favored the most of her three possible suitors. Though they had not danced together as much as she had danced with Lords Dersingham and Lewes, it was Woodward who had been seated near her at dinner at the Thompson's ball last month. And it was her conversations with Woodward that she regaled Alex with during their morning rides.

Like Lady Ella, Woodward held somewhat different opinions of society, and this worried Alex. He did not know enough about Woodward to feel that he was a good match for Lady Ella. And he had no desire to know more about the man or his prospects. He only needed to know where Woodward was at the moment, and what his intentions regarding the midnight waltz were.

Eleven forty-seven. Alex's eyes followed Lady Ella as she slowly separated herself from the other ladies, so as to stand apart from them and make herself available to dance.

"Peculiar, that one, isn't she?"

Alex turned his frown upon an older gentleman who had come up beside him. Something about the man seemed vaguely familiar, but Alex could not come up with his name.

The man inclined his head in Lady Ella's direction. "It will take someone who pities Lady Eleanora a great deal for her to secure any sort of offer by the end of the Season."

"How dare you." Alex grabbed the front of the man's

shirt and shoved him against the wall in the shadow of the oversized plants he himself had lingered behind most of the night. "You will take back that slander and swear never to repeat it or anything else about Lady Ella, or I'll see to it you'll no longer say anything at all."

"No need—to murder me," the man rasped, and for the first time Alex noted his pallor. Alarmed, Alex released him and stepped away. The man leaned forward, hands braced on his knees as he gulped air.

"Do you need a drink?" Alex glanced at his left hand, both astonished and horrified at the violence of its actions. *My actions.*

"No time." The man righted himself, though he was still breathing heavily and did not look well. He eyed Alex with caution. "What your right arm lacks—is made up for in the strength of your left," he remarked with admiration.

"You are far too free with words," Alex warned. "And while I've little concern over those spoken of me, you must apologize for what you said about Lady Eleanora."

"Then it is you who must apologize, for I was only repeating *your* words." The man struggled to cover his deep cough, then tugged his jacket back into place, attempting to cover a frame that appeared too thin. "Heard you myself last October at the Woolpack Inn, when you wagered your horse against the odds that my daughter would make a match this Season."

"Your *daughter*?" Alex glanced over at Lady Ella, then back at the man, believing him to be an imposter. Her father was—based upon his most recent correspondence—somewhere in Africa. And even were he somehow to be here, he had to be more hale and hearty than this gentleman, who looked to be on death's doorstep.

"Ella *is* mine," the man rasped, as if guessing the

direction of Alex's thoughts. "My wife and I were in our later years before we were blessed with a child. As the Marquis of Canterbury,"—He gave a slight bow and coughed once more—"I must say I am pleased to see that your opinion of Ella appears to have changed considerably over the past weeks."

"I did not wager my horse against her odds," Alex said, even as memory of that long ago conversation, and the old man in the tavern who had overheard it, surfaced.

"I'm glad," the marquis said, still sounding unconvinced. "I would hate to see you lose such a fine animal."

"*If* you really are Lady Ella's father," Alex began, "have you any idea the hurt you've caused, practically abandoning her these last years?"

"She was not as abandoned as you think," the marquis said. "It is true that at first I traveled to escape my grief. But soon I did not stay away by choice. Imagine my horror at discovering I was suffering from the same illness that claimed Ella's mother. I have been frantic that Ella might contract it as well, and so have stayed away, attempting to find a remedy to my consumption. At the very least, I wish that Ella does not have to care for me and suffer through seeing me slowly wither away, as she did her mother."

"Perhaps Ella should have been given that choice," Alex said, feeling his opinion beginning to sway in favor of believing the old man.

The marquis shook his head. "As her parent, it was mine to make. And how much better for her these past years that she has been growing into an independent young lady, that she has been well in body and even in spirit, discovering her talents and abilities and enjoying the outdoors she so dearly loves, instead of being cooped up inside, caring for an infirm old man."

"She dearly loves that infirm old man."

"As I love her and wish her hurt no more." The marquis paused, his gaze straying from Ella to the musicians. "But what will Ella feel when the clock strikes midnight and no one has come to claim her hand to dance?"

"What do you mean?" Alex narrowed his eyes. "What do you know about the midnight waltz?"

A smile lifted the corners of the marquis's mouth, and for the first time Alex saw the family resemblance.

"Who has been writing to her?" he demanded. "Where is the man? Why has he not come to dance with her?" Alex took out his watch once more. *Eleven fifty-six.* "It's Woodward, isn't it?" He felt his heart lurch. *I am about to lose her.*

I never had her to begin with.

"Mr. Woodward will not be paying Ella any further attention, as just today he became betrothed to Miss Christina Lyon of Surrey. I have seen them myself and both are quite happy with the arrangement."

"Was he never truly interested in Lady Ella?" Alex could not deny the relief he felt, though he worried over how she would feel when learning of Woodward's betrothal.

"He was interested in helping an old family friend watch out for his daughter, as was the old Lord Benton—not Henry before his passing, but his father. He knew how Elizabeth and I had yearned for a child, and when we were blessed with one so late in life, he agreed to watch out for Ella, should anything ever happen to her mother and me before Ella was of age."

"Agreed to help even to the point of betrothing their oldest son to Ella?" Alex asked.

The marquis nodded. "But things did not work out as I imagined they would, and so I had to take matters into my own hands, planting that book in Lord Benton's library last September."

"You *made* Henry's letter up?" Alex's hand flexed, yearning to grab the marquis by his shirt once more. He'd seen, firsthand, how much that letter had meant to Ella.

"No. No." The marquis was quick to shake his head. "I added the £400 note—£100 for every one of the last four years that Ella's needs have been neglected—but Henry's letter was real. I'd had it for quite some time. He sent it before—" The marquis's mouth closed abruptly. "No time to speak of this now. It is eleven fifty-nine. What are you waiting for?"

"I did not write those letters," Alex said, "and furthermore, I do not dance."

A twinkle came to the marquis's eye, even as his look turned shrewd. "But you *could* have written them. You wanted to. The sentiment expressed in them is your own."

"Do not suppose to understand what I—"

"Do not suppose that my years and forced exile have not made me a keen observer of men," the marquis cut in. "Back in October at that inn, I could see the beginning of your feelings for Ella. You are fortunate that I have been able to watch them develop, and I give you my blessing." He paused, struggling for breath, as if this speech had cost the remainder of his strength. "Now, you want to dance with Ella. So what are you waiting for?"

Twelve

Ella's gaze strayed yet again to the clock high on the wall. Only one minute left until midnight. *Midnight at the midwinter ball. And I am alone.* Her reluctance for the evening and meeting her mysterious suitor had turned to nerves and apprehension as the night had worn on. She had danced with each of the three she believed might have written the letters. And while each had been most solicitous, none of the three had given any sort of hint that he might be the one. Mr. Woodward had confirmed that he definitely was not her admirer, when he'd told her of his betrothal to Miss Lyon. Lord Dersignham had asked if he might call upon her tomorrow, and Ella had been somewhat vague in her reply. Of course, he might call upon her—if he were the one who claimed her hand during the midnight dance and confessed to writing the letters. But if it were not he, having him call upon her on the morrow might prove complicated.

An Invitation to Dance

From the corner of her eye, Ella caught sight of Mr. Darling walking toward her. Her heart did a peculiar little leap. *What if—*

"Your knight in shining armor has not come to claim your hand yet?" Mr. Darling asked, dashing her fledgling hope as he made an exaggerated show of looking around the ballroom.

"He has not." *Thirty seconds until midnight.*

"Hmm. Probably not Dersingham. He seems otherwise engaged." Mr. Darling inclined his head toward Lord Dersingham escorting another young lady to the center of the dance floor. "And it appears that Lord Lewes has decided to forgo the midnight waltz altogether."

Ella followed Mr. Darling's gaze as it landed on Lord Lewes joining a group of men headed into the billiard room. She knew she ought to have felt disappointed. Lord Lewes was the wealthiest of her possible suitors. He was kind and had good manners. Any woman in this room would have considered him a good catch. And yet . . . she had felt nothing for him, beyond that of pleasant acquaintance.

"I think I knew all along that it could not be Lord Dersingham who wrote the letters," she said, hearing only relief in her voice. "And Lord Lewes could not have written them either. When I attempted a discussion on literature with him, he confessed he'd not much use for it and that words on paper held little value."

"A clue, certainly." Mr. Darling nodded his head.

The clock struck midnight, and still she remained alone—or without a partner at least. She closed her eyes briefly, feeling embarrassed, disappointed, *relieved*. In her heart, she had doubted whether she could feel enamored of any of the three men she believed might have written the letters. And there had been no others whom she could have imagined—or whom she would want to imagine—having as a suitor.

Excepting Mr. Darling.

"Ella." His use of her name and his touch at her elbow startled her, though she'd known he stood beside her.

"Yes?" She ceased looking at the couples lining the floor and turned to him.

"Will you give me the honor"—A flicker of fear shown in his eyes, and his Adam's apple bobbed as he swallowed—"of being my partner for the midnight waltz?"

Her heart gave that queer little leap again, but once more she tamped it down. How many times had she encouraged Mr. Darling to attend a ball and dance with her, and how many times had he refused? That he was here was miracle enough and due only to the occasion being at Lord Benton's home.

She felt her eyes begin to water, so touched was she by his gesture, and knowing what such an offer had cost him. "You must really feel sorry for me, to offer yourself up for such discomfort." She attempted a smile and found it wobbly. "But you needn't feel badly that my mysterious suitor has not revealed himself."

A lazy smile lifted one corner of Mr. Darling's mouth. "I feel absolutely no pity for you. As you have demonstrated none for me, *Ella*." He spoke her name slowly the second time and in such manner that started her heart to pounding. His hand slid from her elbow down her arm, over her wrist and to her fingers. These he lifted delicately, then bent over them, placing a kiss on the back of her hand.

He lifted his head once more and looked directly at her. "I asked you to dance because I *want* to dance with you, and because I promised that I would."

"*You* wrote the letters?" She'd imagined but never allowed herself to hope that it could really be true.

"No." He shook his head, but his smile remained in place. "But your father gave me permission to dance with you anyway."

"*Papa?*" She couldn't begin to understand what he meant.

"I'll explain later." Mr. Darling inclined his head toward the dance floor. "*After* we dance." He took her left hand and placed it upon his right. "You will have to help me. And it will be different from a usual waltz." His eyes searched hers, as if attempting to make certain she truly wished for his company, to be seen dancing with him.

She wished for far more than that. Keeping their gazes locked, she entwined her fingers with his and slowly lifted their hands into dance position. His other hand came to her waist, and she placed hers upon his shoulder. The music started and they began to turn, somewhat awkwardly around the edge of the ballroom.

"Look at us." Ella giggled. "Inviting scandal and gossip once again." It was impossible not to notice the many heads turned their direction. Even more impossible was ignoring the delightful fluttering in her middle and the tears of happiness building behind her eyes. *Mr. Darling is dancing with me!*

"Look at *you*," he said, "in your beautiful gown and curls and with those unfathomable eyes that drive me quite to distraction."

Ella felt her heart melt beneath his compliment. "If you are so distracted, how is it that you've managed to steer us quite near the balcony doors?"

"I am not certain." He glanced all about as if astounded to find them exiting the ballroom.

Another quick turn, and they were outside. His hand tightened at her waist as he steered her toward a shadowy corner.

"And did my father give you permission to take me outside?" Ella's heart was pounding so loud she was certain he would hear it.

"No." Mr. Darling stopped beside a set of stately pillars. "This is all my doing—what I have wanted since nearly the moment I met you."

"Truly?" Ella could not help the skepticism in her voice, each having acknowledged previously that their first meeting had not been their best. She loosened her grip on his hand, but he did not relinquish his other at her waist.

"Perhaps it was when you suggested a leaf wish. And then helped me find the courage to make it come true." His head bent to hers so that she felt his whisper upon her lips.

"What was your wish?" Ella asked.

"To be able to do all that a man should." His mouth descended closer. "To help a woman from a carriage or a horse, to dine with her. To dance." His lips brushed hers in a slow, sweet kiss. "To love."

She leaned her head against his chest, feeling dizzy and euphoric.

He brushed his lips across her forehead.

Ella sighed with contentment. "I believe that I have fallen in love with you, Mr. Darling. And not just because of your fine horse."

He chuckled. "That is good. Because he will be away for a while this spring. Dancing with you tonight—loving you—" Their eyes met. "—will quite probably cost me a wager."

ABOUT MICHELE PAIGE HOLMES

Michele Paige Holmes spent her childhood and youth in Arizona and northern California, often curled up with a good book instead of out enjoying the sunshine. She graduated from Brigham Young University with a degree in elementary education and found it an excellent major with which to indulge her love of children's literature.

Her first novel, *Counting Stars*, won the 2007 Whitney Award for Best Romance. Its companion novel, a romantic suspense titled *All the Stars in Heaven*, was a Whitney Award finalist, as was her first historical romance, *Captive Heart*. *My Lucky Stars* completed the Stars series.

In 2014 Michele launched the Hearthfire Historical Romance line, with the debut title, *Saving Grace*. *Loving Helen* is the companion novel, with a third, *Marrying Christopher*, released in July 2015.

When not reading or writing romance, Michele is busy with her full-time job as a wife and mother. She and her husband live in Utah with their five high-maintenance children, and a Shih Tzu that resembles a teddy bear, in a house with a wonderful view of the mountains.

You can find Michele on the web: MichelePaigeHolmes.com
Facebook: Michele Holmes
Twitter: @MichelePHomes

Dear Timeless Regency Collection Reader,

Thank you for reading *A Midwinter Ball*. We hoped you loved the sweet romance novellas! Each collection in the Timeless Regency Collection contains three novellas.

If you enjoyed this collection, please consider leaving a review on Goodreads or Amazon or any other online store you purchase through. Reviews and word-of-mouth is what helps us continue this fun project. For updates and notifications of sales and giveaways, please sign up for our monthly newsletter on our blog:

TimelessRomanceAnthologies.blogspot.com

Also, if you're interested in become a regular reviewer of these collections and would like access to advance copies, please email Heather Moore: heather@hbmoore.com

We also post our announcements to our Facebook page: Timeless Romance Anthologies

Thank you!
The Timeless Romance Authors

MORE TIMELESS REGENCY COLLECTIONS

Don't miss our TIMELESS ROMANCE ANTHOLOGIES:
Six short romance novellas in each anthology

www.ingramcontent.com/pod-product-compliance
Lightning Source LLC
LaVergne TN
LVHW021800060526
838201LV00058B/3184